DECEPTION

FACETS OF FEYRIE BOOK THREE

ZOE PARKER

Copyright © 2018-2019 by Zoe Parker

All rights reserved. No part of this publication may be reproduced, distributed, or transmitted in any form or by any means, including photocopying, recording, or other electronic or mechanical methods, without the prior written permission of the Author, except in the case of brief quotations embodied in critical reviews and certain other noncommercial uses permitted by copyright law.

God, that's rather boring to read isn't it? Kind of like listening to the neighbor give detailed descriptions of her dog's bowel movements. However, the shit is real.

Enjoy!

❀ Created with Vellum

CONTENTS

Deception   vii
Prologue of a big Boob...   ix

Chapter 1	1
Chapter 2	11
Chapter 3	27
Chapter 4	37
Chapter 5	45
Chapter 6	53
Chapter 7	63
Chapter 8	71
Chapter 9	81
Chapter 10	85
Chapter 11	95
Chapter 12	107
Chapter 13	115
Chapter 14	121
Chapter 15	125
Chapter 16	135
Chapter 17	143
Chapter 18	157
Chapter 19	161
Chapter 20	169
Chapter 21	183
Chapter 22	189
Chapter 23	195
Chapter 24	205
Chapter 25	209
Chapter 26	215
Chapter 27	217
Chapter 28	219
Chapter 29	225
Chapter 30	231

Acknowledgments 235
About Zoe Parker 237
Also by Zoe Parker 239

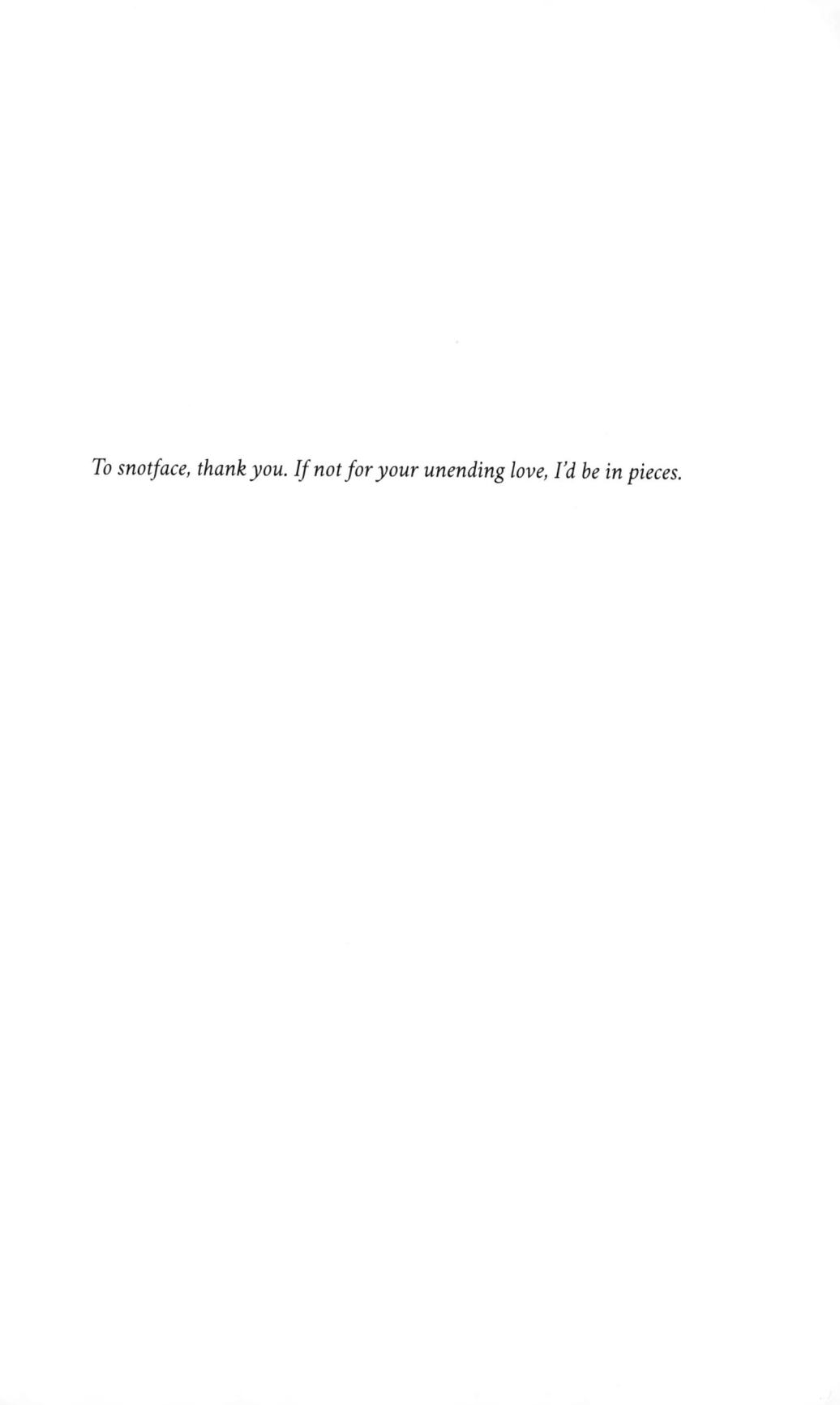

To snotface, thank you. If not for your unending love, I'd be in pieces.

BOOK THREE
FACETS OF FEYRIE SERIES
DECEPTION

ZOE PARKER

PROLOGUE OF A BIG BOOB...

Jameson

"Stupid mud holes," I mutter under my breath while trying to swipe at the muddy slush that's now covering my right pant leg all the way to the knee. Slowing my pace, I scrape off as much of the mess as I can without completely stopping. I don't want to be late. This is the third time something has gone wrong since I left the Sidhe. If I were a superstitious person, this could be considered a bad sign, but there's nothing bad about women and the lovely things I can do with them.

Although, I'll freely admit to myself that this is a new low for me. Meeting a stranger, physical attributes unseen in a public park isn't something I normally do. No matter how you look at it, desperate times call for desperate measures. So much so that I'm overlooking all this cloak and dagger business. She's probably new member of the Sidhe and wants to protect her privacy.

Considering the old, outdated customs of some of the Feyrie, I can completely understand her hesitance to meet in public. With so many people gathered together in one place, gossip is prevalent. People have reputations to worry about, and all that bother, and because of that some of the Feyrie still enforce those customs. I don't feel like getting married this week via a gun pointed at my head.

It's been a few weeks since I've had the company of a beautiful woman. Who am I kidding—months—since I had that kind of comfort, so this encounter shouldn't take long. If I time this right, I can show my appreciation to the tidbits offered to me and still be back before anyone notices my absence. The first one to notice will more than likely be Nika, the one who is responsible for my sudden dry spell in the company of the opposite sex. Slipping past her wasn't easy, the woman is a dragon after all, and for some reason, she guards me like I'm some pretty bauble in her hoard.

And even if I am a pretty bauble, I want no part of that mess.

In this specific instance, Nika isn't who I'm worried about being upset. *Iza* might kill me if I don't show up in time. She planned this day's celebration down to the colors of the napkins and the little paper turkeys on the plates. She spent all night cooking the monstrous bird that everyone will be dining on, without setting the kitchen on fire. She made all this effort is for our family Thanksgiving dinner—and why does that thought make my chest tight?

Stopping those mood-killing thoughts dead in their path, I focus once again on the woman who made this an unexpectedly tedious chase. I hope that she's attractive because it'll make up for ruining my good shoes. Not that her being unattractive is a deal breaker, I'm not leaving unsatisfied. I can keep my eyes closed through the entire thing. I'll also probably keep this little adventure to myself.

All to protect the woman's honor of course.

This adventure is also more palatable than eating Iza's cooking. The plan is to delay it as long as possible because the thought of her cooking scares me more than wandering around in the snow looking for a booty call. The picture of Iza smiling when she's angry flashes through my mind. Those red lips parting to show me rows of pearly white, razor-sharp teeth. I take that back, Iza scares me more than most things, including her cooking. If she smiles at me that way, I'll even ask for seconds.

That's her scary smile, and usually, if she's wearing it, then someone ends up dead or—at the very least—bleeding profusely. I've seen it enough to know. Somehow, I've managed to survive most of them.

Wait, I have survived them!

Has my manly personality finally won over the woman? The next thing you know she'll be singing my praises and telling me how good of a job I've done managing the Sidhe.

"I can't believe he showed up." The amused voice dumps cold water right on my daydream of Iza crowning me the king of personality.

Straightening my shoulders and planting a panty-charming smile on my face I look up to find myself instantly and utterly regretting this decision. Yes, the dark-haired, rather curvy woman standing there with a smirk on her face is incredibly beautiful, but the big hunk of muscle standing beside her with a terrifying, satisfied smile on his face is not my type.

The hair on the back of my neck stands up. *I've made a huge mistake.* As the woman takes the first steps towards me, I'm frozen in place with fear, and the realization of exactly how bad I fucked up hits me. Cold sweat soaks through the back of my shirt, cooling in the cold air. For once I don't care if the shirt is ruined, because I'm more worried about shitting my pants.

"The boss man said not to kill him, but he didn't say that we couldn't hurt him a little bit," the big man says, following close behind her.

Without a word, I turn, and with muscles burning, force my stiff legs to move in a direction away from the scary man. Instead of achieving my goal of magically getting back to the Sidhe unharmed with a macho story to tell the ladies, I find myself face first on the cold, wet ground with a crushing weight on top of me. It's the man who plowed me down like a dragon, taking me down with no warning at all. He laughs while he squashes my face further into the mud with a hand bigger than the back of my head.

A cold metal collar snapping around my neck makes my eyes burn with the desire to weep. I know exactly what that collar is. The

Magiks in it are already working, blistering my skin as the spell in it works its way into my body. Not that I stand a chance with either one of them in a fight, Magiks or not. I'm a mediocre healer who dabbles in herbs and potions. Not a fighter like Iza and some of the others. I've never wished more than right now that I listened to Iza and started training with Alagard because then I could at least throw a good solid punch or two.

Telepathy would be a handy trait to have right now too. I could scream my head off on their wavelength and Iza would come and save me. Knowing this, I still try to do it. Screaming in my mind for help like the pussy I am, begging a god that isn't listening. I'll eat the whole damn bird if she comes to save me, because this is terrifying, and they… are going to kill me.

A thought, foreign to me and completely unselfish flits through my panicking brain. Someone needs to tell Iza that it's a shifter and vampire working with a Light Fey who works Blood Magiks using Feyrie as a conduit for it. Something that essentially created a distorted version of Dark Magiks that can completely null out its own Magiks type. A deadly weapon against someone like Iza, one that they have perfected in my absence.

This is something that can bring our people to complete extinction.

This collar was created specifically to control Feyrie, to make them weak and to truly enslave them. I know this because I helped make it. I realize the error of not telling her sooner, but my insecurities made me hold my tongue. All because I didn't want her to have another reason to hate me.

Now, I'm regretting that choice because she needs to know these things. There's a good chance I won't survive this, and if they are lucky enough to get a collar like this on her, any hope for Feyrie is lost. They will break her then, they will make an example of her and in her death is a herald of the destruction of all Feyrie.

The desperation that I felt mere minutes ago to get laid is quadrupled and focuses instead on the need to do something to help Iza. She might come looking for me, she also might not, but it doesn't matter.

The warning still needs to be there. Thinking quickly, I wiggle my hand up through the mud, gritting my teeth as gravel tears away at my pampered skin, to dig the small tablet out of my inside coat pocket. My arm is shaking from the effort of levering a much of my weight as I can on my left side, especially with 'Muscles' deadweight sitting on me. Sliding it up to my shoulder, I carefully I take a picture of the collar around my neck. Turning my head, I see that he's looking at the woman, I take the opportunity to get a picture of the shifter. Tilting the tablet up, I try for the woman as well, but I'm not sure I get it. Forcing my arm back underneath me I shove the tablet down into the mud. Covering it in the thick stuff to disguise it from view. Gods, I hope Iza finds it. She's smart—somehow, she'll figure this mess all out. Even if I have faith in nothing else in existence, I have faith in her.

The weight on my back disappears, but before I can take a much-needed breath, he picks me up and tosses me over his shoulder like a small sack of flour. I fervently hope I shit all over him. The woman steps around him and takes my face in her hands. The vampires special brand of Magiks comes out of her mouth with her whispers. Without my own to protect myself, I'm helpless to her hypnotic gaze, and the darkness pulls me under.

1

IZA

I can't fucking believe that someone stole Jameson.

Why the hell did they take him? Jameson isn't a pivotal piece in the stupid game they're playing, he's a glorified secretary. He's someone I don't trust, not really. For the most part, he's useless when it comes to the majority of life. As far as using him against me, there are far better choices that would get my attention more thoroughly.

I don't care about what happens to him.

A slight queasiness tightens my stomach and makes the smell of the food around me unpalatable and argues against that fact. I argue back. Jameson betrayed me to save his ass. He allowed us to go through torture because of his cowardice. Why should I care about someone like that enough to worry? I don't give a shit... right?

The realization that I do floods my face with heat. Cradling my burning cheeks with my hands, self-consciously, I look around the room full of confused faces, knowing mine probably has a similar look on it. Shit, this changes things.

"Who saw him last?" I demand of the room, accepting the emotional epiphany for what it is and moving forward. Someone saw something. There are too many people here for no one to have seen him. Jameson is always buzzing about getting into something or someone. Plus, he organizes most of the things that happen at the Sidhe as a good secretary should. Jobs for the people here, chores around the Sidhe, trips to town. Everything.

My instincts are buzzing that there's more to the story. Something else is bothering me about this too. Why was I the first one to notice? As a general rule, I don't pay much attention to him. If I spend too much time focusing on the words that leave his mouth, I end up wanting to strangle him. I don't feel bad about that either.

Nika should have noticed first since she stalks him all the time.

My eyes go automatically to where she's standing, using that ungainly height of hers to look over the heads of people in the room. Why she's looking in the dining room, I don't know. He's not in the Sidhe or anywhere close, anymore at least. The fact that her face has the beginning of panic on it rules her out rather fast. She's worried sick, maybe even a little angry, and it's genuine.

"My lady, I think I saw him in the kitchen a few hours ago. He was in a hurry and was wearing an ungodly amount of cologne," Arista says, standing up at her table to be seen more clearly.

I nod my head to her, glad someone finally spoke up. The Magiks are pushing me to react rather strongly to this situation.

Jameson being in the library isn't surprising, he's always reading something. When he puts on cologne though, that usually means there's a woman involved. In this case, that habit might help me figure out where the fuck he is. My Magiks can't, which is frustrating to it and me. All I can feel is a muted sense of him, very muted. Which is completely useless.

With a quick, selfishly sad look at my big bird—that I won't get to eat—I head towards the library. Searching through the tables covered with the books and scribbled notes, I find nothing. His laptop isn't here either, that leaves one place he'd take it. The place he thinks he privately watches all his dirty movies. We all know he does it.

I head to his room. Just like I hoped, his laptop is on the bed, and papers cover the rest of it. Quickly, I sort through them, looking for something that's out of place or even a little useful. My nose finds it first. A fancy cream-colored piece of paper that smells strongly of cheap perfume and—I hold it up to my mouth to get a better scent—a vampire. Now, why would a vampire be sending Jameson a stinky letter? Unfolding it, I scan over the contents.

In disbelief, I grind my teeth together. Three freaking sentences lured the idiot out of the safety of the Sidhe.

I saw you in town and think you're hot. I'm single, and I want to rub my big, luscious boobs all over you. Meet me at the park at dark.

When I find him, if he isn't already dead, I'm going to kill him. A handful of words from someone he's never met before made him into a fucking moron. What kind of dumbass meets a random stranger at the park because they mention boobs?

'Jameson,' Phobe answers my silent question, drawing an eye roll out of me. Sadly, he isn't wrong. Someone did their homework to know Jameson would fall for this ridiculously transparent rouse. Either that or they know him. Considering that we have a spy in the Sidhe, that's possible, too.

"So instead of eating the bird and pie, I've got to go run around and try to find his ass," I mutter. Glaring at the note, I continue, "I guess the first place to start is in the park." Tucking it in my pocket, I turn and walk out of the room with Phobe's dark presence following close behind me.

The brief, light touch of his fingers on the small of my back relaxes me. Funny, too, because I didn't realize how tense I was until that moment. I glance at him and muster as much of a smile as I can. Letting it drop off my face, I head towards the front door. Without pausing, I pick up speed in the hope of avoiding Nika, who's heading towards us with green fire flashing in her eyes.

Not in the mood for a bitchy dragon right now. I'll end up saying something assholey, I know I will, and this time I'll not have anything filtering it. I don't even feel like *trying* to be nice.

"My lady, we need to—" she begins.

"Nope," is all I say before ducking out the door. Big nope.

Don't get me wrong. I have a small—microscopic—amount of empathy for what she's feeling. The man she has the hots for is missing, but that's as far as my empathy goes. That birdbrain did this to himself, and I'll make sure he's made aware of this when I find him. Because I will find him, and for the sake of whoever has him, he better be in one solid, breathing piece. If anyone is going to kill Jameson, it'll be Phobe or me. No stranger has the right to come in and—

"Iza, where are you going?" Phobe's voice pulls me out of my murderous thoughts of Jameson.

I stop walking and look around me. I have no idea where we are. All I know is the heartbeat of the Sidhe is no longer below my feet, and that up ahead of me the smell of humanity is strong. Looking around I get my bearings. Oh, we're right outside of the town of Moleville. Wow, that went fast. We were hauling ass. By car, downtown is about fifteen minutes away from the Sidhe. Turning to my left, I start walking again. I'm pretty sure the park is—

"Not that way. Come," Phobe says, grabbing my hand.

Rolling my eyes, I let him pull me along. Oddly enough, he's walking at normal speed. Probably because those human spy people are about and know who and what to look for. They did kidnap me, which wasn't nearly as exciting as I thought it'd be, so that means I'm on their radar. They also came to the Sidhe and tried to take the kids.

They're probably somewhere around here making more plans to annoy me. Unless Phobe killed them all already. It's entirely possible, because I know he's been sneaking off and destroying their little bases, but these human government-based organizations remind me of an infection. All it takes is one tiny piece getting away, and it can start a new infection somewhere else.

Annoyingly persistent, too.

It's also possible that Phobe has some other brilliant plan that he, of course, didn't tell me. Him hiding some is just so *shocking.*

'I can do without your sarcasm.'

'Na, sarcasm for life,' I tease back. A smile doesn't crack his face, and no amusement wafts across our bond... well, then I'll try harder. He comes to a jarring stop and swings me around to look at him.

'Iza, you should be taking this seriously, you—'

'—Don't handle things like this well and, unless I use these ridiculous fucking coping skills I picked up during life's wonderful adventures—I'll fall *apart because, despite* everything *he did, I care about the dipshit.'* My tone of voice is all temper and naked honesty. I'm so freaking sick of people, including Phobe, telling me what I should be feeling about things.

I FEEL everything!

His eyes are liquid fire while they search my face and tamp down to embers when he meets my gaze. His mouth opens and then closes, and then he repeats the process, but nothing comes out this time either. Instead, he starts dragging me along beside him again and to be a dick, I dig my heels in to make it harder on him. When he stops again in a small clearing, the amusement fades away as I take a deep breath of the air around me and find myself saturated by the smell of Jameson's fear.

Yep, this is where they took Jameson from. The tang of urine is everywhere, looks like there's a good chance he peed his pants in the process. Sniffing again I wrinkle my nose because I got two nostrils full of that raunchy perfume the vampire wears. The pee smells better than whatever it is she's bathing herself in. How can someone who has enhanced senses wear that awful stuff? The stench climbs in and coats the inside of your nose—wait, it coats the inside of your nose.

"She's hiding something because why else would she wear such a foul scent?" I muse, walking around the disturbed area. He tried to fight, and I'm proud of him for that, but they took him out of action quickly. I'm pretty sure there's an imprint of his face in the mud. There's also the smell of shifter all over that area. I'm guessing that was who knocked him down. The depth of his imprint in the mud signifies that the one standing on him weighed more than the vampire.

"You're correct. There are two of them. That's Jameson's footprint," Phobe points a few feet from me, "He turned to run and was tackled where you are. By someone much bigger than he is."

Studying the impression of him closer, I can see his handprints from where he fought to push back against whoever was sitting on him. They're deeper in the mud than they should be. Like he was using only his hands to lift, which is strange, his legs were free and stronger than his arms.

The lack of drag marks does tell me that he was picked up and carried out.

Turning in a circle, I look for the direction they went. Unlike the 'woodsman'—who is watching me in exasperation—I can't read the signs as well. I didn't eat a tracker or whatever he ate to give him that information. He should know by now that I have a horrible sense of direction.

"They went east. There are footprints right... there," Phobe says, pointing in the opposite direction I'm looking. Seeing them, only because he pointed them out, I follow them with my eyes and then turn back to Jameson's impression in the mud. Something keeps pulling my attention back to it. Whether it's the fact that I feel bad he suffered here, or my instincts are telling me to look deeper, I'm not sure.

When the reflection of something in the dim light catches my eye, I kneel and dig it out of the deadened grass and soil. It's coated in mud, and the screen is cracked diagonally from one corner to another, but I'd recognize it anywhere. Jameson's tablet. My chest burns from the rage that fills me so suddenly it takes my breath away. With a roar of a thousand dragons, the Magiks leave me all at once. When the noise fades, and the trees stop shaking from the force. When I can think again beyond the rage that's so potent my eyes are watering from holding it back, I look at Phobe. All around him is a crater of destruction. The ground suffered from the release of Magiks, tearing up the dirt and flattening the trees at the edge of the small clearing. But not Phobe, he's completely untouched, with the area around his feet still intact.

My eyes jerk to my stinging hand. Well, shit. The tablet, or what's left of it, is now a completely crushed lump of metal.

"There was a chance that someone could pull things off it. Until you broke it like an idiot, who lets their temper control them." I don't miss the lack of playfulness in his tone. He's not thrilled I lost my head, the snideness hides a bit of annoyance with me. Well, buddy, I'm not either.

"Thanks for your support, dick." I'm already mad, something he's fully aware of. His little prod is deliberate and pisses me off even more. The way I see things, he's as good of a target as any. He can survive it. "All those mystical bullshit powers and you can't tell me where they took him?"

"Follow the footprints."

Without another word I turn and do as he bids, because anything that comes out of my mouth right now will be hateful, meaningless junk, and we both know it. Saying it serves absolutely no purpose.

Eavesdropping on my rant, he says, *'Except to amuse me.'* Sarcastic jerk.

Of course, if he keeps running his mouth, I might say all of it, and not regret a single word later. He chuffs, having heard my thoughts loud and clear. Deciding to simply ignore him—barely—I continue following the two sets of footprints that end on the edge of the parking lot at the entrance. I have to bite the inside of my cheek to keep the rage tamped down again. It's the only way to control the Magiks that want to lash out from me like thousands of shards of glass and destroy everything around me.

It's strange that I'm this irritated, I know it is. Yes, I'm pissed off they took Jameson, but being this angry doesn't make sense. I'll admit, to myself, that I care about Jameson. Something about the nerd made him grow on me, but this level of rage? Something's off.

"So, which way did they go now?" I ask, tossing my hands up. They got into a vehicle, and we can't track that. Well, I can't track that. Looking at Phobe staring at me in his Phobe-ness way tells me that he can't track it either.

"Magiks are shielding them from me," he explains.

"That's fun. What fucking now?" His look would make most folks run in the opposite direction. Technically, I guess I do, because I turn and start walking home, at least, the direction I think is home. A few turns later I find myself on the familiar road leading to the Sidhe.

While I walk, I think and chastise myself for my behavior. What the fuck is wrong with me? I have a temper, I know I do—everyone knows I do, but this… this, is different.

"It's your Magiks. Something is affecting them."

"Like, literally?" I realize the question is stupid as soon as it leaves my mouth. I start walking faster, annoyed with the situation and myself.

"I'm starting to suspect that when the Sidhe was Magikally attacked, something was left behind, a trojan horse of sorts," he muses from close behind me.

"How is that even possible? I'm connected with the Sidhe on the deepest levels. I'd know if someone tampered with it." Right?

"Perhaps, perhaps not." His vagueness is always annoying that I can't deny, but this time it's so frustrating I want to turn around and punch him as hard as I can. "That will be considered foreplay, Iza."

Ignoring his remark, I continue, "How very informative of you, Phobe. I just want to find the fucking nerd and eat the fucking bird." I catch myself stomping, so I slow my pace and take a deep breath.

I'm angrily rhyming shit. This is getting absurd.

"Very." His comment is so dry, that dirt could ignite it.

Stopping, I turn to him and exhale in one long breath. "Since I'm not thinking with any amount of sense right now, any ideas?" Fighting the anger that wants to tear his face to bits, I clench my hands in my pockets. Squeezing until the pain of my claws sinking in my hands frees me from the grasp of what ever the fuck this is.

With a smile that's all sharp teeth, he moves in a blur and the impact of his solid body hitting me takes us both down to the ground. On top of me now, he grinds his pelvis against me, his smile big and bright. I'm so shocked my mouth flies open, only to be filled with his seeking tongue. The taste of copper floods my mouth as his sharp teeth take and invade my mouth with no mercy, the fucker made my lips bleed—but I love it. I grab his head and hold his mouth to mine and meet him bite for bite. The wet, tickling sensation of hot blood dripping down my chin and into the hollow of my throat makes me kiss him harder.

Tearing himself out of my grasp, he moves a few feet from me, panting.

"This anger is… attractive. I want you to rage and slaughter, and then I want to fuck you while you're covered in the blood of your enemies." The fire in his eyes heats and parts of me get hotter as well. "This very second, I want to bury my teeth in your bloody skin and feast on you," he sighs. "This is unacceptable. I may want these things, but not with this kind of… Magikal push."

"It's not all Magiks, Phobe," I say quietly, climbing to my feet. I start pulling the leaves out of my hair. Every moment of that was fucking awesome, his words after—more so. I love the wildness of him because something inside of me responds to it. This though… he's right, something is off, because this level is unusual, even for us.

Especially, at such a bad time. Phobe and I are incredibly attracted to each other, but neither of us is keen on having sex given the current situation. We're not that kind of monsters.

Pushing my mind off sex, rather forcibly, I say, "This bullshit is affecting you, too, isn't it?" He nods. Oh, this isn't good at all. Phobe going batshit? That's how the apocalypse starts.

"Anything that affects you affects me," he states, rather calmly, all things considered.

"Does that mean that it's my behavior versus the actual Magiks?" He nods again. Okay, that helps. "Let's see if we can get home without ending the world, all right?" This time he rolls his eyes at me. For some reason this makes me smile, and as I'm turning back around to start walking again, I see the smirk on his mouth.

The shit did it on purpose.

2

PHOBE

The wash of lustful rage that consumed me earlier is easing, but its not completely gone. I want to grab her and fuck her senseless, and the thought is so tempting that it takes every ounce of willpower I possess to deny it. There's still residual heat between us, that never seems to ease, no matter the circumstances. How can I touch her and not feel it? She's the pulse of life for me.

Watching her walking in front of me, oblivious to her surroundings, amuses me also—which helps with the almost undeniable want of her. I think it also relieves her to know that her emotions are what affect me, not the Sidhe mess. Only her. Our essences are so intermingled that I get the backlash of all that untapped violence inside of her—and I love it. I love the chaos of it, and the rage and the desire to destroy, but she doesn't like destruction in the same way that I do. I destroy things and that's fun to me, but she can't tolerate hurting those she considers innocent. This part of me is something that I need to learn to control around her, or we'll both be in trouble.

I see the flash of her black eyes over her shoulder, as I feel her turbulent emotions through our bond like little shocks of static electricity on my skin. No, WE will not be in trouble, but this world she cares about—the people she cares about will be. I can't be the cause of something that she'll regret in such a way. Not because I care about any of them, but because of the guilt she *will* have if she hurts them. Even inadvertently.

Seeing her hurt in such a way displeases me.

Pushing through the last bits of her shield that I think she's barely trying to maintain, I let her thoughts sink into me. A small crowd is standing outside of the Sidhe. Unsure of what has happened to draw them outside. She braces herself to deal with them. She's not good at explaining things and doesn't like having to do it but pushes herself just the same. In Iza's mind, getting her fingernails pulled out one by one is preferable to dealing with more drama. Her thoughts focus on Michael standing at the front of the crowd.

"We found out where Jameson was taken from. Now, who has enough skill with a computer to see if we can get anything off this?" She holds out the crushed device.

Michael steps forward and takes it from her, looking at her, then at the mess in his hands. "What happened to it?" he asks.

"I was a little mad," is all she says before pushing past the group of people to walk inside.

Nika steps into her path. Without saying a word, Iza firmly pushes her to the side and out of her way. I suspect the dragon wants some type of explanation or reassurance, but she won't be getting either one. Grazing the dragon's thoughts, I see that's not all. She has certain expectations of what Iza should be doing and, in her opinion, Iza shouldn't return home until Jameson is found. There are moments when Nika completely oversteps her place in Iza's life, putting importance on herself that doesn't exist. Her demeanor has pushed her to the sidelines of the ones Iza tolerates but dislikes on principle. It's the dragon's own fault, Iza isn't the type of creature that you can push without her pushing you back.

If you're not strong enough for the pushback...

Following Iza to Jameson's room, I lean against the doorframe, watching her mutter to herself while looking on his computer. Clicking around on it, she starts to type.

"What are you doing?" I ask, curious despite myself.

"He has this blog thing, and people read the dumb shit he posts. I figure we can start here." After a few minutes, she closes it with satisfaction on her face. "I think they'll get my point."

"Did you discover anything else?" I ask, simply to maintain the ruse that her shields are still up. I like playing this game with her, even during times like this.

"Jameson has bad taste in pornography, but other than that, no." She sits back and crosses her arms. "I don't understand any of this. It feels like there's a big, important chess game happening and I have no idea what the rules are."

"Do you even know how to play chess?"

"No, it looked a bit boring to play. Too much like life, really. A cruel parody of how so many leaders sacrifice the little guy, to reach your goals. I didn't need a game to teach me that life lesson." Wiping a hand down her face, she looks up at me. "You're awful quiet about the entire thing," she says, the doubt of my lack of opinion thick in her voice.

"Nothing I say will help. I don't have any more information than you do, yet." I give her an honest answer. I don't think she;'l appreciate me keeping anything from her concerning Jameson. She genuinely cares about the imp... all of them. Something I don't understand, especially in Jameson's case. He betrayed us and sacrificed us, much like the king does to the pawns in the chess game. All to protect himself.

"Would it not be better to carry on and let them keep him?" I don't think she'll agree, but the option needs to be put forward.

"They'll kill him, Phobe." I shrug at her answer.

Jameson isn't an important person in her life. He helps her, yes, but they're not tasks that someone else can't be trained to complete, possibly more effectively. I tell her so, "I don't see the big deal, he's replaceable."

She sighs and says, "Jameson does a lot around here, and he deserves the chance to redeem himself. He's been working so godsdamn hard, and he warrants more than to die at the hands of some slutty vampire who bathes in dog piss."

That raises another question. "Why do you think she's trying to hide her scent?"

"You know," she stands and crosses the room to stop in front of me, "I've been thinking about that. I think because whoever is pulling strings doesn't know what I am, only the who." She walks past me heading towards our room.

Yes, our room, even the Sidhe knows it.

"Shifters have a strong sense of smell, but they don't have one nearly as good as I do. The man who squished poor Jameson into the mud is a shifter. I could smell his pheromones all over the place. He was excited about hurting the chicken man. You know," entering the bedroom she strips off most of her clothes and climbs onto the bed clad only in her underwear. "It's kinda strange they didn't try to mask his scent too."

Distracted by her, I say nothing at first. Even with all the clothes stuffed into her closet, she still prefers being nude. Not that I'm complaining. I sit on the end of the bed, close enough to feel her body heat but far enough away to fight the temptation to touch her. Once I touch her, there are other things that will take precedence in my mind, and all of this will be momentarily forgotten.

"He's expendable." I break the thick silence, giving voice to her suspicions.

The small, *other* part of me doesn't care that she's in turmoil, it cares that it wants her, hungers for her. Right now, turning that part loose on her will cause more harm than good. The majority of what makes up the creature I am does care, at least, about her. I feel nothing concerning the rest of her refugee family. That's the only reason I give a shit about finding the foolish imp who got himself captured, over something so absurd, that even Iza can't make up an excuse for his behavior.

Then again, going by one example of her level of ridiculous, Iza does things like lick wallpaper in the store because she thought it would have a flavor like a movie she watched with 'snozberries.' That's the level that very few creatures achieve. I catch myself almost smiling. She had turned to me with the oddest look on her face and told me in no uncertain terms, that the wallpaper did not taste like berries of any kind, and that TV lied, then proceeded to lick it again to be certain.

"What are you smiling about?" she demands.

Letting the smile that is tickling my lips break free I answer, "Snozberries."

Covering her face with her hand, she peeks at me from between her fingers and says, "I feel like it was a perfectly acceptable mistake. It looked like real fruit, like in the movie."

"That's why you are hiding your face?" I tease. Her tongue pokes out between her fingers.

Dropping her hand, her face grows serious as she asks, "Why did they pick him? Out of all the people, why him?" The frustration in her voice makes it deeper, huskier, and her eyes flash black.

Even with her obvious distress, I decide to answer her honestly. "He was the easiest to trick out of the people in the Sidhe. Most of the others are too smart to fall for such a ploy." Not surprised that it doesn't take the frown off her face. "Iza, at least it's not one of your heathens."

"Still doesn't make it right. Jameson isn't very... strong, Phobe. I'm not sure how he'll handle this. It might break him completely." Her reasoning surprises me.

"You're worried about his mental health?" I can't help but ask in surprise.

"His entire health, because they'll probably kill him. Especially if he opens his mouth." In that, she isn't wrong. Jameson talking often makes people want to kill him.

In my perspective, Jameson is expendable, and always will be. Compared to her, all of them are. In this case, she can recover from his rather quickly, I'm pleased they took him instead of one of the children. When it comes to them, I'm not sure she could recover, ever. She's formed an attachment for them that nearly touches the strength of the one between the two of us... she smiles at me, and I know how hard their deaths would hit her. Hers would make me inconsolable. I can admit it at this moment, at least to myself.

The temperature of the room drops, and she doubles over, a hand pressing on her stomach with all the color leached out of her face. The backlash of something hitting her through the Sidhe wafts through our bond. I pull her onto my lap. There's nothing I can do to ease this pain. Expanding my darkness out, I look for a culprit, but there's none. A residual taste that's similar to what attacked her before.

The trojan is showing itself.

"Someone... someone just died." The disbelief in her voice is enough to make me pause, and before I can peek into her thoughts, she's off my lap and up on her feet. Attempting, unsuccessfully, to pull on her clothes while trying to walk at the same time. Grabbing her waist while walking behind her, I steady her to keep her from ending up face first on the floor. Other than this insignificant thing, I'm powerless to help. This is something between her and the Sidhe, something that has already passed, an enemy I can't see to fight. I can sense things sometimes, but I'm only getting echoes of what has already come to pass.

Which gives me no direction to go, no intruder to look out for. When this happened before, I could sense the attack. It was blatant and a show of Magikal muscle by the perpetrator, so I thought at the time. Now, I'm starting to doubt that assumption. The blatant attack was potentially a misdirection, and I fell for it.

I suspect Light, but I can't prove it. Once upon a time, the three of us were equally matched. There would be no hesitation about confronting him. That was a long time ago. I'm not the creature I once was, not yet. One can't replenish all the power lost in a thousand years in a few months. Not at the slow rate, I'm feeding. I'll start feeding more, building my strength. This ensures a confrontation between the two of us, one I need to be prepared for.

My gut tells me he's the one behind all of it. Going after him, if I can even find him, will set off a war that I don't think these creatures can survive. That Iza can't survive. For a thousand years I've wallowed in slavery, my power slowly being starved out of me. In this physical form, I'm also incredibly limited.

Until I am once again at my full strength, I can't take him on.

Unlike me, he wasn't spelled into a physical form and retains his true form and all the abilities that come with it. He's Light incarnate, and it allows him to possess others. I can't hurt him unless I can catch him in a mortal form. In his true form, there's nothing to sink my claws into. It's very frustrating, almost as much as the woman in front of me.

I truly believe that this was always meant to happen, Light and Darkness going against each other. There has never been any form of affection or relationship between us.

The only one who ever shows that is Life. He likes to be sentimental and call us brothers, and I've fallen into that habit and used the term. But we're not even remotely close to being related. We're merely three beings who became aware of existence at the same time. All with different powers, purposes, and strengths. I abused mine, all three of us did and do. Unlike Light and myself, Life, at least, sticks to some semblance of moral code.

Light's only code is to be worshipped by all.

I need fucking facts to move forward, Life on our side is the only way to win this as things stand. For that, I'm at a loss. Perhaps Iza knows something I haven't worked out? Snooping around inside of her head, I find that, although she felt the death of an imp she doesn't know the cause, either. She isn't happy about it, and as we walk through the hallways that the Sidhe creates for her, her mood deteriorates even more.

Val is the one who died, the imp who was sick before. One she doesn't know well but has a bit of a soft spot for because of what happened to his family. This likely means the others who were sick are in danger as well. The sickness was the planting of the seed, and the imp's death is the bloom.

The out of control moments of her Magiks are possibly another part of it, but I'm starting to suspect something else might be the culprit.

First, I need to calm Iza down, because the anger that's driving her is steadily building stronger. She can be very emotional at times, but this level of anger is uncommon for her and will make her act out in senseless ways. It doesn't matter that I like the darkness that's alive and showing its teeth inside of her. Iza always pulls a visceral reaction out of me—this amplifies it, significantly. The deep, primal part of me wants to encourage it. The part of me that's brought out by Iza wants to dissuade it, protect her from the consequences of it.

A conundrum, this war between two fragments of my personality.

The plan I settled on, is to find a way to reach both goals. I haven't found a way yet, but I won't stop searching until I do. Both of the creatures I am… all of the creatures I am, love her—no, it's not simply love, it goes beyond that. So far beyond that even I don't know where it ends.

Iza is everything to me.

"Why do I have a feeling you're having a conversation with yourself about me?" Coming out of my thoughts at her question, I look down into her eyes. She's standing in front of me, her arms crossed. The anger temporarily banked inside of her, raging behind a mental wall. This shows exactly how strong she is, and I like it, too.

Although, her knowing I'm thinking about her is suspicious. Studying her active thoughts, she's incredibly perceptive at times. I check in case she has suddenly developed mind-reading abilities. She hasn't and is merely showing how deep her mind can truly be.

Opting to stick with the truth I say, "I'm trying to decide whether to help you control the anger or let it out." Both of her eyebrows shoot up to her hairline in surprise. It amuses me that, given all that she has gone through with me, I can still surprise her.

"I'm used to your brutal honesty, but that's honest even for you." Her eyes sharpen on me. "Which one do you think is the right choice?" She's seriously asking me my opinion on this subject after what I said?

Squashing the small flutter of flattery in my stomach, I answer, "There isn't a right choice in this situation. You're a creature of the dark, a living breathing representation of it. Letting that part of you out doesn't make you evil. You are what you are. It's why I don't understand your strange concern about being reviled by these people."

A strangely moral one that has no place in her life. She won't go on some murderous rampage if she embraces what she is, at least not against the creatures she has cared for. The masses of Light Fey, though, would be in danger of her doing exactly that. Not only would they become her fodder, but she would also unleash… oh, now I see. It isn't herself she is worried for.

"Control. We will teach you to have it until we find out what is causing your sudden spikes in anger. Is this acceptable?" I offer.

The whole asking her permission thing is new, but in my experiences with her, it's also effective. Even if it's mostly a placation. She responds more positively to requests than orders. Unless we're sparring, that's a different situation entirely, or naked. She likes me being bossy then.

"Did you just think about sex? Because I'm feeling the sex vibe rolling off you." Her anger banks a little more at her question. I shrug. Nothing that I say will make me look like any less of an asshole. Sighing at me she continues, "Come on, the least I can do is find out why he died. His family is upset, and there are no answers to give them. He was watering the lawn and just fell over dead." She turns and starts walking again. "Feyrie doesn't die like that, we all know this."

I say nothing. This is her way of digesting the information. My talking will only delay her from getting what she needs to get out. There's a term for it here in this human world, a sounding board.

"The only conclusion I can come up with, without knowing any facts, is that this shit that killed him is whatever started when he got sick the first time. Like a spell that was hidden or something." See? Her brain will always bring her around to where she needs to be. "Which I'm guessing you already know since you're so freaking quiet about it?" I shrug once again.

Giving me a quick look over her shoulder, in annoyance, she turns back around and goes silent. She's thinking of things I won't like. That horrid wall of blue, singing things goes up in her mind, and I have to work on fighting my way past it. I always get through, and she knows I will, eventually, and when she does things like this it makes me work even harder at it.

Pausing outside of the quarters that reek of grief and disbelief, she takes a deep breath, preparing herself. Iza isn't any more prepared to deal with the mess on the other side of that door than I am. We're not built that way. She's simply better at faking it.

When she opens the door, the sounds of wailing fill the hallway is almost enough to make me turn around away and walk off. If I didn't have to look at the body, I would. Logically, I understand their high emotion, losing Iza would give me that kind of reaction, but the continuing noise, I don't understand that.

'It seems a little... dramatic,' I say, satisfied that I said the right word.

'Everyone handles their grief differently. You went and dragged me out of death land, remember?'

'I did not wail like a child as I did it,' I defend, unable to deny that I did fetch her from there.

'Jameson said you growled a lot. We'll count that as your version of wailing.' She has a point with that, and I don't like it.

I feel like there's more that she wants to say but Val's sister, Mira, falls into Iza's arms, and the noise starts again in earnest. Iza looks at me, clearly uncomfortable despite the front she is putting on and pats Mira on the shoulder. Moving past, relieved it's not me that has to deal with it, I look down at the blue-lipped body of Val.

Delicately, my shadows search him, looking for any type of Magikal signature. Finding a small trail of Light Magiks, I latch onto it, while trying to definitively decipher the source. They're strong, whomever they are. Strong enough to not leave any trace of their actual identity, I still memorize the feel of the Magiks. Even if they can hide their Magikal signature, everyone has a unique taste to their Magiks.

This one I shall remember, and although it feels slightly of Light, I can't say with surety it's Light's Magiks. Which makes everything more complicated. Turning away from the corpse, I give one last, slightly sympathetic look to Iza—who's still holding up the weeping woman—and leave the room. I can't tolerate the noise any longer. Iza's patience is wearing thin as well, but she feels guilty for it. I don't.

'Any idea if this is connected to Jameson?' she asks me.

'More than likely it is related,' I pause, debating on how to broach the rest of what needs to be said. Decision made I continue, 'You could just let them keep him and move on. As you said, he isn't an important piece on the board.'

'He still fucking matters, Phobe!'

Her anger is a blast of heat through our connection. I won't tell her this, but I like these reactions from her, too. 'I understand that you don't care about these people... and I don't expect you to, but you need to understand that I do!'

'His absence is causing you so much pain that you can't let him go?' I ask, knowing that although she cares, it's not much, or used not to be. His death would be filled with more guilt than of grief, but she's acting as if he means more than I deduced.

'He deserves better,' she says more quietly. The guilt speaks.

'In that, you and I don't agree. I'll see what I can find out while you deal with that mess.' There's nothing I can do to help her in that situation. I can, however, look for information concerning Jameson. Even though I still don't think him worth the effort.

I hope that the imp understands that anything I do is for her —not him.

I hope they all understand this, and if not, it's their error.

NOT SURE WHO TO start with, I pick the closest one. Knox is playing alone on his video game when I find him. Briefly, he looks up when I sit on the armrest of the couch.

"What do you want?" he asks, surly as he usually is lately.

"Why has your behavior been so strange?" There's no reason to beat around the bush. Sometimes to get the best answer you ask the source, and in this case, I can kill two birds with one stone. Iza is concerned about his behavior and, using this moment, I can potentially find out if it should concern her.

He looks up at me, his eyebrows drawn together in a scowl, and I watch the emotions chase themselves across his face. Hurt, anger, love, jealousy, and doubt, in that order. At this specific moment, this child isn't under the influence of Magiks, but merely having human-like reactions—insecurity being the predominant one. It's annoying that I can't read this child, and it's suspicious, but for now, I'll tuck it away. This insecurity could be the cause of all his angst concerning Iza that he's too young to express correctly.

"Since you came here, she's been different," he says after a few minutes of silence.

"You're jealous of my place in her life?" I ask, confident his answer will be yes. After staring at me, with that scowl still on his face, he nods.

"That's unnecessary." Now, how would Iza deal with this? Clearing my throat, I take a guess, "You'll always have your special place in her life, Knox." He stares at me a moment, scrunching up his nose. I have no idea if I said the right thing to comfort the child, I'm not even sure why I'm trying to. Iza's influence on me is showing itself, which makes me want to smile and because of that I fight its appearance on my face, but... I do accept it.

The silly woman has her claws in deep, but not just in me.

"So, she isn't gonna leave us because you're here?" His question makes me pause. I know the thoughts going through Iza's head because of Jameson's abduction, and one of them is how special this child is to her.

"She won't stop loving you because I'm here." That will work for now. I have no idea how else to express that without giving away what her intentions are, the ones that haven't even solidified in her mind. This is an awkward moment for me, too. Until Iza came into my life, I can't imagine being in this kind of situation. My solution would have been to simply walk off—or worse.

"Okay, I guess," he mumbles then lifts his eyes up to hold mine, "If you hurt her, I'll kill you." His green eyes flash as he says this, and it becomes increasingly hard to keep the smile off my face. His fierce defense of her makes me a little proud.

"I shall keep that in mind, little shifter." As we spoke, my shadows checked him for any trace of Light Magiks. There's nothing. I think, more than likely, that the 'weird' stuff Iza has been worried about with Knox, is this wash of human emotions going through him. He's insecure about his place in her life and jealous of my presence. He's probably jealous of anyone else who holds her attention for any length of time. In this particular case, there aren't any Magiks involved at all. This will make her feel slightly better, that Knox has been moved farther down the suspect list.

The other shifter, Peter, walks into the room and I give him the same thorough once-over I gave Knox, nothing on him either. There's also nothing stopping me from reading his mind.

Knowing this does not stop the surprising question that pops out of my mouth, "Why did you tell Knox that Iza won't love him anymore?" Iza's influence, absolutely, but the question has already been spoken, and there's a curiosity to have the answer there.

"Everybody leaves. My parents left me and his parents left him." A traumatized child's logic, and for him potentially true. Although more than likely his parents didn't leave him willingly, shifters like to murder each other.

"Not everyone leaves, boy. I think you're speaking from a bad place in your life." Before I can catch myself, I add, "Perhaps it's time for you to change that perception?" Sensing no Magiks from this child either, I turn and leave the room before I can say anything else out of character for me.

"See, I told you so, Peter." Knox's words follow me out into the hallway.

At least this uncomfortable encounter will let me provide a modicum of relief for Iza. The thought of him being hollowed out by possession tore her up inside, pulling on a well of grief so deep inside of her that even I can't see the end of it. I can't help but be slightly relieved myself, especially knowing that I would be the one to have to destroy the child if it were him. Although the truth of it is, that it's not his death that concerns me, it's her reaction to it.

'Your little shifter is more than likely not the culprit.' As an afterthought I add, *'His friend either. In some ways, Knox is incredibly mature for a child, mostly because of what he's experienced. In other ways, he's every bit his age*

and relationships with anyone fall into that category. Be reassured that it's because of these things that he's acting as he is.' Iza is strong, but I think a bit of reassurance is necessary at times with her, it balances her out. She doesn't respond, but I feel her relief. Perhaps she's upset with me for abandoning her to the tender mercies of the grieving women? In this circumstance, better her than I. My patience and understanding of such things aren't at the level of hers. In these cases, it's always better for them if it's her.

She might also still be annoyed that I told her to leave Jameson to his fate. I almost ask and then decide against it. My opinion hasn't changed, to me, he isn't worth the effort she'll put forth to find him because she will find him—one way or another.

Ruthie and Michael are my next stop. The two of them are always together, lately. I've determined it's because they're in a relationship of some kind. One they have yet to admit to anyone, which is stupid because everyone knows. I'm not sure they know what kind of relationship they're in either, or why they hide it. There are a lot of hormones, and awkward faces and they constantly smell of discomfort. The room they're in reeks of it all, so much so that I blatantly cover my mouth with my hand.

After a few, brief questions to them, I conclude there's nothing to worry about—except a possible pregnancy, there's some physical interaction going on between the two. Which isn't my concern, because if that happens, Iza will strangle them for their foolishness and make them do the adult thing of raising their child. Something I'm sure they're both aware of for their sake.

Systematically, I spend the night checking all of those that I suspect and then others that I didn't suspect but check for the sake of checking. At the end of the mind-numbingly awful task, I realize I'm only missing a few. The main one being Nika, who's doing the wailing thing in her room, which I gladly leave her to. I can always check on her later when I don't have to deal with… that mess. Jameson, who isn't here and can't be responsible, unless he's the slyest creature I've ever encountered, and that's impossible. No one can fake that level of inanity.

Circling the Sidhe, I find myself outside, alone. Correction, almost alone, the unwanted company is close by. I choose to ignore it and focus on the night around me. The air is cold enough that my breath steams, but I don't feel the chill against my skin. Finding myself enjoying the silence, I look up at the moon shining like a silver coin, surrounded by pieces of glass in the darkness of the sky. I watch the snowflakes fall haphazardly around me, backlit by the light of the moon in an ethereal moment in time. Even I have to admit that it's rather eye-catching.

"It's strange to see you admiring something as simple as falling snow." I tense, not sure why Life has chosen to show himself to me. I figured he was going to continue to lurk about. "If not for her," he speaks of Iza, and I don't like it, but say nothing. "I'm not sure you'd feel anything emotionally, ever." This is the point I silently wish for him to shut up. Of course, being the windbag that he is, he continues, "Don't get me wrong, you had a certain... curiosity, for the things you made, but never any type of attachment. It's nice to see you love something as much as you love her." I lower my gaze from the view I was enjoying as he crosses into my line of vision, his hands clasped behind his back. The persona he's wearing is that of a wizened old man with a long white beard. This form is a favorite one of his and complete fiction.

"I also have to be honest here, the depth of it scares me a little, too. It will make the things to come even harder on her." He says it with a genial smile on his face, but he isn't everything he proclaims himself to be. In this case, he seems to have a soft spot for Iza, which is strange, to say the least, but beneficial to me as well.

"The prophet has spoken again, brother, and shortly I will come to you and offer my help. Please—for Iza's sake—accept it." In a swirl of snow, he's gone, leaving me standing there full of questions and the strong urge to rip his beard off.

Something bad is coming. He could have simply told me and let me stop it from happening, or at least be more prepared for. Unless telling me will make things worse, something that's entirely possible. I've seen it happen before, that's the biggest downside of knowing the future. Messing with it always changes something, something Life does often but carefully. Reluctantly, I admit that he took a risk telling me this much.

Instead of cursing him in my head, I mull over the brief conversation. He's right, I love her, but it's more than that simple fleeting emotion. I'll feel this way for her to infinity. Nothing can stop me from wanting her, being with her. Nothing WILL stop me. He isn't wrong. I'll do whatever it takes to keep her safe.

Now, I need to find out who's first.

3

IZA

I'M NOT THE LEAST BIT SURPRISED HE RAN LIKE A CHICKEN AND LEFT ME to deal with all this emotional stuff. It does help that he checked in on Knox. Even pissed off, for whatever reason—although, I'm starting to doubt I have a legit one—Phobe's reassurance about Knox took a weight off me that I didn't know was that heavy. He didn't say that it was zero concern, but the fact that he said anything at all about it makes me have faith that it's not Knox. Here's hoping that my faith isn't misplaced.

Honestly, I'm not sure how well I'd handle something happening to the little butthead. I was starting to think he was in danger and that I wouldn't be able to save him. I can't protect them from some sneaky, possessor type. I have no idea how to fight one of those. I'm not even sure you can when it wears the face of people you love.

Now, I know Knox is *probably* not the one being possessed, but I don't consider him safe, we're Feyrie—safe isn't a way of life we understand. In our world, there's always danger lurking about. Safety is a luxury that most creatures never experience. I'll cross my fingers that it'll be the kind of danger I can see—the kind I can fight—and if I can't, Phobe can. Well, if he will, he pretty much does what he wants to. I'm not egotistical enough to think I tamed the beast.

For me, he might fight anything, my gut tells me so. I would for him, and I'm pretty sure we both feel the same way. My stomach contracts with that fuzzy lovey mushy crap feeling, my nose wrinkles and nausea tempers the initial freak out about it. Gods, I've turned into a sop, but my lips briefly lift into a smile, and I accept it with a mental shrug. I move on simply because it's the truth and I'm not ashamed of it. A little disgusted with myself perhaps, but not ashamed.

Speaking of the pain in the ass... Phobe knows a lot more than I do, about *everything* typically. Sometimes it feels like him being a know-it-all pain in the ass is one of his superpowers. There are times he doesn't like to share until AFTER something happens, or he goes off and takes care of it himself without talking about it at all. I don't expect him to suddenly be a conversationalist, but I know I wish he'd stop being so... him and tell me shit. It's hard to deal with things if you have no idea they're happening.

Of course, things like what he did with Knox, being the exception. Doing nice things doesn't come naturally to him, so I can see why he didn't say anything. It's also one of the reasons I didn't tease him about it. Awkwardly patting Mira, who has a death grip on my shirt, I admit—I'm not big on lying, not even to myself—I'm not that great at 'sharing' either, but I'm learning, and I'm a lot better at it than Phobe is.

Not that it's enough to brag about to anyone but myself.

A quick shake of my head brings me out of my grouchy thoughts, and back to the situation at hand. There's only so much of this I can take, and whether I'm an asshole or not, I'm at my limit. I pat Mira, after wrangling her into bed, with help, and leave her in the capable hands of the women standing around the room with worried looks on their faces.

Once outside the door, I take several deep breaths of fresh air that aren't coated in grief and relax a little. It bothers me to see her in pain, and I want to help her, but I don't know what to do about it. This part of the 'normal' grieving process, is foreign to me. The tears and the emotional pain, I can understand—it's the wailing that makes me at a loss on what to say or how to act, so I let her cry all over me until she wore herself out. I'm pretty sure I didn't say a single word to her.

What can I say? Other than that, 'Oh, hey I'll find those responsible and make a belt for you out of their intestines.' Picturing it in my head I smile. Yes, I might, in fact, do just that. This is a way I can help. I'll find out who did this and kill them.

I don't feel guilty about being glad that I finally get to escape. I did my duty to the best of my ability for her. Now it's time for me to move forward with other things. Val's body has been moved, by the Sidhe, to what I'm calling the 'funeral chamber.' It sounded a bit less morbid than the morgue, so I went with it. There are ceremonies that some Feyrie practice for their dead, imps are no exception. This will allow her the time to do so. She has a room full of imp women ready to meet her every need, so she can gather her composure and complete the traditions. She is beside herself, and I get it—mostly, because if I lost the kids or… Phobe—I'm not sure I wouldn't sound like a dying whale afterward, too, but I tend to handle things a tad different from that. Typically, I go looking for something to kill because that makes me feel better.

Thinking about killing someone makes my thoughts move, unerringly, onto Jameson. Now that the ridiculous anger banked itself, compliments of a brew that Arista subtly handed me when I asked about dragon heat, I can think more clearly. I completely understand why Phobe doesn't think that putting any effort into finding Jameson is worth it. A few months ago, I'd have agreed with him, but that was before I came here, because Jameson helps with *everything* in the Sidhe. The shit-head goes out of his way to help others, too. He's surprisingly quiet about it, but he does it. This is the only part of his life where he isn't yelling, 'Hey, look at me.' He's self-conscious about being helpful, the idiot. It's applaudable and helps me work on forgiving him, a little anyhow, for tattling to the magistrate like a scared schoolboy.

I can't say good things about the rest of the shit he does.

I mean, come on, he did go chasing some unknown woman's boobs like a moron. On top of that, he managed to get captured and is being used as bait in a lame ass trap. When it comes down to it, because of what he does to help those here, he deserves for me to try and find him. Even if I end up choking the life out of his ass for being that dense.

Phobe appears out of nowhere right in front of me. The only reason I don't punch him in the face is that he does it so often that I'm used to it.

Sneaky bastard.

"You think very loudly when you're upset."

"Well, you're part of the reason I'm upset, so you deserve my loud thoughts." I start walking, and we fall into step together while passing through the hallways that form, taking us away from the others. The Sidhe is giving us space to talk or argue because my gut is telling me that an argument is coming. Maybe it's the puckered look of his mouth, the one that says his thoughts are distasteful, or maybe it's the static aura around him. When he pauses and puts his hands on my upper arms, my stomach churns.

Fuck.

"Life stopped by," he says. Do what? "The Life," he elaborates. Oh, now I get it.

"And?" I ask, in an absolute shitty tone. For a split second his eyes brighten, he isn't happy with it either. I grab hold of the connection between us and watch it, feel it with everything I can.

Phobe is reluctant to tell me something.

"He said that we're going to need his help in the future." As he speaks his tone warms up.

"Needing his help is never good." And it's not comforting either. Life has a pocket prophet and likes to meddle. Look what he did in my life. "Can't it change things or whatnot if you fiddle with it?" That'd be just fucking great. We try to stop it and make it worse, whatever it is. Which makes me ask even though I shouldn't and had managed to avoid asking for the first minute. "What did he say?"

Phobe's head twists unnaturally to the side. A peek at how nonhuman his form is, as he studies me in the predatory way he has about him. I'm learning that it usually means he's gauging my reactions to something, or that he wants to do me. It can go either way. Although right now I'd prefer the do me part.

"I like that thought," he comments, stepping closer to me.

The warmth of him encompasses me like a comfortable blanket, banking the chaos inside of me that's tearing me apart. Like a greedy bee always in the honey, the familiar smell of him draws me closer to his body. Only he can give me that feeling of safety that all creatures crave but don't admit to wanting. The softness of his shirt under my cheek is a brief relief as my eyes drift shut. I exhale long and deep, and for this second in time with his heartbeat a steady drum of comfort in my ear, I completely relax.

Phobe's planet-sized presence serves as the world's greatest dampener. The mess with Jameson and the random deaths are pushed back, but just far enough to give me some breathing room. Leave it to him to know what I need when I don't even know what I need sometimes. I kind of like it.

Like most good things in life, the moment of peace is short and sweet. The question that sent me off the mental cliff resurfaces. Why did Life tell us something bad is coming, but not what that bad thing is? Exactly how bad is this supposed future going to be?

"I'm not sure it's something we can change without making it worse." Phobe's hand slides up my back to press me more fully against him. "It's a sound assumption that he didn't tell me specifically what it is because making it worse is a higher probability. Because of this fact, I shall be more vigilant, because I think it is all we can do right now."

"I feel like there's a big, fucking conspiracy going on all around me, and I have no idea what the fuck it is or who's doing it." My voice is muffled against his shoulder and sounds a bit whiny. I'm completely annoyed with myself for it but can't seem to stop it from creeping in.

"There will always be conspiracies when it comes to people of power. That's something you need to accept and get over." He sounds so fucking matter-of-fact, the jerk. I bite his shoulder and laugh when he tenses in that sexy way that pulls at my gut. Biting isn't a punishment for my dear Phobe, he loves being bitten or vice versa. Fact is, I like it too… when he does it.

Instead of giving him the reaction he wants, I say, "You're always so blunt." Which I happen to like about him, most of the time. I pause and then say, "You know communication is the key to a good relationship? The magazines and talk shows say so."

"Then it is fortunate we are so good at... communicating." Laughing, I wrap my arms around his waist. Although, he means that in a completely sexual way, it's the truth in other ways as well. We are good at communicating, too good sometimes.

"Does this mean you'll stop looking for the imp?" At his question, a fresh wave of anger shoots through me all over again. The potion has worn off already. Great, just great. Gritting my teeth, I fight through the almost overwhelming feeling of it, careful to keep my mouth shut. I need to find out why it's doing this shit.

"Why?" I get out between my teeth, looking up into his face—seeing dark amusement. He's completely serious, but he also knew what my reaction would be too.

"We need to discover the reason for your current issue, Iza because it puts you in danger. That's more important than worrying about an imp who was foolhardy enough to get himself captured." He says it so reasonably that it makes me automatically want to agree, but I don't because he's wrong. Jameson matters. He might not be someone I love or someone I think about often, but he matters, and because of that I'll keep looking.

"I'm still going to find Jameson," I say, stepping out of his embrace. "I know you don't care about anyone, but I do. I have to fucking care because it's built into my godsdamn brain!" Biting down on the stupid words that would've followed and been nothing but worthless, mean shit, I grit out, "The problem that's wrong with me, is my heat cycle." Turning away from him, I say, "I think you need to stay away from me for a while." Fighting the temptation to punch him in the face, I stomp off. I know I'm overreacting, but no matter how loudly I yell at myself in my head... I'm still irrationally pissed off at him and the world in general.

I want to scream, and break things and the Magiks inside of me is damn near encouraging it. I'm acting like a moody teenager. My goal is to find Arista and ask some more questions, maybe get some more of that potion. This is the absolute worst time for this to happen to me! While we were in the room with Mira, Arista calmly told me she smelled it on me and as a female dragon she'd know. It explains all the symptoms. The moodiness, the sudden bursts of anger, and the increase in my already substantial appetite are all warning signs that I should've picked up on right away. With everything going on it didn't enter my foggy brain, and it's been a while since I had one, years in fact, so I had almost forgotten what it was like.

My heat times tends to lead to violence, however—the one good thing for everyone around me—it's short-lived. Five days at the most, but it's not painless, especially for other people. I don't bleed like humans do, I never have, instead I go into a hormonal cycle that's all dragon. My libido multiplies by two million, and I get a lot more aggressive. Something that would've been nice to know about growing up, but the whole suppressed memories thing kept me from knowing what my mother told me as a child.

I'm incredibly violent when I have it, all female dragons are violent, but I'm more so. My mother told me that when in heat, dragons put out pheromones, to draw members of the opposite sex to them—like any creature that has similar physiology—but they'll only mate with the one they deem strong enough. Unless they love someone, then there's no issue about choice, the lover always wins. Mom said you must be the strongest to win the love of a dragon.

Secretly, I think that being strong bit is for no other reason than to survive the heat cycles. If a female dragon doesn't want to mate with you, no matter how strong you are—yeah, she'll kill you. As far as mine goes, I don't think I put off the pheromones because I've never had creatures lining up to mate with me when I hit my heat. They run from me, sure, but running to me? Never.

At least now, I have an answer to one problem and have probably added more, but we'll work on those when they happen. I know how to sort out some of my anger issues when it comes to the heat, I need to eat lots of food and beat something up. That always seems to help the anger, hitting things—even if it's a wall. Maybe I can get Phobe to—

The pain that pulls my chest tight and makes me feel like I'm falling off a cliff drops me against the wall. I know what that feeling means now. Someone else is dead, the thread that once held their presence, their vitality is empty and cold. This time there's one glaring difference, Rido's—a dragon— death was violent. The force of it traveled through the web before his heart stopped, I can still feel the echoes of it. I can't see what he saw before he died like you know—his killer, but the Magiks are still whispering, and the Sidhe is singing to me.

Fuck.

Pushing myself to my feet, I run towards the source of that ache burrowing into my heart. Not stopping to tell anyone, I bolt past without explanation. There's no time and no point, them coming along changes nothing. When Adriem appears out of the shadows ahead of me and then falls in behind me, I'm a bit surprised. He's a lurker that one, but normally it's his mother and father who are right up my ass in situations like this.

No, wait... *normally* it's someone else, but I told that person to fuck off. Grimacing at my stupid decision to do that, I move faster. The sense of urgency pulls me towards the lake, that's a shimmery blur as I run by it, but I still see how the moonlight is reflecting off it and find myself a little sad that on such a beautiful night a good person like Rido died. He's kind of...no—he was kind of a simple person. Sweet, liked to smile a lot—not a violent bone in his body. The other dragons from the enclave teased him for his nature. I admired it because he was the type of person I'll never be.

Pushing against the sadness of it all, I make myself think of other things. I can grieve later. This is not the time to mourn the loss, because it's a grave one, but its time to see what I can find out about who killed him. Maybe even why, there needs to be a why, Rido wasn't one of the Feyrie who got sick before.

The first thing I need to do is see the body because this time the intent behind the death felt different from before. Anger was present this time. There was so much of it involved that I can almost smell it. As far as I can tell, none of it was coming from Rido—at least not in the beginning, he got angry eventually. Gentle or not, he was still a dragon. It came too late to do much, but he didn't go down gently. It's why I'm hoping that maybe there are some clues to the identity of the attacker. Something blocked me from knowing anything else, and that something is incredibly strong.

That possibility worries me because if whatever is working against me is stronger than Phobe, we've lost before we even began. I can run my mouth all I want, and I'll not back down, but I know without one shred of doubt that Phobe can hand my ass to me without breaking a sweat.

Someone stronger than him? Yeah, I'm fucked, we all are.

4

PHOBE

THROUGH HER, I FEEL IT, ANOTHER DEATH, A RATHER NASTY ONE THIS time. Iza is shocked about it, but it doesn't surprise me. I was expecting more. This is the beginning of a war, and in war there are always casualties. But, for her sake, it concerns me, when normally it wouldn't. This second death strays from continuing on the same path of Val's death, which I know was a result of the initial attack.

This one is different, related but not at the same time. There's no doubt in my mind that it's connected. There will be more, probably many, I'm guessing all the ones who were ill before. Rido was not one of the sick ones. Usually, a death like this is because they saw something, that's a reason I would kill someone unprovoked.

This attacker, because I think it's the same person, has no particular reverence for anyone. No one is safe, several children were ill in the initial wave, and if Rido's death is hitting her this hard, I can't even imagine a child's. I suspect she's starting to realize it, too, but right now she's angry with me, and considering this I'll wait to comment. Once she's ready to speak with me again, without being emotionally overwrought, then we'll discuss it.

Keeping my distance, I follow her, not caring if she knows. Adriem is following her as well. Pretty sure she is aware of it, I saw her tense when he fell into step behind her. I'm not sure that Adriem is aware, he's focused completely on her.

Her body language isn't giving her thoughts away either. She's better at controlling her expressions than she realizes. Her emotions, not so much. Anger, cold and biting with fangs of ice, are dug in and seething in the bond between us. The realization of why she is having it is… entertaining to eavesdrop on. The options she's not considering, are as well.

The smell of her anger mixed with pheromones, wafting through the air towards me—even at this distance, touches the monster I am at heart. Touches it and arouses it. For now, I have control, but it's not something I can guarantee. Iza manages to pull me to places I can't always stop going. Fraying my control like no other creature in existence, especially now. The exception this time is that the result will be incredibly pleasurable. I won't mourn losing control in that regard.

Her little love bite is only the beginning, and she has no one to blame but herself.

The smell of blood hits me first and pulls me out of my thoughts. Those more pleasant thoughts, I'll revisit later. This situation needs my full attention if I want to get any answers. She zigzags all over the place like a blind hummingbird with her emotions high and bleeding out through her aura.

Moving close enough to get a whiff of her shampoo, but distant enough to remain unseen, I watch her through the bushes. As Iza looks around her, her eyes turn pitch black, shining with the Magiks fueling her rage. Stepping carefully, she circles the torn-up area where the air and ground still smell of death. Kneeling, she touches a dark, wet spot—blood—and looks around at the rest of the small puddles of it strung throughout the mess. Absently she rubs it between her fingers. With a frown, she scrubs her hand down her pant leg, and then stands and walks towards a tree that's bent and broken from the violence that happened here.

The victim fought, hard, but his opponent was not beatable.

Unfortunately, there's no body. Bizarre that they took it, but perhaps it's part of their game. I know from the smells around us that the dead Feyrie was a male, one of the dragons to be precise, Rido, she called him. The torn green scales strewn on the ground are evidence that he managed to take on his natural form. The damage is another. There are claw marks on the trees and large gouges on the ground.

Walking around the clearing, barely out of sight, I study the path of destruction. I have no idea why he was out here, perhaps taking a nightly walk or he was tricked out here. Whomever it was he trusted, initially. The violence starts in the center of the clearing, leading me to believe that he was surprised after encountering the person. The trees towards the center are torn from their roots and overturned then trod upon. Fire scars the ground and broken trees. His opponent somehow escaped injury, the only blood in the clearing is the dragon's. The only claw marks are the dragon's.

In fact, there is no sign of the other attacker at all. No smell, no footprints, no claw marks, nothing. *How odd.* Turning towards Iza, I attempt to enter her mind again and find myself blocked. Frustrated, I start to whittle down her shields. She knows I'm trying to get in and will eventually. I have once already since she tried to shut me out. I think she likes to make me work for it.

"Are you okay?" Adriem's voice breaks the silence of the clearing.

I skim over his active thoughts and catch myself torn between amusement and annoyance. I think Iza would call this a case of 'bad timing.' Adriem has a crush on her. Everyone is aware of it—even Iza. The extent of it is something I don't think anyone is aware of.

Iza already has a mate, and I don't share well with others. However, if anyone else were to appeal to her, it might indeed be the rebellious Nightmare. My eyes sharpen on him, taking in his entire person. He's young—for a Nightmare—and she likes the grungy types, this is something she's told me before, but… I don't think that she reciprocates his feelings.

Iza is angry and—what is the human word? Pondering the various words that come to mind, I settle on, hormonal. That's the most common term they use to describe women during their period. At least, the humans I have consumed called it that. I suspect that term might piss her off and that's enough to keep me from saying it. The last thing I want to do is upset her further. I am… uncomfortable with her being distant like this. The anger I can handle, and I enjoy inciting it to her at times, but her anger usually burns hot and fast.

Not this cold shit that makes me feel… weird.

At some point, very soon, she'll hit the peak of her woman's time and the hint that her scent is giving me will be a full-blown invitation. Finally, something else will take the place of the anger. I'm not sure whether I'm looking forward to it more or dreading it a little. It's not the violence, I love that about her, it's not the unadulterated lust—that's a perk. Quite simply it's the timing. There are other factors in play that can harm her. Ones that I can't see, can't stop, but I'll find a way because I refuse to allow them to take her away from me.

"What do you want, Adriem?" Iza asks, her gaze remaining on the ground instead of looking at him. Her voice isn't harsh, but it's not welcoming either.

"I'm concerned for you, Iza." He isn't lying, he is concerned, but he's more worried about her anger and outbursts than the people dying. That's not something I fault him for, I feel the exact same way. He steps closer to her, and I force myself to stay put. The emotion—jealousy, I know now—is short and sharp and fades as fast as it came. When it comes to Iza, I have to learn to navigate the emotional minefield that accompanies her.

"Be concerned for the dragon that died here. I don't need or want it." Her tone has softened slightly, but it doesn't completely hide her irritation.

"I can't help it," Adriem mutters.

Iza turns to him, and the familiar smirk appears on her face. It's the one she gets right before she bites, I love that smirk. In this case, I don't think the intent is the same—or at least the result.

When she speaks, I'm proven right. "You realize that whatever weird shit that's in your brain about you and I isn't going to happen, right?" Adriem looks up from the ground, meeting her glittering black gaze.

"Because of Phobe? We know what he is, Iza, and he's trouble for you. A creature like him doesn't care about us." She tenses at his impassioned speech.

"He cares about me, and that's enough." She says it quietly, but I hear it. I hear it, and my nails dig into my palms to remain there, hiding. She sighs and continues, "Adriem, I'm flattered that you wanna see me naked but as tough as you are, I'd still tear you to itty bitty pieces." Her smirk turns into a slightly sad smile that makes me dig my claws further into my hand.

"I'd enjoy every minute of it." Adriem counters, smiling in that self-satisfied way that only someone who's ignorant of something can pull off. Iza turns her head to the side and the sad part of her smile vanishes, the sharp teeth replacing it again.

"You say that, now. Would you say that while I'm fucking you and digging my claws in so deep, I almost gut you? Or when I bite too hard, and my teeth go all the way to the bone, only to have me chew on it and like it? You're a monster, we all are here, but can you survive that?" Her tone is soft, coaxing.

Sexy.

She continues, "Can you survive it and *like* it?"

A short, completely unexpected laugh burns my throat... leave it to her to surprise me. Not that her refusing him is at all shocking, and I freely admit that I enjoy being proven right in this circumstance, but her description of one of our many, highly satisfying encounters is accurate and erotic at the same time.

Her eyes are on me now. She heard my laugh, Adriem did not.

"Is sex with you really like that?" Adriem asks, disbelief thickening his voice.

Scoffing she says, "I have no idea why you're so surprised about it. You eat people... most Feyrie do. Why is having rough sex any worse than that?"

"Iza, that is... the most incredible thing I've ever heard." His mind fills with various fantasies of him and Iza, some of which I have lived with her.

His response is not the one she was expecting, and she says so. "That's not the answer I was expecting." Sighing, she turns back to the mess on the ground in front of her. "You're cute and all, but I like my monsters to have bigger teeth." It is a dismissal and Adriem realizes it.

The emotions crossing Adriem's face in those first few seconds are bizarrely rewarding. The final one that remains for a split second before his face goes stoic, one I know well, is defeat. I like it, especially since it's now replacing that look of interest he was wearing moments before. The Nightmare isn't giving up entirely. He's going to recoup and think about these new things he learned about Iza.

I'm not sure how I feel about it.

He nods his head at her and turns to walk off, but he doesn't go far. The Nightmares take their guard duties seriously and won't leave her alone, powerful and angry or not. I'm starting to believe that this encounter between Iza and Adriem is the main reason Licar and Auryn aren't here. They know Adriem's feelings and perhaps knew his intentions today.

'I'm surprised you're not rubbing this in.' Her voice in my head is unexpected but as always, a welcome intrusion.

'It's amusing.'

'Well, I won't lie to you... if you didn't exist, he'd be my first choice, but since you do he'll always be the second one. That's not fair to him.' Her honesty is something I appreciate about her. So many creatures deceive, me among them, but not her. She tells things exactly how they are, whether one wants to hear it or not.

This time though... her honesty hits me in a soft place that she created.

'What if I no longer existed?' I'm not sure what makes me ask but now the question exists, and I want to know the answer.

She pauses mid-step and then turns her head to look over her shoulder, directly at me. "You will always be the first choice." Her softly spoken words hit me like a fist to my gut. Pride, love, lust all intertwine and make the urge to cross to her and take her in my arms almost unbearable. Watching her begin to walk around the clearing again, her shoulders tense like she is ready to throw a punch at any second makes the decision for me.

Appearing behind her, I pull her into my arms and rest my chin on the top of her head. The strands of her hair are happy to see me and tickle my chin and cheeks. They're a good indicator of her actual emotions. With a deep sigh, she relaxes back against me.

"I'm on the first day of my five-day heat cycle," she whispers.

"I know."

"How, exactly?" she asks, but already the answers are forming in her mind.

"I can smell it." It's not super strong yet, but the call of her scent is growing by the hour.

"Do you have any idea how we're going to be when I hit it full throttle? Which will be soon, I need to add." The tone of worry in her voice makes me want to reassure her, but I think it would be a falsehood. Instead, I opt to be as honest as she was.

"I'll keep control as long as I can, but with you that never goes as planned." Her snort of laughter makes me fight to keep a smile off my face.

"It came at a bad time," she says.

"Is there ever a good time for this type of thing?"

"I'm worried that it's all tying together into whatever bad thing Life is on about," she muses, all amusement gone from her voice. My answer is to pull her against me tighter because I have the same concerns. Now is not the time to let her mood go back onto the dark path.

"You think Adriem's cute?" I ask instead.

5

JAMESON

For years I worked to avoid ending up like this. I kissed countless asses, doing everything I was told. I betrayed so many people, including the only one that can save me. Karma really does exist because I'm in the very position I put many of them in. I'm such an asshole. The guilt hurts almost as much as the random shit they're doing to me to entertain themselves. So far, I've lost all my fingernails on my right hand, compliments of the vampire slut and her fancy toolbox—which I still think has a nice... *you idiot get your head out of her vagina*. She thought my screaming was fun, and it turned her on, too, I could smell it.

The big idiot broke my right foot, and I'm relatively sure he shattered my knee too. Scarily enough he did it with his hands. I'm also sure that I have a skull fracture and a few new holes in it tool. They poked me with the random tools from the toolbox that she left open on the floor at my feet. Every single injury, every ounce of pain is less than what I've seen inflicted on others.

How the fuck did Iza survive this shit?

The guilt threatens to drown me, and I'm not sure I'll ever be able to rid myself of it, because there's so damn much. At this point, I'm not sure I'm going to survive this, but I have this feeling that Iza is looking—that she's coming—and I need to hold on until she gets here. I don't think my faith is misplaced. Whether she likes me or not, she's part dragon, and they don't like to part with what they consider theirs.

Which would be every Feyrie there, including me.

One way I feel like I can redeem myself a little is by finding out everything I can in the process. It's why I'm hanging here by arms that have gone numb from lack of blood flow. The concrete pillar I'm chained to, like a butchered animal, is the only thing keeping me on my feet. Without support, I'd curl up into a crying man-puddle or die, and there's a good chance of the latter if I keep bleeding like a leaky faucet.

Gods, Iza is going to kick my ass so hard when she finds me. I can't believe I was dumb enough to come looking for an unknown woman who left me a note, with the promise of boobs. Where did I go wrong? Have I been in denial of my reality for so long that I've become a complete moron? Looking at my recent actions, there's a good chance that this is true.

Fucking retrospection, this deep thinking is another side effect of my situation. I hate it. It's something I've always tried to avoid in the past but can't avoid because that's all I have to do. It's preferable to them stabbing me with the screwdriver again.

Cut off from my Magiks, I can't heal myself. I'm stuck in this perpetual cycle of physical and emotional pain and the thought of it all ending occasionally makes me cry.

Iza never cried. I feel so ashamed.

"Why did you take that one? He's useless." The familiar voice makes me perk my ears but keep my eyes closed. I passed out hours ago and then kept pretending to be that way, in the hope they've grown bored with me.

That owner of the slightly nasally voice is Kael, Iza's uncle. The red dragon who named himself king after, more than likely, murdering his sister. I don't think he's the ringleader though. He's clever but not that smart. He's a weapon wielded by someone else. Now that my brain is out of the haze of the life I've been living I can think with some modicum of sense. I'm not surprised he's part of the plot against Iza, not at all.

He's a coveter that one—greedy.

"He's the one we were told to take. If you don't like it, check with him." The vampire sasses from somewhere off to my right.

"Are you sure he didn't mean a different one, Sharon?" Kael's voice moves closer as he talks.

"He specifically said the dumb one that will chase anything he can fuck." Well, that's rather demeaning, I'm not always dumb, and I don't chase anything, not typically—this time I was a little harder up than usual.

Okay, I'll admit it was dumb to do this.

"That's this one. I figured he would ask for one of her guards or that quiet one that's always at her side, the blonde one."

I almost choke out a laugh. Their night would've gone much differently had they tried to snatch one of the Nightmares or Phobe. I wouldn't be hanging here like a side of beef, that's for sure, and they'd all be getting digested.

"Why are you here?" Sharon asks suspiciously. I can imagine her face in my mind, I've seen it enough in the last day or two I've been here. She has beautiful brown eyes the color of whiskey and a perfect cupid's bow mouth. Her face is as stunning as any I've seen in this human world. She's also a frigid bitch, and I feel bad for anyone who sticks their dick in her freezer burnt twat.

She's also strangely proud of her little-pointed teeth. I get why Iza makes fun of them for it now. The version of me that is waking up out of the dumb-fog yells, *pay attention, dumbass*. At least part of my brain is working, pulling me back to the conversation that's probably important. Kael comes so close to me that the smell of his cologne stings the inside of my nose. He smells like he rolled around in it before gargling with it.

"I admit I was curious why he involved base creatures like you in his grand plan." A growl echoes in the room. "I suggest you control your puppy or I'll roast him." It's said so flippantly that for a moment

I'm reminded of Iza. She's very assured of her place in the world and the food chain. In some ways, this asshole is too.

"You're a shifter too, why should you be any more important?" Sharon says, rather snidely. Brave of her, considering how scary Kael is.

Kael chuckles, and his stench moves away.

"You think I'm a blood-muddled shifter?" He chuckles again, and with that chuckle, I hear the growl of the dragon that he is. "Don't fuck up. He'll kill us all." His absence is rather sudden, the slamming of a door is the herald of his departure. What was the purpose of his trip here?

Unless he's not sure of what's going on completely either. This visit was enlightening to me though. Kael isn't in charge—honestly, he's the one I had pegged for the mess with Magiks that made a bunch of people in the Sidhe sick, but it's not him. I think the most important question of all is, who is the puppet master that has Kael afraid?

The sudden pain in my midsection, brought on by the fist that took the breath out of me, is a very solid reminder of the situation I'm in. One of my folly, that maybe I can do one good thing with.

Find out who the bad guy is.

Once I can breathe normally again I raise my, now open, eyes to look up into the face of the shifter who's standing in front of me with a shitty grin on his face. Two gold teeth dully glint in the swinging light above us. He reminds me of one of those wrestlers on TV that wear the neon underwear and body oil, lots of it. If Iza were here, she'd be making fun of his tight pants and chicken legs. I can hear her now... this thought makes me laugh.

"What's so funny, loser boy?" The intended insult, which widely misses the mark, makes me laugh harder. I'm probably a hundred years older than this idiot. Unfortunately, I'm not a fighter, and after this, I'm probably not going to be a lover anymore either.

"I was thinking about how Iza would make fun of your itty-bitty legs. Knowing her, she'd probably rip them off and then laugh while she beat the vampy bitch to death with them." Laughing, I choke up blood, that I spit on his shoe. In my mind, I can see her whacking him with his severed leg while chastising him for wearing his pants so tight.

The punch is solid enough to roll my head back on my shoulders and bounce it off the concrete behind me, filling my vision with black and my mouth with blood—and quite possibly a tooth. Still, I keep laughing, because if Iza can stand what was done to her, the years of torture, then I can take a few fists to my face.

"Aren't you a surprise, imp. I expected you to be begging for your worthless life at this point." The new voice sucks the laughter right out of me. I know a Schoth accent when I hear one. Blinking, I center my fractured gaze on the tall, golden man standing beside the shifter. The unique markings on his bare arms and hands signify who is he immediately. The sinking feeling in my stomach sucks what little energy I had left out of me.

He's the Guide, Iza's Light counterpart, and by looking at him, I know he's as powerful as she is. This is a problem. I had no idea that he even existed, there were rumors, but the Guide stays with the king, and I've never laid eyes on any royals. I'm so glad that Iza and I read through the old tomes, because of them we know the tattoos that represent signs of her counterpart. His golden eyes sharpen, and the calculation in them is enough to make my already wobbly knees give out and leave me to hang by my already strained arms.

Is this the boss?

"Has he told you anything useful?" At his question, Sharon steps forward to join the group looking at me like I'm a bug stuck to their shoe.

"Are you sure he knows *anything* useful?"

"Oh, I bet he does. He knows her and her weaknesses, her secrets… get them out of him before we move onto the next part of the plan."

"Who are you to tell us what to do?" The shifter, forever argumentative, asks. He's not the boss, that's disappointing. As the shifter goes flying across the room, moved by Magikal means, the thick, oily feeling of dread makes me gag.

Panicking, I rack my brain for a way to not tell them anything. I'd like to say I won't break under torture, but I know better, and although I don't know many secrets of her secrets, I know some of her weaknesses.

Oh dear, One-God I beg you…

"Here is your chance, imp. Tell me what you know, and I'll make things a lot more pleasant for you." His smile is blatantly false but beautiful. I can't believe I wanted to be like him once upon a time.

I decide to play along. "Can I fuck the vampire?" At my question, his smile broadens to one of amusement.

"You can fuck both of them if you want to." Days ago, I'd probably have sex with anything offering it, but I don't think I'd ever be desperate enough to fuck stick legs.

"You know, I learned recently that women could have more than one orgasm, but I'm not sure that stiff bitch can have one, let alone multiple." As I speak the amusement drains from his face. "Do you have any palm leaves around? Between them and the human's blue pills maybe I can make some Magiks happen."

"Beat him until he talks." Dismissing me, he turns away and disappears in a flash of light. Iza would be so annoyed. She has to walk.

The first blow, even though I expect it, hurts enough to make me yell. I have a goal though. I want them to keep hitting me. If they hit me I can't talk, if they knock me out, I can't talk.

Great plan.

"I bet you have a little dick, too, I mean all that upper body strength has to be compensation for something." I taunt. When he hits me this time, I feel something in my face break. I try to smile, but my jaw won't work right to form it. This doesn't stop me from running my mouth or attempting to. Something I wouldn't have dreamed of doing before I met Iza.

Unfortunately, the words don't quite sound right. "Eye not… weep it out eh puve me woong?" Even though I sound like my mouth is full of rocks, his face reddens, and I know that he understood what I said just fine. Fire races across my jaw when I try to smile again.

There's an audible crack when he hits me again. Yeah, my jaw is destroyed now, possibly even ripped from the socket. The first attempt to talk makes me feel like puking. Channeling my inner Iza, I force sound out of my throat, and the pain wrings everything that's in my stomach onto his pretty, blue shoes.

The smile, a mental one, comforts me as another strike to my face sends me into the darkness of blessed unconsciousness.

6

IZA

Even though there's no evidence of Rido's body, because of the gossip hounds, everyone knows his death happened. They hear it word of mouth, I felt it in my soul—I can still feel it inside of me, stinging and burning like a small splinter that I can't get out. Normally, I'm rather pragmatic about some things in life, one of those is Death. It's a fact of life, everything and everyone dies. Even the supposed gods die, but that logic doesn't make this situation any easier. Looking around me at the rampant destruction of a place, where a man fought with everything he had to survive, and lost, takes the fire right out of me.

Rido wasn't a fighter... he didn't even kill bugs, and he cried when he stepped on a flower. Rido was a special person, one of those unique creatures that have the gift of seeing everything through the eyes of a child, even at a hundred years old. For someone born into our world, Rido was uncommonly kind and sweet, and now he's dead, and it's my fault. The guilt of his death, and Val's has my guts wrapped up in knots and the only way to appease it is to find the fuckers that did it.

No matter how I look at this situation, I can't seem to wrap my mind around their choice for this kind of violence. Val was sick before —an obvious target and his life was snuffed out like a whisper, but

Rido, he didn't get sick. This is completely random, and he was physically attacked—with rage. Just seems so strange that they'd target him with such ferocity when I don't think that was their intention. At least the intention of the one who started this shit. They're related, it'd be stupid of me to assume they weren't. Even though I don't know how many people are involved in this fucking mess, there's got to be at least two. The bipolar reaction signifies that. But did they mean to do it this way or was this an accident?

Did Rido see something he wasn't supposed to?

"That's a safe assumption." The voice timbered to make you want to hear him talk, pulls me out of my thoughts. Looking around, I find that I've wandered to the lake. I don't remember heading here, but it kind of makes sense that I did. Whenever I need to think I come here or the tower room and that makes me think of my dad.

"You know, it's strange he hasn't popped in. Normally, he's here the minute he feels that I'm super upset about something or simply to visit. I haven't seen him for days."

"I can go look for him if you wish." I muse over Phobe's offer. It's unusual for him to be gone so long but it's not completely unheard of.

Still, with everything that's going on, I ask, "Yes, if you don't mind. I need to head back and get the Sidhe settled down. People are freaking out." I look over at him, and he nods, those hypnotic eyes searching my face. I can also feel his dark presence he's embedded in my thoughts, shift. He's like a persistent tick that won't let go.

Honestly, I kind of like it, even when I say I don't.

In two steps he's in front of me, his cool lips lightly brush mine, hinting to the heat of his mouth, and then he's gone in a whoosh of a portal. My mouth spasms like a fish. Well, then. For a moment I smile, but it vanishes as quickly as he did. When he reappears a few minutes later, the last vestiges of humor vanish. The frown on his face and the flare of his eyes makes my chest tighten, and my heart turns into a lump of terror-filled ice.

"Dad?" The voice that says that single word sounds like the young child that I once was.

"He's locked in his realm, someone with more power than either one of us holds him captive." As he speaks his eyes flare brighter. Phobe doesn't like the fact that he's blocked from doing something, not at all. I don't like the fact that my dad is trapped like a rat in a cage.

"Is he okay?"

"Yes, he sends his love." Which means he's telling me to stay the fuck out. "He's working to escape, but it will take time." Roughly translated, he's beating the shit out of things until they break. I'm my father's daughter. The corner of Phobe's mouth twitches, hinting at his amusement with me.

When I exhale my heart picks up a normal rhythm again. For one awful, absolutely terrifying, moment I thought something had happened to my dad. I'm not sure how I'd handle that, not at all.

"He said for you to stay here, that he's safe and will see you soon." This is Phobe's nice way of saying that there's danger, but my dad can handle it.

I open my mouth to ask more questions, then stop. I have other things I need to deal with here. If he's safe, then I don't need to worry. Instead, I need to trust their judgment, right? Frowning, I look up at Phobe, my decision already made.

My common sense lasted a few seconds, that's gotta be a record. "Take me to him?" It's a demand as much as a question. I want to see for myself what kind of condition he's in. Phobe wouldn't lie to me, but his version of bad off and mine differ, slightly.

Growling low in his throat, he hooks his finger in a belt loop and pulls me to him. The portal opens up behind me, the force of it blowing my hair into my face. The strands are not happy about the disturbance and hiss at Phobe in protest. With a grunt he lifts me, and the abject cold of the NetherRealm is a shock, one that affects even me, but before I can get off one shiver we're out again. Phobe releases me and steps away as I look around at the land of the dead.

It's dark and rather dull looking. Bare rock makes up the majority of the landscape, and the only light in the sky is a moon that looks like someone painted it black. Talk about setting a tone.

"She doesn't listen very well, does she?" I turn at his voice and walk towards him, only to hit an invisible wall. What the fuck?

"You didn't expect me to listen, did you? What is this shit, Dad?"

He puts his hand up against the barrier and smiles at me, and even though his eyes look tired and his face is a bit bloody, the smile is a happy one. I can't help but smile back and match my hand to his. The shield snaps and crackles under my hand but doesn't hurt me. The Magiks in it feels weird, familiar but in a bad way.

"Who is this person that can do this to someone like you?" I muse, out loud.

"They're strong enough that I can't even put a dent in it and Phobe couldn't break it completely. Although, he did a good bit more damage than I managed to," he says, sounding more jovial than he is. In fact, he sounds exhausted.

The frown on my face is so tight it pulls on my scalp, as I say, "It's the other one isn't it, Phobe? Your other, brother person." He's the only one capable of it, a god, just like the One-God aka Life, like… Phobe. Turning to him, I look past the outside, deep into those eyes of his, that flame when I stare at them.

How did I forget that the man I love is a god?

"No, I'm merely something different from you are. Don't give us a title we do not deserve." He sounds a bit angry about it, making me glad I didn't make the 'god' comment out loud.

"Iza, you and Phobe need to go. There's nothing that you can do to help me, right now. I can manage fine down here, and as soon as I get out, I'll come to find you." I turn back to him as he speaks hurriedly, then looks behind him at something I can't see. Frustrated, I punch the shield. He turns back to me and smiles, in that sweet way that only a loving father can smile. "I'll be fine, dove. Now go take care of your flock." His eyes flash black, and he grows into the creature that earned him his deserved title in life and vanishes into the mists behind him.

Before I can comment or argue—or beat myself mindlessly against the shield, I'm pulled against the rocks that make up Phobe's abs, and we're sucked into another cold portal. As soon as we're stationary, and back at the Sidhe, I turn on him prepared to throw a royal tantrum. The look on his face stops me dead in my tracks.

Control yourself, idiot, some voice of reason inside of me chides. To calm myself, I take a deep breath in through my nose and exhale through my mouth. I do it twice just to make sure. Much calmer now, I say, "I wish you'd have let me help him."

"Other than standing there yelling fruitlessly, there's absolutely nothing you can do." I don't like his logic, at all. He leans down a little to put his face even with mine. "That's a frivolous thing to waste time doing."

I make a face at him and bite my lip to shut myself up before I say anything else. Pushing the loudly roaring, hormonal teenager inside of me down—as far as I can stuff her—I gather the scattered bits of my composure. I hope this shit is over with soon. It's frustrating and unpredictable. Half of what I say or do doesn't make complete sense on a normal day, let alone in a hormonally fueled temper tantrum.

"Stop grumbling about something you can't change and work at something you can," he says. Sage advice, it is, and the first thought that pops into my head, because of it, is the one that pops out of my mouth.

"I'm going to send the Sidhe away. I feel like all of this is my fault, that somehow, I've failed to do my duty as this Shepherd person." Taking another breath, I continue, the words coming out of my mouth burning my throat. "They'd have been fine if I hadn't come along thinking I could make a difference."

"These things happening are... unfortunate, but this is war. War isn't peaceful and kind, Iza. It's cold and bloody, and lots of things die." He continues with his damn logic, "Things would be much worse for them if you weren't here. You gave them peace while they were at the Sidhe. Only you could do that, Iza."

"So, you agree with me then?"

"Of course not, don't be ridiculous. We have no idea what separating you from the Sidhe will do to you. I believe that you will weaken because of the symbiotic relationship you have formed with the Sidhe. This is a guess only. I'm sure the truth of it is much worse."

He straightens, hooking a thumb in one of his pockets. He looks so nonchalant, talking about my potential demise, but I see the tight line of his jaw. The seething shadows around him are another giveaway. I might not be able to read minds, but I'm learning about other tells.

"Maybe nothing will happen?" I don't believe that anymore than he does.

"It will happen, it's how things like this work." He crosses his arms over his chest, no longer looking nonchalant. "What about the possibility of the deceiver going with them?"

That's a question I can't ignore. "We'll keep those suspected separate from the Sidhe."

"How do you propose to do that?" he asks.

"Carefully?" Why does he have to go and ruin a perfectly good idea?

"You could ask the Sidhe to leave a sliver of itself here, enough to trick the occupants and keep them safe and away from the main group. It will still have the traits of the Sidhe but if it's attacked or invaded won't hurt the main body. The Sidhe is an incredibly powerful entity. I imagine it can keep them fooled for a time." Okay, that's a good idea, and while I'm thinking about it, I ask the Sidhe. The song of its answer takes a bit of the burden off me.

"It doesn't fix the issue of you being separate from it. Why do you have to set your mind on a task that will result in you suffering for them?" There goes my smile.

"Because it's the only worthwhile thing I've ever done in my life. It has meaning and makes me feel like I matter." My voice raises with each word, but at this point, I don't care. The last word echoes in the clearing and his eyes flare, right before he kisses me full on the mouth.

Like a romance novel heroine, my eyes flutter shut, and I lose myself in him. For those glorious few minutes in time, I feel nothing but *my* Darkness. The heat of his mouth suffocates the chaotic emotions, making me focus only on the undeniable presence that is he. The flick of his tongue against mine fills me with a different kind of fire, and it lures me away from the burning pain of loss. I kiss him back with everything I'm worth, greedily taking his solace. When he breaks apart from me, a low moan escapes from my still open mouth due to the loss of him.

"Did you compare yourself to a romance novel heroine?" he asks.

The laugh that claws its way out of my tight throat surprises me. Throwing my arms around his waist I bury my face in that lovely space between his neck and shoulder. I swear it was designed for noses, and... for hiding tears. His arms snake around me and hold me tightly against him. This is the kindness that no one else sees, a monster that holds his blubbery girlfriend.

"Hey, I figure that since I'm a damsel in distress and you're my gallant hero, that it fits." His huff of laughter tickles my hair, who of course tickles his face in return. The humor that makes him soft and warm and, almost, cuddly... drains out and I tense and pull away.

"You're still going to send the Sidhe away?" At his mood-killing question, I step completely out of his embrace and put some distance between us. Studying the serious look on his face, I nod.

I realize how committed I am to this decision when no urge to argue appears. "Yes, I think it's what's best for them." Removing them from sight might remove them from being targets. "You're right, it's a war and people die but if I can delay it—give them a few more months of peace, I'm going to."

"Even at the cost to yourself?" I nod again. "Since that's your choice there are some things I need to prepare for." He half turns away from me. "Don't leave the Sidhe until I return. It's not safe for you out there alone."

As he disappears into a portal my eyes narrow, did he just give me an order?

♥

A HOT SHOWER is the first thing on my agenda, then food, lots of it. Leaning against the counter, eating my third sandwich, I watch Michael run into the dining room. He looks around like a lost kitten and then ducks into the kitchen, stopping when he spots me.

"I've got some images off Jameson's tablet." Dropping the last bits of sandwich on the counter, I go to his side to look down at the tablet screen in his hand.

A fuzzy picture of a large dark-haired man, eyes amber with the change, fill the screen. A shifter. The picture looks like it was taken from the ground, Jameson took this on purpose. Shit, Jameson, you took a chance taking this picture.

"There's two of them, but the other file is so corrupted I couldn't recover it." He taps the screen and looks at me hopefully. "Will this help find him?" Nodding, I memorize the face on the screen. The woman, I'll know, because that nasty smell alone will help me, plus vampires are all connected to their Prince. I just need to find him, to find her.

The shifter is another matter. I frown at the picture. Jameson took a big chance taking it, but I think it's more than me seeing this guy's face. I think it's because of how strange it is for a vampire and shifter to work together. They don't get along all that well. The vamps had enslaved them all at one point—pretty sure some still are. Looking at the amusement on this shifter's pudgy face, though, makes me relatively sure that's not the case here.

He likes what he's doing. Hurting my poor chicken man.

"Thank you, Michael. You did great work." Michael blushes a little and smiles, then his face sobers.

"Have you talked to Ruthie?" I shake my head at his question.

"Why?" I ask. His face reddens even more.

"We had a bit of a fight, and she's mad at me." Oh, well that's normal for them to have disagreements from time to time. Plus, teenage girls are the devil, I see it all the time on TV.

"Get her something shiny and sugary. She'll forgive you. Also," I take the tablet from him. "Let's not tell anyone about this yet."

"What about Phobe or one of the Nightmares?" I shake my head and tuck the tablet in my waistband. It's too big for my pocket. I don't think he'll keep the secret, but it will give me a little while to look for myself. And maybe it'll give me a chance to wrangle in all this crazy emotional crap that the heat is bringing on.

"Now, go make up with your girlfriend, there's some chocolate in the cabinet." I turn him around and push him towards the right cabinet and scurry out of the kitchen before he realizes it's a distraction. Not that I think he'll notice, Ruthie is occupying his attention rather well.

Getting out of the Sidhe unnoticed is easy without Phobe around. I have years of practice from sneaking around while I was in prison. The only one I can't shake is Phobe, and since he isn't here I'm set. Adriem followed me for a while inside of the SIdhe, but I still lose him in the maze of hallways that he can't follow me in.

Stepping outside, I look around me, noting the absence of everything that makes up life at the Sidhe. For one gloriously freeing second, I enjoy the silence of the cold night air around me. The gentle falling snow that flows and dances around me in a curtain of fluff, is a welcome white silence. I even experience a teeny tiny piece of joy kicking my feet through the snow. For that one freeing second… but only for a second.

Reality, the asshole that it is, crashes in on me way too quickly.

Focusing on where I need to go, I kick the ground a little harder than I need to. The wave of snow that bursts out in front of me, followed by a chunk of dead grass, does nothing to improve my mood. I'm unsure of what I can do to fix this, and I'm also choosing to ignore the sharp stab of guilt that's starting to dig into my brain like a small shard of glass. He has no right to tell me what to do any more than I do him. Besides, he doesn't want to find Jameson anyway. I do.

Tucking my hands in my pocket, I focus on the prince that's doing everything he can to hide from me—and failing. It's time he and I talk. Although, it'll mostly be me hitting him with something instead of talking, I'm sure there'll be words mixed in there somewhere.

Maybe.

7

IZA

Iza

Riding on a bus, probably isn't the best idea for someone like me. It's something I've never done alone, but I can't deny that I'm enjoying myself, a little bit. The diversity of people who ride these things is incredible. Everyone from mass murderers—the fiends know the flesh of the damned—to religious women who forgot what soap is and have awful dressing habits. To single moms who're running from an abusive relationship.

Unlike Phobe, I can't read minds, but the woman across from me is definitely running. She has a black eye, and a busted lip to prove it. Those aren't nearly as important as the haunted look in her eyes. I also don't miss the way she keeps looking around her like someone is going to reach out and grab her any second. The brown-haired, little girl beside her has the same look about her and keeps looking at her mom with hero worship. Makes me wonder if the woman put the fucker who beat her in the ground somewhere in the woods.

People like her abuser doesn't deserve to breathe. Especially not after beating on people who love them too much to leave. This one did though. Something finally pushed her over the edge. It's probably the little girl. The woman gets up and looks around like a trapped animal, before grabbing her daughter's hand in a shaky grasp. Carefully they make their way to the bathroom at the back of the bus. You'd think there were landmines in the aisle, the way she steps so quietly and cautiously. Kind of makes me want to find out where she came from and visit her former address.

After a few minutes, she makes the return trip, smelling of the hand wash in the bathroom. As she walks by me, I subtly stick a wad of cash in her purse, winking at the girl who caught me. Everyone needs help occasionally, especially those who'll actually do something with the help. This woman is one of the strong ones, she'll survive, and maybe when she finds the money, she'll be able to have a better start.

The little girl darts another look at me before sliding back into her seat. I put my finger against my lips. Surprising me she smiles and before I realize it, I'm smiling back. Her smile doesn't last long, but it makes me feel like I accomplished something because she gifted me with one. She gets a nudge from her mom and disappears from my sight onto the seat. I hope these two humans do well. If there is a human god that no one knows about, I hope he or she is listening and gives this deserving person a chance.

When my cell phone buzzes in my pocket, I ignore it. I have a good idea who it is, and I don't feel like talking to them right now. Snuggling down into my coat and the incredibly uncomfortable seat, I lean my head back and close my eyes. There is at least six hours before I'm at my destination, I might as well catch some rest in the meantime.

♥

SLEEPING on a bus isn't comfortable, but I've slept on worse, so I rested rather well. Standing and stretching, I squeeze out into the small aisle as soon as there's an opening. My skin feels grubby and the desire to take a shower is getting intense, but it's not something I can deal with right now. When I climb down the bus stairs, slower than the smelly man behind me likes, I blink at the early morning sun. The fog is still lingering near the ground, curling and moving with the people walking through it in their rush to depart the buses in front of the station.

"Lady, get your ass out of the way." His breath is heavy with the smell of old onions and processed cheese, as it wafts through my hair —that hisses at him. Looking over my shoulder, I let my eyes shine. I think it's past time the humans know what walks among them. I've never really agreed with that entire, 'hide your true nature' shit anyhow. I'm not afraid of their tanks and guns.

His gaping mouth snaps shut, and he takes a step back up the stairs, his pupils dilate, his breaths are coming fast and sharp. Oh, I scared him—poor thing. Smiling, I give him a good eyeful of my teeth, and then without another word, I step completely out of the bus and breathe in that nice fresh, exhaust-filled air.

Bus stations are foul places.

Pulling out my phone I summon the Google God and look for maps of the area. In my mind, I grab the thread that attaches me to the prince idiot, and turn until I'm physically facing the direction. The map says I'm heading east, so east I'll go. I'm sure that I'll smell the vampires when I find them, for now, I'll try to enjoy the walk.

No way am I daft enough to try and drive in this unfamiliar place. Plus, I only do that when Phobe is with me. I enjoy watching him hold onto the handle above the door like a scared old woman. That's the only thing that makes driving worth it because I always end up wrecking the vehicle. Always.

As I walk at a human pace, because there's no real reason to hurry, I notice that a lot of the buildings and houses are rather decrepit. It's a shame to see houses that were once beautiful turned into trashed wooden skeletons. This human world has issues with homelessness, yet they have all these houses sitting empty. I don't understand it. Why not put people with jobs in the homes and homeless people in the apartments?

Haven't they thought of these things? The solution is right there and being ignored. I'm not sure I'll ever understand why they don't help their people more. Of course, I doubt they'd understand a Feyrie either. In a perfect world, we'd all be able to get along without any bullshit issues. Thinking about all the different ways that a relationship between the humans and Feyrie would work or fail, I settle on the worst one because it seems the most likely. War. Unless, you consider they're going to need us to help stop the Schoth, that are planning on invading this world.

The smell of old blood and desperation pulls my attention away from the various dreamy scenarios of Feyrie conquering the human world, to focus on the group composed of vampires and shifters standing slightly ahead of me. If the smell is any indication, there's a bunch behind me too.

Now, why are there Light Fey—well, half Light Fey—in the prince's city? It stands to reason that his loyal people, who are more powerful with him here, would have chased them out by now. Something is fishy with all of this. It's like with the vampire and shifter that took Jameson, working together even though they're sworn, enemies.

Is the Blood Prince involved? I feel for his thread inside of me. Initially, I thought he was hiding and being a pansy, but now, I'm not so sure. He's mostly masked from me Magikally, but it doesn't feel all sneaky like someone trying to be deceptive. Now that I focus on it—with a clear head—it more like someone else is trying to hide him from me. Some mystery person is tinkering with shit, except this is something they can't completely cut me off from. The Feyrie are mine.

We can't let them hide him, can we?

The fiends hum in anticipation, vampires are their favorite snacks. *I like a good buffet too girls, but this time we need to wait—there are more at our destination.* I think I'm going to need them more at the end of this little stroll than the beginning. These guys are young, barely any power to them, they're the equivalent of a Magikal mosquito.

And I'm a big fucking bug zapper.

Instead of waiting for some weird sign for them to attack en masse, I dig my feet into the ground and leap, landing on top of the 'leader' type guy. The impact of my body weight on him catches him off guard and causes him to wobble and totter around on his feet. Grabbing a handful of his hair, I start punching him in the head, and smile when I feel his body give underneath mine. When he's on the ground, I bounce up and down on him like a trampoline. He's soft, and his body gives easily underneath my shoes like those squishy little air bubbles in that plastic stuff that I keep stealing from Jameson. The smile fades, and anger surges through me, it pisses me off thinking about Jameson. When I hop off the vampire's battered body, I give him a solid kick in the face. The bones give way, and I'm pretty sure that I toed his brain.

Just a little bit.

Turning to the larger group, I let my glamour drop, completely. I'm sick of hiding behind masks, sick of letting others think they can walk all over me... over all of us. Let them see what we are!

"What the fuck?" One exclaims, stepping back from his buddies. Grabbing the purple haired vampire in front of him, I lift the man up —one-handed—and slam him down on the ground. Fucking vampires, they need to be afraid of me. They need to know that I'm not one of their stupid elves. That I'm tired of these—earthbound, weak ass motherfuckers, fucking with my life.

I pick the man up by his shirt and slam him down again. Smiling at him in the process.

"I'm Iza and," grabbing his arms, I lever my foot on the shoulder of the vampire in my hands. Pushing down with my foot, I pull both of his arms out of the socket, "I'm tired of you assholes getting in my way." Putting more effort into it, I pull one arm out entirely with a moist, meaty pop. The screaming starts and he fights harder against me. Standing with both feet on his stomach, I pull the other arm out with that grinding, bone cracking sound that makes the rest of them stop in their tracks.

He goes limp because he's probably dead at this point. Good. Swinging up one of the severed arms like a wet noodle, I point at another vampire with it. He hisses at me. I'm not kidding... hisses.

"If you have any brains in your head, you'll tell me why there are shifters in the Blood Prince's territory, and why—the—ever—living—fuck you all think you're scary. All I see is a grown ass man hissing at me like a grass snake. Who the fuck does that?" I throw the arm at him. Reflexively he catches it, and then with a look of open-mouthed horror on his pale face, throws it down on the ground and skitters back from it.

I'm pretty sure he's gagging, yep… I step back away from him as he pukes all over the place. Including on the dead guy whose arms I ripped off. Speaking of arms, I still have one of them. Swinging it like a scythe, I smack it into several of the closer vampires. It isn't my fault they were distracted by their puking buddy. Pulling back like a pitcher from TV, I lift my leg up, and I throw the arm as hard as I can at the closest one. The thud it makes when it hits him makes me giggle.

When the first one turns and flees, yelling that I'm a crazy bitch, my smile comes back. Three more joins their friend, running away from me as fast as possible. They look like little roadrunners from the cartoons, dust flying behind them and everything. Those little suckers are fast. I had no idea they could move like that. They always seem so slow when I'm ripping their body parts off.

The hair stands up on my head and hisses, see now—they're a relative of serpents, it's normal for them to do it and much more realistic. Ducking forward, the board passes harmlessly above me. Kicking out backward with my leg, I catch someone in their soft belly and sidestep to kick them again, landing in a squat.

Rolling to the side, I come up with an undercut that takes one several feet off the ground. His jaw cracks under my fist and his teeth snap together with a clacking sound that probably means some of them broke. I hope it's those two little ones they like to abuse people with so much. He lands in a lump of unconsciousness. Straightening, I look around at the two remaining vampires, they're both unconscious… well, one is unconscious—I'm pretty sure the other one is dead.

The unconscious one happens to be the one I punched into tomorrow. Squatting down beside his head, I slap his face. I need some answers, and he looks like he might have some for me. When his eyes finally open they immediately fill with fear. His mouth opens, and I see that one of those canines are in fact gone. I smile at him, all my teeth showing my appreciation... and the fact that I'm going to kill him afterward.

"Hello, sleeping beauty. I've got some questions for you."

8

IZA

It took a few severed fingers, but he eventually talked. I think the fact that I bit the last one off assured his cooperation. I've also picked up a sort of stalker. A human who's probably not even shaving yet, but is brave enough to follow me with his cell phone leading the way. I'm pretty sure he recorded everything with the vampires. Which means it'll end up on the tube and the Google God.

Good.

For the moment, I'll let him follow me—maybe once he gets an eyeful of what's going to happen, he'll have enough brains to grab some pictures and run. The part of me that likes to stir up shit considers stopping and giving him an interview, or maybe the finger I bit off that's still in my hand. But there are too many vampires for me to contribute to his viewing count. I can smell them ahead of me now, the old apartment building is full of them. They remind me of an infestation of cockroaches crawling in and out of the decrepit rooms and decaying hallways. Scurrying away from the light like the bugs I'm comparing them to. Totally creeps me out, I hate bugs—especially cockroaches. Honestly, I should burn the building down and go home, because that would be the simplest, easiest way to do things. It's how Phobe would do it, in-out and then home.

Good thing he isn't here. The easiest way isn't as fun.

Standing at the bottom of the concrete stairs that climb the building like old spider webs, I take a deep breath to prepare myself. The stairs are mostly crumbled, but there's just enough flat area for me to jump a few times, to get to the top floor. That's where I need to go, I'm pretty sure that's where they're keeping the Blood Prince hostage/hidden.

Before they came here this place probably looked nice but now there's trash strewn everywhere, newspapers and old magazines. Soda bottles and half eaten food. Some of it is piled high with a body or two hiding underneath it. I can smell them. The vampires didn't clean up their victims.

Pushing off the ground, I jump up a level and then another.

A vampire makes a half-hearted leap at me, and I kick him away mid-air. The surprised look on his face is amusing. Why doesn't anyone ever believe I'm capable of whipping their asses? Vampires can move fast, the runners earlier demonstrated that, but these are younger—fodder, rather easy to kill. They're also in my way.

The room ahead of me, with a bright red door, still has some semblance of nicety. For one there's electricity, because I can see the lights are on through the window. It's cleaner and unlike the other rooms, guarded. That's what sets it apart the most. That's where I need to go and none of these fuckers are going to stop me from getting there.

This time I don't play around, the daggers come out, and I slice through the bodies with a solid, steeled determination to reach my goal. The Prince is hidden from me for a reason. The people doing it also know where Jameson is, because the little squealer I chewed on told me as much. I know that it's a woman in charge of this lot, I'm guessing she belongs to that awful perfume. Not a very smart one. She used because she was stupid enough to think that it will trick my sense of smell.

To give her some credit—I suppose—a lot of creatures would've been fooled, unable to get past the chemical smell. Her mistake is not knowing her true target, me. I spent most of my life in prison with some of the most foul-smelling motherfuckers in the realm, but I could still smell a piece of stale bread hidden under a rock.

Speaking of smell.

That awful perfume wafts towards me, brought by the vampires running at me in a constant wave of sacrificial flesh. Smiling, I push myself faster. *Now you guys can eat.* I encourage the fiends, who are salivating over the living, dead flesh of the vampires. The screams, oh the screams. The beautiful symphony fills the air as it echoes off the empty walls around me. Only to cut off when they're sucked into the NetherRealm to become a feast for the ones waiting behind.

Underneath the dissonance of death and pain, I hear one phrase repeated over and over. Ohmygod. Ohmygod. Ohmygod. The human kid is still here, he's still recording on his little phone, and he's going to be eternally scarred. If he has any sense, from this point on he'll be very afraid of things that go bump in the night. After all, he just discovered that monsters are real.

"What the fuck are you?" The woman's voice grabs my attention.

In damn near slow motion, my gaze zeros in on her. She's standing behind a fresh wave of vampires, a smirk of arrogance on her face. With long curly, platinum blonde hair and a pair of bright blue eyes, she cuts a striking figure. Her face is all Norwegian supermodel and reality star.

I got to stop watching so much TV!

"Where's my nerd?" I ask her, calm, smiling and letting the fiends clear a path for me to her. I stop to lean against the wall a few feet from her.

"Your nerd?" She repeats, with a bit of a duh look on her face. The minute the realization hits her, she smiles like a cat in the cream. She eyes me up and down. "You don't look like much." Then, like the total skank she is, she opens her lips and languidly licks one sharp tooth.

Snorting with laughter I dismiss her as any kind of threat. What's up with these vampires and their two little teeth? It's like a dog showing you it has a tail, or a siren making that obnoxious eek noise. It's just not that big of a deal.

My skin feels heavier, apparently my glamour is back up again. It's become a reflex of sorts, the minute I stopped fighting it reflexively returned. Well, we can't have that. I let it slither off me like a slinky dress, slowly, revealing what I am, fully, to her and what's left her of cohorts. The fiend armor, gifted to me, from the legion of fiends, flips out of my skin like scales. Tearing what's left of my clothes in the process. My hair grows and writhes around my head as my mouth stretches and pulls to make room for all my teeth.

With a serpentine tongue, I too, languidly lick all my sharp teeth. Now the paleness of her face is more pronounced, the cocky look and arrogant smile are gone. The pinpricks of her pupils stare at me in terror. The smell of it makes me smile again… the perfume stinks, but her fear smells divine.

"I'm asking you again… where's my nerd?" Her eyes travel down my arm to the glowing dagger in my hand, then back up to my face where her eyes flicker back and forth as my agitated hair waves around and hiss at her.

"What the fuck are you?" she repeats. Her voice is shaky, breathless. It's the voice of someone who is about to—she turns and takes off at a pace that knocks over her bodyguards, she just abandoned.

What a great lady.

I realize the mistake I made, in that very second—I stopped paying attention. There are so many vampires around me now that I can't even begin to count them. With one brief look of longing towards the woman I want to chase down, who's getting away I might add, I turn my full attention to the problem at hand. There's no way I'll catch her and avoid these fuckers, which leaves me one option.

With a roar I dive into them, the fiends echoing my war call.

It's moments like this that I understand why people smoke after a big fight scene in the movies. Looking down at my—mostly naked—blood-covered self, I shake my head. All I have left is one boot, my socks, and my underwear. My armor destroyed most of it, but I have no idea where the missing boot went. I hope it's stuck up one of the vampires asses. That's a fitting end to a good boot.

Tired, I hop up on the concrete wall of the parking lot, situating myself to get as comfortable as possible. Fuck, I'm exhausted. There were so many vampires that I lost count at a hundred or so. For a while there I thought they might get the best of me too. If not for the fiends, they might have. Looking up the broken stairway, towards the walkway of the former apartment building, I see the broken and bloody bodies littering the walls, the crumbled stairs... some are even hanging off the few, intact balconies. That's not even counting the ones the fiends fed on. They ate so much that most of them are bloated and lethargic.

The ones left are waiting in reserve.

Honestly, I have no idea how they all fit in that building. It felt like there was a never-ending supply of them. They were coming out of every nook and cranny, even from the roof. That's not counting the shifters that were mixed up in the group. Although much fewer in number and not as tough as the vampires in this case, I still noticed their presence.

This all smacks of some lazily thrown together trap. Whoever planned it was sure of its success and not the sharpest spoon in the drawer. All it accomplished was to let the one person who could give me information get away.

"Ma'am, get down on the ground and put your hands on your head." The yelled order surprises me. Looking at the police officer—who's pointing a gun at—I hop to the ground and put my hand on my hip to regard him standing a few feet from me.

His pale face and wild eyes tell me he probably saw enough of the encounter to be a bit freaked out, and although my glamour is mostly up—I'm covered in blood and damn near naked. It's safe to assume he saw things he can't unsee, and it terrified him.

No normal human wants to know that things like monsters exist here, and I'm a fuzz scarier than the baby toothed vampires. I think it's time they know; it's why I let the little human follow me. The one who called this gentleman here, I imagine. The kid is still lurking too, on the sidewalk behind some bushes on the other side of the police officer.

I smile and wink. He's lucky, if I were a bad guy—a little gun wouldn't stop me from getting to him. They're all lucky. This group has probably been feeding on people here, so me killing them saved human lives. Dozens if not more a force this large would've required a lot of food. I decide to tell the cop that.

The man startles when I start talking. "You should pay me for killing them for you. I bet you've had people going missing left and right lately. Probably good people, and maybe even kids. Am I right?" After a moment of regarding me, he nods.

Then he says, "Lady, you're a monster too. I saw you." He licks his lips nervously, the gun wavering in his sweaty hands. I can tell by the white-knuckled grip he has on it that all it will take is one hint of movement and he'll shoot me.

"Yep, I am, but I'm a different kind of monster. I kill ones like those, the ones who hurt innocent people." I keep my voice soft, non-threatening.

"What are you? Some kind of vigilante demon?" His voice is getting stronger. I think he's becoming less afraid because I haven't tried to rip his head off. If he sprays that poison in my face, though, I can't make any promises.

Sighing, I flick a random piece of flesh off my arm, I think it might have been a slice of an ear, but I'm not entirely sure. The leather of his belt creaks as he twists his arm around to take the cuffs off the hook. I genuinely don't want to hurt him. Their motto is to protect and serve. That's something I can mostly get behind, but I don't like handcuffs, and I'm tired. I want to go home and bathe and deal with the fallout of sneaking away without telling—

The forlorn appears in front of me and roars, a loud demonstration of his master's displeasure with me. The fiend's immediate response is to attack it, males of their kind or not its being aggressive towards me, but I know that it won't hurt me. The forlorn like me. To be fair, I'm betting Phobe is worried and this is an example of it.

"Hi, big guy. You can tell him I'll be home soon, so he can get his panties out of knots."

"What the fuck is that!" The retort of the weapon echoes off the walls and drowns out the words he's yelling. The bullet hits me hard enough in the shoulder to send me a few steps backward. They won't kill me, but it still stings like a motherfucker. The forlorn turns to him and roars again except this time it's a different kind of roar. This is one of rage, not annoyance.

"No, don't hurt him! You scared the shit out of him, he didn't know that the bullet would go right through you. Now go on, tell Phobe I'm coming home." I put force in my words. The human simply reacted, I can imagine how scary a forlorn is to him. All teeth, red eyes, and demon-like visage. I think they're adorable but I'm not human, either. With one last look at me, the forlorn disappears.

Letting my fingernails grow I dig the bullet out with a grimace and throw it at the police officer. "Why'd you shoot me?" I demand, hoping that talking to him will calm him down. The forlorn is gone, and it's just the three of us now. Oh, and the dozens of fiends hidden from his view. I think it's best not to mention those to him.

"Put those on. I'm taking you in… I have no fucking idea what they'll do with you, but my vest cam caught the entire thing. At least they won't call me crazy." I'm not sure if he's talking to himself or me. He keeps muttering under his breath about going to church.

He turns and digs around inside of his car. I catch the shirt he tosses.

"Put that on first, can't have you… naked." Then he goes back to muttering. I almost feel bad for him, but ultimately this will be good for everyone involved. I hope the humans don't get ideas about military occupations and shit. They've learned that lesson I think. I hope.

Sliding the shirt on, I ignore the smell of cologne and human sweat. I smell much worse than the shirt. I'm pretty sure I have some vomit on me too. Probably worse things, I did gut a few of them.

"Well, officer," I look at the name on his badge, "Monroe, I need to get going, but that kid caught everything on camera, so I bet we'll both be famous by tomorrow." The gun comes back up at my words.

Moving fast I stop in front of him and grab the barrel of the gun, bending it up. I get right in his face, and say, "I have faith in what you do, and I'd rather not hurt you in order to leave. So, the short version of what happened here is, these were what you humans call vampires and shifters. They fed on and indiscriminately killed humans under your protection. There are stacks of bodies in that building behind me to prove it. I killed them because they took a friend of mine and in the process did you humans a favor. Now, I'm tired, and I want to go home. If you'll—"

He faints, in my arms, out cold. Gently, I lay him in his car and motion the camera boy out of the bushes. Immediately, he walks over to me. Kids have no brains, I swear.

"Never just come out... what the fuck, kid? I could eat you or something."

"No way, you killed the bad guys. I heard everything that you said to that one you—" he clears his throat nervously, "Chewed on."

"Oh, yeah. I'm looking for my friend. They took him."

"This video will be everywhere tomorrow. I'm sure someone will know." I look right at the camera when he says that.

"I'm going to get you, assholes." Turning, I start heading back the direction I came. He jogs to keep up with me, rapidly firing questions at me, that I mostly ignore. It doesn't matter that I agree with this world discovering we exist but I'm not in the mood to play twenty questions, either. Stopping, I turn to face him, catching him when he almost runs into me.

"Look, there are creatures coming here... ones that want to kill humans or enslave you. Hell, worse things than that I imagine, but it's my kind that stands in defense of this place. When the time comes, you and your internet minions need to remember that." Then I turn and jump back towards the room that the Prince is trussed up in. Leaving the boy standing there trying in vain to catch sight of me on that camera phone.

Once I free this guy, I plan on going home. There are too many things I need to get done and not enough time. Plus, Phobe is mad at me, and well, I've got to fix that. It outranks everything but taking a bath, because man, I stink.

Busting open the apartment door I stand there gaping at the man tied upside down in the chair, naked. The blue of his eyes is super bright in the dimly lit room. His *other* nature peeks out of his human façade. This guy is one-hundred percent Feyrie. Overlaying the average looking human face, I can see the monster he becomes. Michael might be thrilled to know that another of his kind exists here. How did they catch such a powerful Feyrie and hold him so easily?

"Are you going to stand there staring like an idiot or are you going to free me?" Well, what a pretentious twat, maybe I should leave him like that with his man bits just hanging out all over.

"I think I'll take option three," I answer.

"What's option three?"

"I could cut your dick off and shove it in your mouth BEFORE I leave you there to die." His body tenses, his brain has kicked in now.

"Shit, you're her." He sounds so happy about this fact.

"Of course, I'm her. Now, I have some questions for you, Mr. Blood Prince."

"Can you untie me first?" He sounds much more contrite now, but I'm still tempted to leave him tied to the chair. Instead, I cross to him and grab a handful of the chains holding him. The Light Magiks in them turn my stomach, but it's not too much for me to deal with. With a hard pull, they snap in my hands, and he slumps down over the side with a grunt of pain. Of course, I leave him there in the man mush pile on the ground.

Slowly, he climbs to his feet and dusts himself off like he's wearing a five-piece suit. Pretentious twat was a dead-on observation but... the Dark Magiks say he's not so bad. He's loyal, and he cares about his people, our people. Whispering as I walk around him, the Magiks tell me all that they can about the Feyrie who escaped the slaughter of his people by coming here.

The Magiks push at me to tell him where to go, and I do, but reluctantly. People like him and I don't get along well. The scenarios of us butting heads are already playing out in my head. Dane, yes that's his name... here anyhow, is an arrogant know-it-all who's used to doing things his way. Well, that's not going to happen.

"How did you end up naked in a chair?" I ask, snooping through the papers on the desk in the room. There's nothing but magazines and nudie pictures. No receipts, no detailed directions to Jameson. How annoying.

"I foolishly trusted that bitch that ran away." I can hear him behind me, it sounds like he's putting clothes on.

"Stinky? Yeah, she seems to be in the thick of things. Any idea who's pulling her strings?" I turn and discover he is dressed in a pair of bright pink sweatpants. It's a genuine struggle not to laugh because they're at least three inches too short and skin tight from the thighs down.

"No. My father was a firm believer in the prophecy… are you really her?" Walking closer to him I pull the glitter covered strings holding up his pants, tight and tie them. Don't need his little buddy poking out again.

"You're going to want to gather anyone that's loyal to you and take them with you. The Sidhe is one of the few safe places for us, at least for now." I decide that answering the question is pointless. He can figure things out on his own.

"There aren't many, but I have a child."

"Is she safe?" Because if they have her, I will leave Jameson to rot a little while longer to get her out.

"Yes, for now."

"Good, do you need money?" He stares at me, weighing me with his gaze, then nods.

"Let me go find my wallet. I'm sure it's out there somewhere." Turning, I go back out to the bloody walkway and dig around in the bodies for my wallet. Eventually, I find it and hand him a wad of money. Without another word, other than the address of the Sidhe, I turn and leave. He can make his way there, I've got a pissed off god man to go home to.

9

PHOBE

When the forlorn found her, my annoyance traveled through him. She stood mostly naked and bloody, with a fucking smirk on her face—while a human stood there with a gun pointed at her. There were dozens of corpses scattered around, mostly in pieces. She killed them all, alone, and even though I was momentarily proud of her for that, it pisses me off that she snuck away while I was gone. If there had been someone waiting for her… someone more powerful than her, I would have lost her. All because of her foolish stubbornness.

Plus, she got the pleasure of killing things while I was stuck reading dusty old books and dealing with a pissed off records keeper —that I could not kill—all for her. It didn't dissuade her from going off like a complete simpleton, half-cocked, all for of an imp that's not worth any of this.

I want to bloody strangle her!

The hours I have spent pacing in front of this doorway, waiting for her to come walking through it, only made me think more about the situation. There was no point in my going after her, not when she's coming here, but in hindsight, it might have been better for both of us. All this waiting, pacing, and thinking has made me angrier than I might have otherwise been.

When the door creaks open, echoing along with a guilty muttered curse word, I lean against the wall and watch her try to tiptoe inside. Of course, she trips over someone's shoes, the rug, and manages to somehow knock pictures off the wall. Full on cursing now, she runs a hand through her hair and her eyes land right on me.

"Hi," she says. Guilt and ire war in her eyes and I watch guilt win. This is interesting, she acted out like a child—and somehow managed to make it home, looking like she does, without ending up in a human jail. Then she holds her arm up, and I see the handcuffs dangling from her wrist.

"Did you have fun?" I ask, no longer angry, because after searching through her thoughts—I find myself rather amused. Iza exposed our existence to the world. I agree with her decision, hiding was a stupid endeavor to begin with. Nonetheless—she felt the same way and rectified it. The reasoning of it's rather solid. She's preparing them for what is coming.

She then came all the way home, bloody, monstrous and proud of it.

"A bit, well, up until the twentieth cop tried to arrest me. He sprayed me in the face with that awful shit and managed to get cuffs on me before I ripped his car door off. Which," she takes a drink of water that a goblin hands to her, "I left cuffed to the door with those plastic things they carry. They're much more effective than these metal things," she says, holding her wrist up and shaking the broken cuffs. She takes another long swallow of water. "Thankfully they have the instructions written on them, or I wouldn't have been able to truss him up so effectively."

The image of the human spread eagle on the car door flits through her head. It's a small battle to keep the smile off my face. Once I start to study her, it's less of a battle because the urge to smile fades away. Her skin is coated in flaky dried blood, with some patches of darker blood, which tells me it's an injury she was given. The large shirt she's wearing is stiff in places with it, a testament of how much blood her skin was coated in before she put it on. There are bits of guts and flesh in her hair and stuck to her in various places. She has on one shoe, a dirty, bloody pair of socks, and her underwear under the shirt.

"Where are your clothes?"

"The armor tore most of them, the rest I'm not entirely sure. Once I started fighting... I kind of hyper-focused." Finally, giving in to the creature that wants to assure itself she is safe, I step forward and pull her into my arms. For several seconds she stands there, stiff, but then melts into me, wrapping her arms around my waist and tucking her head under my chin.

"You stink." I say into her smelly hair, then ask, "How did you acquire transportation?"

"I had a return ticket for the bus. I told them I had slaughtered dozens of vampires and needed to get home to my angry boyfriend," she leans back and smiles up at me, "I'm not sure they believed me because they let me on the bus after the driver laughed so hard he about wet himself. They thought I was playing some sort of prank." She sighs and continues, "I will tell you that the lady I sat next to didn't appreciate my fragrance. She sprayed awful perfume in the air every ten minutes. It was a long ride."

"You should have waited for me." I don't want to word it in a way that will make me come off as her master, because that's something I'll never be, but I want her to understand the chance she took going alone. There's also the fact that it pissed me off.

"Probably, but I survived so don't worry about it."

"Did you find out anything useful?"

"Well, I found the vampire, but she ran away like a fucking coward. There were so many of her lackeys that I couldn't bust through to get to her. I did manage to rescue the prince twit though, so he should be coming along soon. He had to go fetch his daughter in his pink sweatpants." Her face lights up, and she steps back, out of my embrace. "I found him tied upside down, naked, in a hotel chair. Then when he started running his yap, I considered leaving him, but these stupid Magiks wouldn't let me."

"He sounds like a winner." She laughs at my sarcasm and then turns and walks away. I know where she's going, the bathing pools are a beacon in her mind. She can't stand the smell of herself anymore. Several minutes pass, while I wait for her to slide into the hot water. My mind conjures images of her lathering soap over her pale skin as the water runs red around her. Then as she stands to rinse and wash a second time... I'm walking before I complete the thought, and when I get there, I'm not disappointed. She's the most stunning creation in existence. Standing, the water sleuthing off her muscular body, her hands run slowly up and down her sides, then her stomach and my eyes follow them like a starving man.

"I'm going to tell them tonight that I'm sending the Sidhe and everyone in it, away." The seriousness of her voice pulls me out of the more lascivious thoughts I'm having about her. If I pursue them, while she's having such a highly emotional moment, it'll make her angry with me.

I need to stop letting my baser instincts control me around her. It makes me no better than Jameson.

"Most of them won't react well." Mainly her circle of children.

"It doesn't matter. It's happening whether they like it or not." I want to argue with her again, I want to beat it into her thick head that she's putting herself in danger, but I don't. It's a pointless argument and will only put us on the outs again. We need to be a unit, not divided by this kind of stupid shit.

"You still don't agree, do you?" she asks quietly.

"No, but I don't think that will stop you." She shrugs and starts to wash again. Iza is simple about some things when her mind is made up, and there's no changing it.

I study her a moment, her sweet scent pulling on me, all of me. As the water touches my bare feet, then climbs farther up my calves, I move closer to her. Her breath hitches and her heartbeat increases, her pheromones filter into the air. This will ease her heat; it's what her body is demanding... what mine is demanding.

Her smile, slow and full of fire is all the invitation I need.

10

PHOBE

After our bath, that left her much calmer and her heat temporarily sated, she calls everyone into the dining area of the Sidhe. A hum of tension projects from the Sidhe and fills the air. Boomeranging into the inhabitants and returning in full. It's so thick that if I wanted to, I could reach out and cut it with my claws. They know something bad is coming, something I still can't agree with her on.

The research I left to do wasn't as helpful as I hoped. No matter how far back I went in the history books, spell books, even storybooks, I found no answers. The Sidhe is too unknown by everyone. It wasn't created by any of the 'gods,' because it existed before they did. When my 'awakening' happened, there were already other lifeforms existing in many, many worlds. The Sidhe was one of them. Floating around, from place to place looking for its anchor.

Back then I didn't have thoughts in the way I do now. Everything was instinctive and borderline preprogrammed. There were intentions but not actual words to go with them. One thing I knew then that I still believe now… was that there was *something* before Life and me, and Light. Before the three of us *were*. The Sidhe also came from that unknown entity. The Sidhe was already old when I was still young, but different from it is now. Whatever that may be.

It simply *is*.

There's nothing other than vague references and useless folklore about it or what made it. I dislike being uninformed, but this time there's no choice. The information doesn't exist to find. We have a small chance that she won't suffer any ill effects, but I'm not holding out for that. Things are never that simple in our lives. There are endless complications and plans going wrong at every corner we turn. Fate is against us, and that is a fact.

One day I'll hunt down those old bitches that meddle in fate and eat them.

The room falls silent as Iza straightens from where she leans against the wall, moving to stand in front of the confused mass of people. Slowly, she looks around at the faces of those gathered, keeping her own carefully blank. I see the truth of it, those sparkling eyes of hers are brimming with emotion. Her thoughts are dark, and angry, and even a little sad. She hates this but truly feels like it's the best way to protect them.

"Two Feyrie have died senseless deaths, deaths that I couldn't stop. I couldn't fight what killed them, because I'm failing as your Shepherd. I don't know who our enemy is. I don't know if I can defend you against them. The *only* thing I do know is that there are only a few things I can do to delay—to hide you from them. Tomorrow morning, I'm sending the Sidhe and all of its occupants away."

The room erupts in noise and shouts, several louder than others. Knox, among them. He's standing now, in the front, yelling at Iza for all he's worth. Her shoulders stiffen, but she doesn't look directly at him. If she looks at him, she'll give in to the guilt that's threatening to overwhelm her. It'll eat her up, make her doubt herself—cause her pain.

"Enough!" My shout instantly silences the room. In a more normal voice, I continue, "It doesn't matter if you agree with her decision, because it's her decision to make. So shut up and allow her to explain what will happen next."

Iza doesn't hesitate, she jumps right in. "You'll all be leaving in the morning. Once the danger has passed, then I either join you where you are or recall the Sidhe here. It will be up to the circumstances at the time." Other than the ones she's leaving to be safely separated from the others. Unfortunately, her Knox is among them.

"I hate you!" Knox yells and runs from the room. Pain flashes in her eyes but is quickly hidden.

"Don't try to leave me because I'll follow you wherever you go," Michael says, sounding much more mature than he did when she first found him. He too then turns and leaves the room. Ruthie looks at Iza with bright eyes and then follows suit without saying a word.

"My lady, we cannot allow you to go on this journey alone, it is our—"

"Auryn, I appreciate it, I do, but that little bundle in your arms is way more important than I am, and I need you to keep them all safe. You and Licar will be doing something super important for me." Her eyes steadily hold Auryn's who after a few seconds, nods.

"Take Adriem, at least," I say quietly into the room. If I told her through our minds, she'll ignore me. This way calls her out, and the dirty look she shoots at me lets me know she's aware of it.

I know she wants to argue, and even if I couldn't read her mind, the intent clearly on her face. Her quick agreement makes me instantly suspicious. Her mind was full of arguments before I found myself blocked off from some by that obnoxious blue wall of singing creatures. It makes me want to hunt down whoever created them and rip their fingers off one at a time.

'Temper. Temper, Phobe,' she teases, instantly calming my brewing irritation.

'Why do you insist on always hiding things from me? It fucking annoys me.'

Of course, she doesn't reply, instead of continuing to answer the questions of the Feyrie. Most revolve around their welfare, something I find unsurprising. They aren't thinking about the sacrifices she's making, they're thinking of the ones they need to make. One that have been few and far between since they came here.

The silent ones are concerned for Iza, worried about what she's taking upon herself. These are the people she's truly doing this for, putting herself in danger—hurting herself, it's all for them. As I skim their thoughts, they're centered on how they're going to sneak and help her anyhow. Some are planning on gathering others to provide support in any way they can while still seeming to obey her commands because they're loyal.

Subconsciously, her gaze skims over some of those silent people, and I watch the resolve harden in her eyes. Yes, these are the people she does this for. The ones she gets stupidly emotional for. That's why I hold my silence. I can't fault her for having honor. It's not something I posses in any measured amount, but it means a lot to her, and I'll respect her beliefs.

This time.

"For those of you that think you're going to ignore my orders and remain, your loyalty is appreciated, but I can't allow it. The Sidhe will make sure you go." Her words start up a clamor of denials and arguments.

"Does this mean you're going to leave Jameson to rot because you selfishly want to run away?" The voice cuts through the murmur of voices like a knife. Iza's head snaps up and focuses with steady ire on the tall form of Nika.

Why is that dragon so determined to piss her off? I try to skim her thoughts and find nothing but anger over the lack of Jameson's presence. Nika is a rather shallow creature who, for the most part, is good and capable of great compassion. There are times when her thoughts are full of nothing but her desires, ones that Jameson doesn't share for the woman. Her desires are unhealthy and moments like this demonstrate it. She doesn't love the imp. She obsesses over him.

And it's not just about being a dragon.

"I don't see you out there hunting for him, lizard." Iza's eyes flash black and then back to her normal undulating purple. Nika wisely keeps her tongue, in both circumstances. "Now, I suggest everyone severs any connections to the town in preparation for leaving." With that, she turns and leaves the room. Every head in the place turns to watch her leave and then turns to look at me.

I shrug and follow her. They want an explanation that I will not give them. My version is not one they'll like.

♥

I'M NOT SURPRISED about her destination. Without pause, she travels to the exact spot where the dragon died. Snow has fallen again and covers most of the evidence of destruction, but you can see the bones of it poking out through the mostly undisturbed white powder. There are only a single set of faint tracks circling the area, her tracks. Why is she allowing her unnecessary guilt to draw her back to this place?

"You're arrogant to believe this is your fault," I say into the silent snowfall.

Without turning, she says, "Maybe, but that doesn't change anything. He still died because of whoever is chasing me."

"Iza, whoever is chasing you is directly related to all of them. If you want to cast blame, lay it at the feet of the one who murdered him. Not at the feet of the one who tried to save him."

She turns to me. "You actually sound like you mean that."

"Trivial words aren't something I bother with." Leaning against a tree, I watch her walk around the clearing, squatting near the place that Rido met his end. "Your plan has a mile wide flaw in it." The wall of annoyances has fallen, and I see bits and pieces of the scheme she's cooked up in her head, one that will fail.

"Every plan has flaws, they're useless when it comes down to it, but it isn't the plan that matters—it's the planning." Tossing a piece of branch onto the ground she says, "You know there was a time that I dreamed of something as simple as getting married and having a dozen kids."

I have no idea what makes me ask, "Do you still wish for those things?"

"I'll admit I've daydreamed a time or two of a wedding with a certain monster," she says. She's trying to hide the fact that she more than dreamed of it, Iza has planned the entire thing out.

Her thoughts unfold for me like a colorful painting of white dresses and bright purple flowers. This is something she uses to keep her heart happy when the world is pressing down on her.

This is something that I can truly give her.

"Give me a few moments, please. They're too loud in my head." She suddenly stands, and after giving me a long look, takes off into the darkness. My muscles automatically tense to follow her, but I stop myself. She wants time alone, and she'll have it. I know something new, that I had no idea about it, and it leaves me with much to think on.

Turning, I walk back to the Sidhe, taking my time with it. I can hear the voices of those outside, gathered in wait for Iza. Perhaps this is why she needed time to herself, to gain her composure. She pulls off the social interactions, but I know it costs her. Iza was isolated most of her life, and she's no better in most social situations than I am. Her fake persona only goes so far.

At the lead are her three children, Ruthie, Michael, and Knox. Knox's mind is unavailable to me but he's standing silent, wringing his hands nervously. His green eyes are steady on the path in front of him, sad and still wet from tears. The immeasurable love he has for Iza is shining like a beacon in them. I'm not surprised that the anger he reacted with was short-lived, and now he just wants to be reassured by the woman he looks at as a family.

Ruthie is mostly thinking about Michael. The looks she's casting at Iza aren't the friendliest but her thoughts don't mirror them. All I can glean is that she's staying because he's staying. None of her thoughts are about Iza's welfare or what's in the near future. She isn't even concerned about her own safety. That's odd but not too out of character for the emotional teen.

Michael is nervous and worried, wondering how he'll follow if Iza leaves without him. The kid genuinely cares about what happens to the woman he looks at as an older sister. His love is much stronger than his anger, to him she's his family, and he refuses to lose another one. Michael will grow to be a strong man one day soon.

As I skim the other's thoughts, finding a broad variance to them, I keep my gaze on Knox. Is that what it is like to have a child of your own? One minute they hate you and the next they love you so much that it can move anything with the strength of it? Is this why she aches for the loss of one? I'm not sure that this is something I'll ever understand, but it's why I will one day find those responsible. That scar on her soul is more than enough encouragement.

It's not something I need to share with her when I do, because, in her way, she's made peace with it. Upsetting the precarious balance inside of her isn't something I'm willing to do, but I have no issues making them pay what's due in her place.

Moving off the darker thoughts I end up studying Ruthie again, who, for the most part, has been rather silent about everything. Skimming over the thoughts about Michael I push a little deeper and strike gold. She's pissed off that Iza is keeping him from going with her and the rest of the Sidhe. Her anger at Iza is deep-seated and hidden by the shallower thoughts of a typical teenage girl.

Something inside of her has changed concerning Iza. Pushing to go even deeper I stop when she looks around in confusion, very perceptive of her. She's furious with Iza for leaving, for causing this issue between her and Michael. A fight they had that isn't Iza's fault.

They had their first lover's quarrel. She also mad that Iza is leaving this place and making her lose her home again. A perfectly acceptable reason to be upset for a child that's had everything taken from her. From the memories I possess I know that a lot of teenage girls are highly unstable in their behavior, it's considered a normal behavior for them. In Ruthie's eyes everything will be Iza's fault. Until eventually she'll realize how big of a shit she's being and they'll bond once again.

It's unfortunately not as easily remedied as Knox's issues. Since I can't go deeper into her mind without causing her harm, only time will tell. She goes on the list of suspects. The fact that she feels so much anger at Iza seems misplaced in the scheme of things. I can understand some anger, Iza is sending them away—or trying to—and it can potentially cause a rift between Michael and Ruthie. Then again, females are incredibly complicated when it comes to their thoughts and emotions, so the logic I'm using could end up being completely useless. As Iza teaches me again and again.

There are no Magiks around her, no taint of something that I can see. That is enough to temporarily satisfy my suspicions, but she will stay on that list, as a precaution… mostly.

When Iza enters the clearing, it feels like feathers tickling across my skin. My awareness of her has quadrupled over the years, and now I can't deny that I… like that feeling. Dipping into her mind, I discover she's not overwhelmed any longer. There are tinges of sadness swirling inside the churning mass made up of her conviction and stubbornness to continue down her path. One can't help but admire her tenacity, even if she's doing something stupid.

At least, this time, she won't travel it alone.

The instant Knox spots her he runs to her, launching his small body at her like a bullet. She catches him easily enough and swings him up into her arms, holding her against him, tightly. Even at this distance, I hear the words he's whispering into her hair.

"I'm mad at you, but my heart hurt too bad not to say goodbye. I'm scared something will happen to you." Iza says nothing to this and simply kisses the top of his head. She knows enough about life not to make foolish promises, although the thought was in her mind. She wants to promise him she'll return but she doesn't believe she will.

Spinning away I step into a portal. I have more musty books to read before we leave in the morning. I'll return when the goodbyes are passed, they have nothing to do with me, and I can't stand by silently watching them play emotional games with each other. If you will miss someone you say it. A simplistic, easy approach to socializing if you ask me. Iza lives with this philosophy, but her Feyrie don't.

As I step into the portal, my eyes flicker over those gathered to speak with Iza. Perhaps this is their version of simplistic. The area is full of their love and sadness, it's apparent she's beloved by most of her people. This isn't an interaction that I understand, but there are a lot of things about these creatures that I don't. The portal closes behind me sealing me in darkness, she's safe for the moment, and that's all I need to go about my task.

11

IZA

Two days later, I find myself sitting on the floor of my hotel room attempting to watch TV. Picking out the hotel was easy, I went for one my Dad owns. One that I can get away with the activities that I'll be participating in. The staff will keep their mouths shut, and I when I told them to remove all other guests, I was obeyed.

One thing is ticked off my list. The Fake Sidhe is intact, and the ones on the suspect list are there under the watchful gaze of Auryn and Licar. Knox included, if nothing else he's safer being with them. One less thing to worry on and it gives me more room in my cluttered brain to figure other things out.

Saying goodbye to all of them was harder than I imagined it to be. My chest still aches from the emotions I could feel from them. They're my people... my family but sending them away still feels like the right choice.

Including the two moody teenagers next door.

Michael was true to his word and left the Sidhe land so it couldn't take him with it. Ruthie, of course, followed Michael. Against her rather obnoxious protests, I got them separate rooms. That girl is in full teenager fueled hellish mood swings, she's worse than me, and I'm in the end stages of my heat. Phobe fucked me out of the majority of it. There's a hole in the bathroom wall to prove it. He was impatient to reach me from outside.

I'm glad I'm not as wound up as her, it's messy enough as it is.

I snuggle farther into the soft blankets that I've used to make myself into a burrito with. I don't need their warmth but they provide another type of comfort that I need. The emotional bits aren't nearly as intense, and the outbursts are less and less. Plus, I don't feel like I'm constantly going to explode. I owe a lot of this calm to Phobe, he knew what I needed, and he gave it to me without question, without reserve. A reluctant smile pulls at my stiff face. I don't want to be smiling, considering everything, but it's a happy memory and should be celebrated. Even if only with the hint of one.

Ugh, emotions. Why the fuck am I feeling guilty for one of the small, happy moments in my life?

"Are you okay?" Adriem's soft voice pulls me out of my self-lecturing tangent. Oh, yeah, I forgot about him. His question makes me realize that someone asking me constantly if I'm all right makes me feel worse, and apparently, I'm not over all the irritability. I look over at him, sitting on the end of the bed, remote control in his hand. Looking awful comfortable in *my* room.

Why is he in my room? So, I ask, "I'm fine, don't you have your room?"

"I'm guarding you, remember?" Waiting for him to give an explanation that makes sense, I stare at him. Sighing, he says, "There's no cable in my room, so I'm borrowing yours. I have to say," he smiles in an obnoxious way that makes me sort of want to smack him. "Watching you wrap yourself up in a cocoon while wrestling with guilt you shouldn't have is... entertaining."

My response to his unwanted humor is my middle finger standing proudly at attention. I ask, "Where did Phobe go?" Shows how deep in thought I was not to notice his absence.

"He said something about feeding his monster." Another smile tickles my lips. He went to get me something to eat. Whoever said a man that eats people can't do nice things?

"Do you think what he feels for you is real?" The question catches me off guard.

"Why are you asking that?" I ask.

"Mom says that Phobe created us, I'm not sure I believe her. But if the stories are tree, our creator is exactly a creature of sentiment. If that's the case, then how can he care about you?"

The question is rude, there's no other way to look at it. I'm trying to decide if he cares for my well being or his penis. Staring into his eyes I settle on the former. At least, it's mostly the former.

"Phobe created you, never doubt that, but that doesn't mean you know anything about him other than that. He's so much more than any of you will ever see or understand," I pause and make my tone even out. "Thanks for the concern but if you insult him again like that, I might rip out your tongue."

Adriem laughs as he nods. I'm dead serious. I'll rip out his tongue, whether he thinks I will or not.

The scuff of a shoe outside the door brings my eyes to it. Adriem is on his feet, standing to the right of it seconds later. A knife is already in his hand, and his form is wavering with the Magiks of change. I know from experience he won't shift forms unless he wants to but it's something they all do when their emotions run high. I'm sure I have a version of it too. I know my hair makes a lot of noise, the little brats. Reaching up I pat them affectionately.

I can't say I've actually seen what I look like as a whole without glamour. My body changes but not into a dragon. Well, not entirely a dragon. There are parts of me that are definitely along that vein but no awesome wings or tail. Yeah, I didn't get those because whatever decided on my weird mesh of DNA chose to leave those cool features out. Instead, they gave me weird looking feet and—

The knock on the door pulls me from my ridiculous thoughts. My brain trips me out sometimes. I'm pretty sure that there are parts of it that are gone in crazy land, and this is the way it copes. Oh, and killing stuff, it copes that way too.

"It's the hotel clerk," Adriem whispers.

"Yes?" I call to the door, shaking my head at Adriem standing there looking all menacing and shit.

"Message for, uh," he clears his throat nervously. "The red-headed bitch." That's definitely a message for me. I nod at Adriem to open the door, he does and smiles cheekily at the clerk. Who, unknowing of the knife Adriem tucked in his shirt somewhere, smiles back.

"What's the message?" I ask. He turns to me, with a line of sweat on his forehead and a quiver to his mouth. I have that effect on humans, the only ones that don't react that way are usually children and the occasionally mentally ill person. He holds up an envelope. Adriem plucks it out of his hand, passes some money to the man and promptly shuts the door in his face.

Handing me the letter, he sits once again at the end of the bed and waits for me to read it. I smile a bit sharply when I see the scrawl on the envelope. It does indeed say, 'The red-headed bitch.' It's unopened so the clerk didn't read it—it also means it was delivered here, meaning they know where we are.

Not that I'm trying to hide. I was relatively obvious about things, because I want them to know where I am. Much like the video of me circling around on the internet, that in two days it has gotten two-hundred-million views. Adriem told me that's a lot. I haven't watched yet, but I will, eventually.

Opening the envelope and unfolding the single piece of paper in it, I read the address and simple message.

COME TO THIS ADDRESS; *we have information on your missing associate.*
P.I.T.

"WHAT DOES ARMPIT WANT, I WONDER?" I muse out loud, climbing to my feet. It's a guarantee that they want something from me, it's not the type of group that offers something for nothing. Jarvis is a total twat and as far as I know, still the leader. Phobe may have dismantled —well, ate—a good bit of their members, but it didn't stop them from existing. They're like a hydra, cut off one head fourteen grow back. With Jarvis, the fat head, remaining untouched, other than that bit of a love tap I gave him.

Maybe he's due for another?

"Why do you call them armpit?" Adriem asks.

"They call themselves PIT, Paranormal Investigations Task Force—catchy, huh? I decided that I like calling them armpit more."

Slipping on my shoes I head towards the door, not surprised when I find Phobe resting against the wall outside of the room. Standing, he leans inside of the door and sits a box on the dresser inside. I know the smell of the contents—it's cake, I love cake. I know what I'll be doing when we return.

You're very predictable at times.' Phobe muses. I shrug, it's true enough not to argue with. He falls into step beside me, while Adriem falls in behind us.

The cell phone is a wonderful, human invention and putting in the address provided gives us directions to our destination. One that we're going to by car—I try to talk Phobe into letting me drive, but Adriem slides into the driver's seat without a word.

He's only been driving a few months! He's better, way better than I am—but it's still not fair.

'I'll have you know that I hit fewer things now.' It's partially true, I can drive straighter. I merely have a tendency to press my foot too hard on the gas pedal.

'The fact that you still hit anything is a deterrent, Iza. As well as how you forget the brake exists.' He's not wrong, so I say nothing as I climb into the back seat of the car. Phobe pauses a second or two before climbing into the front.

Listening carefully to the instructions given by the accented voice on the phone, we manage to only get lost once or twice in the two-hour drive. I've noticed that with GPS you're directed to bizarre places sometimes. Like left-hand turns that are supposed to be a street, end up being someone's living room.

Eventually, we end up at a warehouse. It's like a bad TV drama. It looks deserted and forlorn with pieces of paper flapping around in the empty parking lot. Climbing out of the car I walk quickly to the front door. Kicking it open without pause, I go inside and stop when I see a group of men, women, and children huddled together in the center of the cavernous room. They're chained together, like animals. Filthy and scared.

The minute the Magiks touch them, I know who they are—the wingless dragons. Jarvis has left them like a badly wrapped present to butter me up. Giving them to me is bribery, if he had Jameson he'd be here too. Not that I thought the humans had him anyhow. Taking in their clean but pale forms, I study the chains around them, dampeners, they're humans use to control Magiks users. The chains aren't strong enough to take away all their Magiks, but it makes using them a bit painful. The level of that pain depends on the strength of the user.

Without me even asking, Phobe moves to them and starts breaking the chains. I know why—the Light Magiks in them hurts me. I can tolerate this amount, but it will make me weaker. A problem that I'm already experiencing and keeping to myself, I don't need an 'I told you so'. Since I sent the Sidhe away, I've noticed a definite drain on my abilities, my body. I hate admitting Phobe was right, I do, but being away from the Sidhe—even in this short time, is taking a toll on me.

We traveled to the city to be more visible to the ones who're holding Jameson and I slept most of the trip. I napped off and on coming here and still, I'm fighting the tiredness that makes my steps heavier, slower. No matter how much I sleep I can't get rested enough.

Good things have come out of it though, partially, I have the wingless. They come to me in trickles, one or two at a time. Some stand and stare, others reach out to touch my shirt. The younger ones boldly hug any part of my body they can reach.

"Have you seen an imp named Jameson? He's yay tall," I hold my hand up above my head. "He likes to hump random things."

"We're sorry Shepherd, we've seen no one like that." A woman steps forward answers. My gaze zeroes in on her. She's strong, Zafrina is her name. She strikes me as the caretaker type too. I nod in acceptance and start explaining about the Sidhe.

"There's a safe place for you to go, we'll get you to a hotel, and I'll have Adriem's kin pick you up from there and take you to a safe place," I say to her. She nods and without prompting, starts to gather the younger ones up. Something she's done many times before, given the smoothness of it.

My heart pangs a bit that they've gone through what they have, but now it's over—rather anticlimactically at that. I guess in my imagination I figured I'd have a grand battle with tanks and rocket launchers. I'm only somewhat disappointed. For the most part, I'm relieved. This situation allows me the time and energy to keep looking for the dumbass imp and discover who took him.

For the moment, they'll be safe. Which is all I can do. I can't promise that there won't be worse things in the future. I can only slow it down, by standing in the way as long as possible. It's not a feat I can do forever, I'm not immortal but with Phobe at my side— who knows how long I can hold the tide of assholes at bay. My goal is a few decades, let them have babies and experience life at peace. I'll do whatever I need to, to ensure that it happens. Even if it kills me.

Who am I kidding? Of course, it will kill me.

Phobe pokes my shoulder, and I realize that I've been staring off into space for several minutes. Shaking my head at my distracted mind, I watch the last of the wingless dragons leave the warehouse. Some of them are even smiling. Well, that's something off the to-do list. Now I can work on the next thousand things on there.

Turning around in a circle I study the mess of a room. The furniture is overturned, and the phones dangle off the haphazardly placed desks. Paper is strewn everywhere, most of it torn or shredded. In the corner is an area of screens, and one of them is so large that it takes up the entire wall. While I'm staring at it—wondering where I can find one this big, it flickers and turns on. Jarvis's bulldog cheeks fill the screen.

"Hello, Iza Black. I see you've gotten my peace offering." He looks over my shoulder at the empty room. I say nothing in response, people like him like to hear themselves talk. "I was hoping it would make you more amicable to lend your assistance in a certain situation."

"Why would I want to help you?" I say into the silence; I can't help it if I'm a bit curious.

"There have been patterns of strange weather all over the world, entire towns are disappearing, and otherworldly creatures are popping up everywhere." He clears his throat nervously. Good old Jarvis doesn't like asking me for help, and this amuses the shit out of me. "Our military is responding and quarantining the areas, but they've taken a wait and watch approach."

'The invasion has started.' Phobe supplies in my mind.

'There goes the ten years Jameson predicted. What do you think, do we help them?'

'That choice is yours. I think in one way or another you'll end up helping them regardless, simply by dealing with the threat to your people.'

"Because of your video debut, there are roving groups of rednecks out monster hunting, some of which have met unfortunate ends." Licking his lips nervously he continues, "We can't combat some of the threats that are emerging." He sounds a bit desperate, and I get it, he wants to protect his home.

"What about your pain in the ass chains and shit?"

"Mostly no effect. Whatever these things are—they're immune to it." Its because the chains contain Light Magiks and aren't nearly as effective against someone who can wield the light.

"It's the beginning of the Schoth invasion. They're turning against any alliance you formed with them and plan on taking this place for their own. They'll send their scouts, then their assassins, next will come their mages... you can't fight them. Your bullets will be useless against those who can control the elements." I see no point in not telling him the truth, he's an asshole, but he needs to know. I like the Earth realm. I don't want to see it fall into the hands of the Schoth.

"What do we do?"

"I suggest you beg every Feyrie and dragon and the dark creature you have locked up in your dungeons for forgiveness and hope to your god that they'll help defend this place."

"Does this include you?"

"I'll protect the innocents of this world, but I won't help you butchers save yourselves." The look of relief on his face surprises me a little. I told him all his secret people could die and he's happy about that?

'But you also told him that you would help save the rest of the world, Iza.'

Oh, there's that, I guess.

"That's good enough. By the way—there's information in the folder there on the desk. It might give you a clue about where to find your lost friend." With those parting words, the screen goes blank, and my eyes are immediately drawn to the folder.

The folder is a dull red and unassuming. Uncaring that I may look desperate myself, I snatch it off the desk and tear it open. In it is another address and two pictures. One of the stinky vampire supermodel and the other is the shifter from the picture Michael pulled off Jameson's tablet. Both pictures have them coming and going out of a house marked with the number on the written address.

"Let's go," I say heading out the door. My instincts tell me Jameson's time is limited and it's ticking down quickly. I've wasted enough, waiting. I refuse to be responsible for his death, not when I can stop it. I hand the folder to Adriem who inputs the address into his phone.

We get the wingless loaded up in a transport van and sent to the hotel where they can be picked up. Our drive will take significantly longer. The four-hour drive stretches on for eternity. No ones talking, a good thing because I'm not sure that small talk is something I'm capable of now. My mind is already ahead, hoping that we'll find Jameson there.

That small hope is immediately dashed because the lights are all off and the house is screaming abandoned. We're too late. That doesn't stop me from hopping out of the car and heading to the front door. It's unlocked but I fight the temptation to kick it anyhow, and move farther into the house.

As I walk my eyes scan over the refuse and the broken furniture, the bits and pieces of things people leave behind, scattered on the stained hard-wood floors. I look everywhere downstairs for signs of

Jameson. My nose is leading me upstairs, where the smell of blood is fresh enough that I can tell it's his. There's enough of it to cause me to pick my pace and take the trash-strewn stairs two at a time. At the top of the stairs is a hallway and I slam each door open as I pass it, heading for the one on end. The smell is strongest from that direction.

For two breaths I pause outside the door, dreading the fact that I might find him in there dead. Swallowing the lump in my throat, I open the door and find it empty except for a chair and a plastic-topped table in the center of the room. The frayed rope dangling off the back of the chair is stained and cut. The pool of blood underneath the chair is at the congealing stage and looks like more tragic than it really is. The table next to the chair has three things on it, a pair of bloody pliers, a bloody knife and a tool I don't recognize.

"Those are bolt cutters," Phobe supplies as he walks past me to inspect the chair.

With his finger, he touches the tool and then smells it. "They cut something off, finger or toe is my guess." He leaves off the fact that we can both still smell the fear and pain. The smells are faint, at least a day old, and there's no indication of where they went when they left here.

Casting my eyes around the room, I look for something that can give me a clue, but there's not a lot. Wandering into the bathroom, my nose wrinkling from the smell, I try the faucets. No sounds, no water. The shower door is broken, and the tub is full of shit and worse. The floor is covered in food wrappers and drink bottles. The garbage can is what finally snags my attention, or rather the receipt sitting on top of it.

Rather ironic when you think about it, there's shit all over the place, but someone threw a receipt in the garbage can. I pick it up and see that it's a hotel restaurant receipt, dinner for two, in a familiar town. Dragon town. I tuck it in my pocket and walk back out into the bedroom.

"There were at least a dozen people here at any given time in the days Jameson was here. Including your stinky vampire and her shifter companion," Phobe says, his eyes on the chair in the center of the room. So, they're traveling with friends, that's good to know.

"Do you think he's dying?" I ask.

"The wound isn't life-threatening, and not my greatest concern." Frowning at him I move closer. "There's a strange smell here, and I only noticed it because of this—" he points at the seat of the chair. Words are scratched into the chair, stained from his blood.

collar hurt iza

"What does it mean?"

"The stone had similar properties, although made from different things. The Schoth were working on one with Jameson's help to specifically tamper Feyrie nature. Looking at this message makes me think they were successful," Phobe explains. A collar like that would keep him from doing something simple like healing himself. Essentially, he's human and now susceptible to infections and worse.

"He helped make a slave collar?" I ask. In answer, he nods. Well, that's fucking spectacular. Pulling out the receipt I hand it to him and watch the realization hit his face.

"I'm not that surprised, Kael has been involved from the beginning. I take it we're going to visit him?" I give him a duh look, of course we are. His smile, shark teeth and all, makes me laugh a little. He's not going to argue. He gets to eat a couple of asshole dragons, that should top his batteries off for a bit. With one last long look at the chair, I turn and leave the room, Phobe in my wake. Time to make me a pair of dragon hide boots.

12

PHOBE

Without asking, I have Adriem stop at a fast food place. Against her shocked protests, I manage to get her to eat by shoving the food in her face. However, it doesn't remove the dark circles under her eyes. The beginning of separation sickness is showing, and she *thinks* she's hiding it from me. All she's doing is delaying me finding out things, she's not nearly as secretive as she believes herself to be. We're too enmeshed together for her to hide everything from me for very long.

It's something I've not told her yet, probably never will. There are times I practice hypocrisy and hide things too.

With a long sigh, she rests her head against the window and is sound asleep within seconds. Carefully, I climb into the backseat to sit beside her. The fiends hover near her and are trying, and failing, to bolster her with their energy. Iza needs the Sidhe, they have a symbiotic relationship and with the distance her energy isn't being returned. Not that she'll listen to reason of any kind, she's determined to destroy herself saving her Feyrie. I wish that I could muster up some jealousy, at least then I could have a leg to stand on in an argument with her. She might respond better to it.

"You actually care for her, don't you?" The surprise in Adriem's voice is borderline insulting. I meet his eyes in the rear-view mirror and then turn back to Iza. Under his breath he mutters, "And this is why I stand a better chance of being crowned king than being with her."

It's true, so I say nothing.

"We'll be at the dragon place in less than twenty minutes. Are you going to wake her?"

"Yes. she'll want to kill things." An oversimplification perhaps, but true. Iza will be cross if I don't let her have fun and vent her frustration. The woman genuinely cares for her wayward imp, that fact bothers her even more. The idea of getting to smash a few heads always appeals to her. And distracts her.

Bloodthirsty, stubborn and—although there are splotches of color under her eyes and her face is pale—sexy. She'll always be these things, and I'll never ask her to change them. Even if she frustrates the fuck out of me, a good bit of the time. Unable to stop myself—I never can with her—my finger slides softly down her cheek, and I smile when a strand teases my finger with a playful nip.

When the car stops I realize I have been staring at her for several minutes. Not wanting Adriem to make it uncomfortable for either of us, I slip out the door and walk around the car to get her out. Knowing that time is of the essence I simply open the door and watch her barely catch herself from hitting the ground. Rolling on the palms of her hands she flips to her feet, her eyes glowing with her ire when she looks at me.

"You couldn't tap on the window?" I shrug at her question. That idea was not as entertaining as watching her roll out of the car. "Oh, look, they're throwing us a welcome party."

That's all she gets out before the first dragon attacks, Romiel the coward. Iza meets him half-way, her claws long and sharp. Easily she dodges him. Even as he shifts to his much larger form, she holds her own. I lean against the car and wait. Adriem dives in, his true form roaring and flinging saliva all over the place. As large as he is, compared to some of the dragons he looks small. They're outmatched and severely outnumbered. Iza can hold her own, much better than Adriem, but she's running on fumes and from the looks of things is barely trying. Every punch, kick and swipe of a sword looks half-assed.

What the fuck is she doing?

This continues for several minutes until finally, she lays down on the ground looking defeated and at the mercy of the gray dragon looming above her. She's bleeding all over the place and from what I can see, the cuts aren't healing.

Exasperated with her I leap across the clearing and land at her side. Pulling Romiel's clawed hand off her, I hold it effortlessly and wait for her to open her eyes. They pop open and with the audacity that I sometimes love and sometimes hate, she winks at me and shuts them again.

'How else can I get my dear old iguana uncle out here? He has to think he's guaranteed a win or he'll keep hiding.' The urge to kick her ass is strong, and the only way to resist it is to take a step back from her. Deciding instead to take my anger out on something deserving, I turn to Romiel and twist his leg until it snaps.

Iza remains on the ground, eyes closed, and as predicted Kael makes an appearance, thinking his opponent weak and easy to destroy. The foolish creature, his arrogance is his downfall. The large red, scaly form of the dragon now dubbed 'iguana,' lands in the middle of the fight and roars his fury. She was dead on; he planned the entire thing—this way he looks like the gallant hero coming in to save the other dragons from the evil Feyrie. Avoiding most of the fight in the process. What a load of shit.

I can't stand cowards.

Iza flips to her feet and goes straight for him. Stepping back, I avoid the tail whip of Romiel. I almost forgot about him, a dangerous habit that I have around her. Iza was right when she said a dragon would help charge my batteries. Smiling I jump up and land on his head, and the shadows come out to play. Romiel is a weak dragon but he's still a dragon, and he tastes like power.

As he screams and thrashes below me, I watch Iza. Quick as a snake she climbs up Kael's long neck, going straight for his face. Iza is impulsive, and sometimes flighty and other times, utterly reckless, but when it comes to fighting, she's as tenacious as it gets. Watching her sink her daggers into the dragon's big eyes, hearing his piercing screams of pain as he thrashes around trying to dislodge her—is a beautiful thing to behold. It's so engaging that the people are trying to reach her stop in their tracks and watch, as mesmerized as I am.

What is that saying they have when the previous king or queen dies? Oh, yes... long live the queen. Something she looks every inch of as she scrambles around the blinded dragon's head, using her daggers as handholds, deftly avoiding his claws. Claws that are strong enough to slice through his thick hide into his neck—causing rivulets of blood to form small streams as they flow down his body to the ground.

He's doing more damage to himself than she is. Iza's touch is stopping his healing in its tracks. Her death touch does not work on every creature, but it is working on Kael, and given his desperate grasps for her, he knows his end is coming. My shadows touch him, and I try to read his thoughts, curious if his weakness would enable it, but nothing happens. I'm still blocked.

Iza's smile shines through the blood on her face. The little shit is enjoying herself. Bit by bit she's toying with him and drawing it out. This betrayer doesn't deserve a clean death in her perspective. I don't disagree with her. To betray your sister over something as paltry as power is an egregious mistake. He deserves the suffering she's inflicting.

She isn't planning on stopping either, her thoughts are full of maiming and killing him. Sergean won't get this kill after all, but it should satisfy his need for revenge that his daughter—their daughter —spilled the murderer's blood and will soon take his life.

In a way, it's her right. The deception perpetuated by this creature and his puppet master led to the painful life she's lived. She's suffered the most, and with his blood, she will extract the life debt he owes her.

My feet touch the ground, temporarily pulling my eyes from Iza and her one-sided battle with Kael. Rather anticlimactically, Romiel is no more, his body was devoured completely. His memories swirl around inside of me, and they're as hollow and useless as the owner of them was. Dragons are good to eat, but I'm still hungry—I want more.

Thinking of Iza's reaction, I search the thoughts of the dragon coming at me with his teeth bared, claws out in front of him. I smile. He's as rotten as Romiel and Kael, a willing participant in their stupidity. He's also powerful, more so than Romiel.

How would Iza say it? Snack time?

Amused by my absurdity my smile broadens. The pinprick of one of my teeth digging into my lip encourages my tongue to flick out to lick the drop of blood off. The dragon's eyes widen in shock, but he is too committed to moving forward to stop. A plain imp would not have a tongue such as I. Exhaling, I let my glamour ease a little, let some of my true self-peek out. It's enough to hear his exclamation of confusion as I meet him mid-air and bury my hands in his neck. Dragon does taste good, and there's an entire buffet of them here—no reason to let all that food go to waste.

'Don't eat the good ones, some of them don't want to be here.' Iza chastises as if I didn't already know this. I say nothing and continue playing with my food. I'm already 'quality' checking each dragon as I move forward through the mass of them. The ones who don't want to fight her but were ordered will be knocked out or hobbled enough to take them out of the fight. The rest... well, they'll all meet in the darkness inside of me.

'Are you going to continue batting your mouse around, Iza?' I decide to tease her back. A quick at her to see Kael thrashing around on the ground with a laughing Iza dancing on what was left of his wings. The smile falls from my face as I turn mid-air to see a white light shoot straight for Iza. Her black eyes are wide with surprise as she flies halfway across the town square to crash through the wall of one of the houses.

Landing lightly on my feet I study the newcomer, instantly knowing what he is because I can see it around him. For every inch of darkness that Iza possess this man possesses double the light. He's Iza's counterpart in her place in fate and her Light's equivalent—the Guide—who, in a fair world, should have power equal to that of Iza's. However, this cheater came here with borrowed Magiks. I can see the sickly color of them suffocating his own. He's stronger than her with this boost, one that will ultimately cost him his life. Something like this always comes with a cost. I bet his master left this out of the offer of power.

His presence isn't too big of a surprise to me either. I knew there were more players in this game, and now one of the big ones has shown his face. The desire to cross the distance between us and rip the skin from his skull is so strong that I dig my feet in to remain still. If I go after him before she has her chance, she'll be livid with me. I'd rather her get her ass kicked, and she will, versus her being angry with me.

I won't let him kill her like he plans to do. I don't need to read his mind to know, the look on his face is evidence enough. Plus, he has the same protections that Kael has, implying they are plotting with or protected by—depending on how you look at it—the same person. No, not person... a supposed god.

Gritting my teeth, I watch a shaky but still standing Iza come strolling back into the clearing. Her face is pale, and the wounds she suffered in the initial assault are still very much present.

"Well, hello there. I'm guessing you're the Guide fellow?" She calls to him. Her smile is sharp and mocking and full of piss and wind, but inside she's a little bit worried. From somewhere she pulls on inner strength and straightens her shoulders.

Iza and Jameson researched many more things than I realized, for her to know who he is purely on sight. Iza also knows she'll lose against him as he is, but that won't stop her. Even knowing defeat is inevitable that recklessness in her is coming out. Frustratingly, the Guide seeks me out with his golden eyes and smirks. There are times that those used by the more powerful don't know the truth about their enemies, because they rely on their master too much. His master doesn't know me as well as he thinks either.

The fact that I must stand here and allow Iza to fight her fight is something that he will pay for as well.

As she walks by Kael—who's on the ground huffing in pain—she makes a move I don't expect. Smiling that vicious smile that I love, she jumps on him, and while holding the Guide's gaze—stabs the downed dragon through the heart. Kael's roar turns into a scream as death stakes a claim. It'll be slow and painful, and no Magiks of any kind, can heal the wound she dealt him. Iza put a fiend inside his heart to devour it as he dies.

Clever, clever.

The Guide slings his arm out and says a bunch of useless spell words—natural Magiks don't require spell work—it comes from the desires of the wielder, not the words spoken. The white light flies towards Iza again, but this time she's prepared and already moving. With a hard kick to the man's face, she rides him down to the ground. Two more kicks to his bloody face and he finally manages to push her off him, with Magiks rather than his arms.

The man has no idea how to defend himself physically from her. Iza picks up on immediately. With a grunt, she flips back to her feet and goes after him again. Over and over they play this game, she hits him or stabs him, and he blasts her away with Magiks. This conflict is taking its toll on both of them but in different ways. Their exhaustion has made them equal, and now they stand face to face as such.

Adriem stops beside me, breathing hard, his clothes ripped and torn—dinosaur or not he's still fighting dragons—and says, "Aren't you going to help her?" I shrug.

If she genuinely needed me to, I would, but for now I'm going to eat more dragons. Turning away I go after my next... snack.

13

IZA

I'M NOT SURE I CAN KEEP IT UP, MY BODY HURTS AND MY VISION IS FULL of black spots. Any minute now, I'm going to barf all over shiny man and there's nothing I can do about it. The one good thing out of this shit is that he looks as bad as I feel. My wounds aren't healing at all anymore, and I'm pretty sure that my Magiks pool isn't refilling either. I'm fucked nine ways over.

At least I killed my fucking uncle. Dad might be a bit pissed off, but he'll get over it. I owed that motherfucker a lot. Dad lost his mate, my mother... I lost everything. So maybe some little part of me thought it only fair I get to kill him. I'll get Dad a Christmas card or something, isn't that what families do to say I'm sorry? Maybe that hooker I asked him about getting.

'Pay attention.' Clenching my teeth I focus on the Guide.

This guy cheated and filled himself full of someone else's power. My Magiks knew immediately that something was wrong. Even with the current imbalance between the dark and light, there shouldn't be that big of a difference between the two of us. Hell, if we had been on Sidhe land, I'd be the one with the upper hand, instead I'm the one about to pass out. I'm getting my ass handed to me by a guy who probably can't do a single pushup.

The Light Magiks burn when they hit me. He might be a complete wuss when it comes to a bit of hand-to-hand, but he isn't when it comes to slinging that light shit around. The good thing is, he's tired too, enough that this—I punch him in his mouth—hurts more. When his Magiks hit me again though, I'm laid out flat.

Spitting the dust out of my mouth I roll to my side to try and climb to my feet only to fall back on my face. Well, this sucks. Pushing myself harder, I try again and fall again. Blood coats my hands and arms, it's also running down my stomach to pool at my waistband. I'm fucking spent. Every part of me is tired, even my hair that is now singed and injured. The silly things tried to bite him, and he fried them.

I hope they can heal.

'Are you quite finished?' Phobe's using that pissy tone. I want to tell him that I can keep going, I want to so bad, but we both know I can't.

'Yeah, for the moment. Can you smack him once for me though?'

'I shall deal with it—'

'No! Don't kill him, it will fuck things up and will more than likely kill me. The only one who can take his life... is me. That's if those fucking books are telling the truth.' His frustration bleeds through to me. He's not the only one, but Jameson was crystal clear about it when he showed me the old books he found in the library at the Sidhe and well, one day I was bored enough to read them.

'You trust those books?'

'Yes, the Sidhe directed Jameson to them.' Lifting my sore, tired head, I watch him cross the few yards between him and dumbass and smack him with a Schoth's dead body. Laughing, I fall back on the ground and continue laughing when Phobe's familiar arms wrap around me to lift me from the cold ground.

Since my finger is in such fine form from all its use lately, I use it to salute the Guide, who's laying on his back with a stupefied look on his face. I rest my head against Phobe's shoulder and pass the fuck out.

♥

Jameson

It takes genuine effort, but I turn my head enough to the side to peek through my swollen eyelid at the commotion. We've moved again. First, we were in the warehouse, then that horrible house where they tortured me until I could no longer scream. We're holed up in some sort of boarded-up storefront now. There are chairs that resemble those from the hair salon, I indulge in them often. There's honestly nothing better than the feeling of someone else washing your hair and massaging your scalp.

I'd give everything I own for something so simple as that.

"That fucking bitch has killed me!" Kael's roar of anger fills the small space. Followed by groans of pain and the scraping sounds of someone rolling around on the floor. My one good eye adjusts enough for me to see him, in human form, sprawled out on the floor covered in blood and little else. Biting the side of my tongue barely keeps the smile off my face. I know Iza's handiwork when I see it.

"Something she did trapped me like this... in this fucking frail form. That two-faced motherfucker promised me I would heal... I'm not—" deep wheezy breath, that has a rattle is never good. "—healing. Nothing is healing."

"From the looks of it, you're not going to live long enough to kill her. What the fuck did she do to you?" Sharon asks coming into view. She eyes Kael's battered body and then rolls her eyes. "I don't understand how a mage or whatever she is, can do what she does. She took out my entire nest and I plan to kill her for it."

Kael surprises everyone by laughing. The deep, wet coughing that follows doesn't stop it either. He laughs right through it.

"You idiots. You think she's... a... fucking mage?" The laughing gets louder and sounds grossly wet. Something inside of him is loose and bleeding. The instincts that allow me to do my little bits of healing are screaming at me. The Feyrie inside of me senses more, something dark is inside of him. Something that's part of Iza.

"Iza isn't a mage. Iza is half dragon and—"

I can't help myself, it's hard to talk, and there's a good chance they won't care about a word I say, but I have to interrupt, "Yeah, your niece," I laugh a little and mine doesn't sound much better than Kael's. "She's going to kill all of you because that's what Iza does, she kills things. You're too stupid to see it, yet." The big lug, Reggie, must have understood well enough because he crosses to me in a few long strides and punches me in the face. I'm tied to a chair against the wall, so there's not much space for me to go anywhere except the wall, my head thumps against.

"For someone so strong, she lost well enough to our boss," he says while standing over me with a smirk on his face. At least, I think it's a smirk. It could be a frown, the room isn't orienting quite right. Its spinning, I wish they'd stop beating on my face—up until now it was my best asset.

I attempt to smile up at him, and say, "She must not have been trying hard."

"Why in the world do you think that? Boss said she's severely injured."

"You sound like one of those cheesy henchmen from the movies. You know the one who dies in the stupidest way?" He raises his hand to hit me again and stops when Sharon grabs his arm.

"If you hit him again, Reggie, you might kill him. I don't want to end up being the one tied to that chair in his place." She cautions him. Through the blur of blood in my eyeball, I can see the strength of his desire written on his face. Oh, yeah, he doesn't like me, and he's almost stupid enough to hit me again and tempt fate. Almost. He lowers his arm and steps back, his eyes on Sharon.

He has a crush on the vamp. That's an interesting bit of information to have and maybe use later. I suspected it before, but he's looking at her with big dumb doe eyes now. That's a weakness that can be exploited. The Schoth taught me that. He's not that smart and easy to rile up. Sharon isn't always around to calm him down, either.

When the door slams open, admitting the Guide and his bodyguards, I cough instead of laughing like I want to. He looks rougher than Kael, and his wounds aren't healing either. The exception is, he's not dying like the dragon.

Turning to Reggie and Sharon, he says, "You two gather your things. I want you to go give her a message for me." He hands them something in a brown envelope. "I did the hard work already, she's not a threat anymore," he orders, with power in his voice. But I catch the grimace of pain as he sits down in the chair at the scarred desk across from me. "Tell her either she meets us at our next safe house or I kill the imp." The two nod and leave me, and both bloody men in silence.

"You told me I'd heal," Kael asks from the floor, breaking the tension.

"And you believed me?"

"She'll kill you too, you know. I think by the time it's all said and done she'll kill all of us." Kael wheezes and falls into silence.

"My master says differently. Her death will free us to rule all the worlds... well, me. You'll be dead, dragon." It's said snidely. This man isn't surprised Kael is dying. "As angry as she was, I expected more of a fight."

Kael's sudden laugh ends with wet cough, then he says, "That girl is just like her mother... she wasn't angry at you."

"How do you know that?" The doubt in the Guide's voice is comical.

"Because you're alive," Kael says, with such smugness that for a moment I don't realize he's stopped breathing. The utter stillness of his body clarifies his demise. This time I do laugh, one down.

14

PHOBE

"You know, I was hoping that the motherfucker didn't exist. But I could feel something out there in the world, something dangerous to me. Whatever it is, revolves around that man," Iza says, then runs to the bathroom her hand covering her mouth. The sounds of her retching tighten my stomach.

This is her third trip to the bathroom to vomit, to dry heave and suffer because there's nothing left to come up. The first two times she didn't make it that far, the floor and my lap felt the wrath of her upset system. I cleaned us both up and gave her cool rags to place on her wounds and face. No human medicine will work on her, and there are no healers that can heal her now, not with her separated from the Sidhe as she is.

There has to be something I can do. Perhaps it's time to ask the Sidhe itself? Michael is lost in his computer land, looking for information that may help us while Ruthie is brooding in her room with the TV turned up too loud. She came and checked on Iza once and then said to give her some type of drink and it would help. Teenage females are odd, there was some concern for Iza in her, but she's so blinded by her desires and frustrations that it's not enough to be here helping Iza now. Selfish child.

That leaves only one capable of caring for her, "Make sure she rests, I shall return—watch her closely." Adriem stands from the chair he has been broodily sitting in and nods. If something happens to her in his care, I'll kill him, and he knows it.

Hours later I find the Sidhe. It's one of the few things that I can portal to, if it's not trying to hide from me. I don't make it inside but I do manage to come out near it. Finding it wasn't easy, it hid well, and Iza refused to let any of us know about it. Rather smart of her to keep that knowledge only to those who have gone with it. It's why she had to call someone to pick up the wingless, instead of sending them herself.

Standing outside in the dark, I watch the man and woman, hands clasped, walk right by me. It's two Nightmares, and they look relaxed and smiling while making small talk to each other. For all appearances, like a couple taking a stroll. That's not the case, and anyone who attempts to get inside will discover that. Hidden deeper in the shadows are more of their brethren watching with sharp eyes, and other creatures mill about even more hidden. They're taking the security serious.

A note of sound fills the night sky. The Sidhe knows that I'm here, I greet it by brushing my shadows against it. Carefully, I show it what I came here for, and I also show it the condition Iza is in. The sadness I get in return is palpable, this creature—energy, whatever it is, cares for her. The ground rumbles beneath my feet and the Nightmares gather near its source, prepared to take on the enemy, but this isn't an enemy. A crack appears a few feet from me, and a root unfurls upwards, the end glows an eerie purple color, much like Iza's eyes, holding something.

A ring.

Peeling out of the shadows I step forward and take it. Gently, I place it in my pocket and look around at the startled faces, and say, "Be thankful for the sacrifices she's making for you." Turning, I wrap the dark around me once again and begin to run. I can't portal back to her and time is precious. I don't want her on her own for any length of time. With the state she's in it's dangerous. Iza believes herself to be dying and, with the emotions entangled in this belief, is unpredictable, incredibly so. Adriem can help guard her, but he can't keep her from doing the things she wants to do.

I'm not even sure I can.

Impatient with my progress, I stop as great leathery, black wings unfurl from my back. The humans have seen the monsters, hiding is no longer necessary. Flapping them experimentally, I jump and use them to lift into the air. With great flaps I move towards the pulse of her pulling me unerringly towards her.

As I fly I think of what I saw on the news stories as I journeyed here. Militaries from around the world are gathering, joining together to face the Schoth threat. There's no doubt at all that the Schoth are invading. A war unlike anything humans have ever seen is coming, and without the help of the Feyrie—they will all die or become the slaves of their soon-to-be conquerors.

Iza is the only one who can save them.

15

IZA

WAKING WITH A START, A SCREAM OF PAIN CAUGHT IN MY THROAT, I immediately roll over and bury my face in the pillow. The dampness is cold against my skin, but I ignore it, using the suffocating feeling of the pillow to modify my breathing. Gods, I was dreaming of Jameson and... no, I was Jameson, and they were torturing him. Jameson has no idea how to be resilient to such things, no way of being prepared for that type of pain.

All he did was scream in agony.

How can I not feel a little sorry for him? Especially since in that dream-that's-not-a-dream he wasn't breaking, he was screaming, crying, and begging, but not breaking. *Bravo, Jameson. You're so much stronger than I thought you'd be.* How much longer he can keep it up is the biggest question on my mind. I have to find him, he needs help.

Rolling onto my back I scrub my hands down my face. The nausea is still present but lessened, probably because I don't have anything left to puke up anymore. Sitting up gingerly, to the protest of the various cuts and bruises on my body, I move around to test out my limits.

A few broken ribs, probably a fractured right arm, if the limitations of movement and sharp pain are any indication. Also, a couple of deep gouges in my stomach don't appreciate me moving around. They're bandaged but sore as hell.

Climbing out of bed, I lean one hand against the wall and grit my teeth as the world swims around me. I need two things... no, three things. Shower, food, and water. Grabbing a bottle of water while using the wall to hold me up, I slowly make my way to the bathroom, I chug most of it in one drink. Tossing it on the floor towards the garbage can, I pull my sweaty clothes off. Three times I try to turn the taps on and miss, damn things keep moving. A masculine arm moves past me and turns on the water. The shower fills with the cleansing steam of blessed heat.

"Do you need help getting in?" Adriem sounds nervous asking and it makes me laugh. Well, the noise that came out of me was supposed to be a laugh but sounded more like a weird wheezy snort.

"Yeah probably." I manage to stutter out. A chuckle follows someone lifting me and carefully sitting me on my shaky feet.

Leaning my shoulder against the wall, I wave him out and bury my head under the hot spray of water. I have no idea how long I stand there, letting the water take away some of the aches and pains, but it's long enough that the water temperature cools.

With the tepid water I soak the bandages to make it easier to remove them, but taking them off still stings like a sonofabitch. I toss them towards the garbage can too. Mustering up some energy I grab the small bar of soap and a washcloth and start scrubbing. Removing the filth and dried blood reveals exactly how damaged I am.

There are abrasions, claw marks, skin tears and bruises marring most of my body. Twisting around I see that even my butt has bruises on it and none of them are healing like they normally would. They're not lethal, but they're not much better than when they were inflicted either.

Phobe just had to go and be right, didn't he?

Hurrying as fast as I'm able, I finish washing up, including trying to wash my poor hair that is lethargic and still—concerningly so. Drying off is a painful experience and I give up halfway through. Cursing under my breath, I walk out into the room to hunt for some band-aids. Some of the wounds are bleeding and taking another shower is out of the question.

Adriem is sitting on the edge of the bed with bags full of first aid supplies sitting beside him and a worried frown on his face. The once over he gives my nude body has nothing but concern in it.

"Sit down and let's get you patched up, you're a fucking mess."

"I had no idea," I reply sarcastically, laying flat on the bed so that he can start with the worst ones.

"Where's Phobe?" I'm asking that question a lot lately.

"He went to run some errands. He should be back—"

"OW! Motherfucker!" I give him a dirty look but wave for him to continue. I'm pretty sure he dumped acid on my stomach and not antiseptic.

"Sorry, I'm not the best at this." He doesn't sound sorry, the little sparkle in his eye belies that fact.

"Any news?" He opens his mouth to answer me, but the door flies open and Michael, with Ruthie mid-yell behind him, strolls in.

"Holy shit, you're naked!" Michael exclaims.

"Oh, my gods, are you serious?" I say in mock shock. He crosses the room, cheeks red but his blue eyes are serious as he studies the wounds that Adriem is cleaning, except now with a lighter touch.

"Iza, you're hurt."

"I told you she wasn't indestructible." Ruthie sasses from the foot of the bed. I look past Adriem's shoulder at her. The smile of triumph she has on her face fades, and she turns away from me. Someone save me from teenagers.

"Thanks, Ruthie. I remember a time you were the beat up one in the trunk of a car." I see the moment that my jab hits home, her face pales, and she looks guiltily at me.

"I'm sorry Iza... I—" She wrings her hands and goes to step towards me.

"No, it's okay, I get it. Hormones and all that. Why don't you and Michael go get something to eat, I'd love something greasy and bad for me." She nods and grabs Michael's elbow, dragging him out the door.

"She's a good girl. I think loving that boy has her fucked up," Adriem says, finishing up the last bandage.

"I heard love does that to you," I say distractedly while sitting up and digging through the bag on the floor for clothes. A simple shirt and jeans work and with a little help from Adriem I get them on.

"Does it?"

"Does what?" I have no idea what he's talking about.

"Does love fuck you up?" Oh, that.

"Yeah, yeah it does." Especially if it's a fucked-up love to begin with. Then I add, "But in some situations, it's worth it." I wouldn't trade anything to change what I have with Phobe, as odd as our relationship is, it's also unique and special to us both. Love isn't always roses and soft kisses, like in books or TV. Sometimes it's teeth and tongues and... wow, that went south fast.

A laugh bubbles out of my throat, its rough and sounds like an old woman's, but even in the condition I'm in, the fact that I can still think of Phobe in a sexual way—amuses the shit out of me. My chest constricts in pain, but I press my hand to it and keep laughing, I've had worse.

"What's so funny?"

"My lady hard-on for Phobe." I look up as I answer and laugh harder at the look on his face. His nose is all scrunched up like he smelled something rotten and his eyes are wide and full of disgust. Best look ever. My laughter turns into coughing, but I make it through it and ignore the taste of blood in my mouth. Laughter is precious, and I refuse to let something as mundane as pain stop it from happening.

"Is that even possible? A lady hard-on?" He still has that wrinkled up look going on his face, and because this little moment of levity is helping me, I decide to extend it.

"Wanna see?" I tease. Not that he didn't see all the good bits when I was naked. He still smiles like he won the prize, arrogant shit.

The hair on my arm stands straight up, and my eyes jerk to the door. Mister Big and Bad is standing on the other side of that door, I can feel it. Hmm, I wonder how far I can push this to entertain myself without him eating Adriem?

"I know you're joking, but it's hard not to say yes."

"You've already seen, you know—earlier when we had our moment on the bed." The cocky smile drops like a hot rock. His face pales, and he glances at the door. All that arrogance and power, yet he's afraid of Phobe. Shows that Nightmares were born with brains *and* brawn.

"Iza, wait... what moment?" He scoots back away from me, putting a few feet between us.

"You know... our moment. I was naked. Your hands were on my body." I stand, wobbly as a baby dragon, and start walking towards him in a limping seductive sway. I'm sure it looks more like a pirate walking on a ship, but I'm sticking with seductive.

"I was bandaging your wounds and..." he sputters and then sputters some more. Walking backward until he hits the wall he stares at me the same way he was staring at the door. I stop in front of him and pat his cheek as the door opens.

Phobe, who was obviously reading my mind and probably Adriem's horrified one as well, knows what I was up to and he knows why. Playing along, he stops near us and looks Adriem right in the face and growls. Adriem gives me a dirty look and slips away from me to head out the door. Unable to contain myself any longer I lean against the wall and laugh/cough.

Phobe grabs my shoulder and spins me around. Pulling my hand up, he slides something warm and familiar onto my finger, and instantly I feel better. The coughing stops, the pain starts to recede, and familiar itch of skin knitting together relaxes me. What the fuck?

"The Sidhe sent this for you, a small part of it is enough to help you for now. It won't last forever, Iza." Taking a moment to stare down at the dark stone ring on my finger, glowing a little purple with the essence of the Sidhe, I take a deep breath and close my eyes feeling the power surge through me. Beautiful dark power. Stretching my hands over my head I let it flow through me, fill me and make me feel the best I've felt in days. When I open my eyes, I leap on Phobe, who easily catches me.

"What exactly is a lady hard-on?" he asks as soon as our mouths part.

Laughing I say, "Wanna see?"

♥

"Where are you going?" Pulling on my socks, again, I smirk over at him.

I feel better, so I don't want to sit in the room with my thumb up my ass, plus, my rumbling stomach is reminding me that solid food and I are estranged. Michael and Ruthie didn't return with any, probably distracted by their tiff. "I'm hungry, so I'm going to go to the restaurant they have downstairs. Do you want anything?"

"No, I am going to look up a few things on your Google God."

"Anything interesting?" He shrugs, so maybe. I slide on the other shoe and head towards the door. "After this, I want to try and find that hotel on the receipt we found. If nothing else, it can lead us in the right direction." He's already absorbed in the computer screen, so I'm ignored.

The story of my life. Shaking my head, I close the door softly and stop outside of Ruthie's door, I raise my hand to knock, but the sound of raised voices stops me.

"Can we go home now? She doesn't need us here. She has Phobe and Adriem. She doesn't need you to get in the way, Michael." Ruthie's voice is shrill and clogged with tears. Part of me aches for her, she's not having an easy time with things, young love and hormones and her life-changing so drastically.

I need to kidnap her for a movie or something, maybe that will help.

"Ruthie, she's doing this for us, but you're too worried about yourself. She gives you everything you ask for, and all you care about is making our relationship work. Do you know how fucked up that is?" Michael doesn't sound like a kid anymore, and the frustration in his voice sounds like it's been there awhile.

If there's a way to help them, I don't know what it is. Ruthie is swinging hard in both directions and from what everyone has told me, especially the mothers in the Sidhe, its normal behavior for a teenage girl in love. I wish that hating me wasn't part of the deal. I miss spending time with her. I miss her hugs and her humor. Gods, all this shit is just a regular mess now. I wish they all came with instruction booklets so that I could cheat and read the directions.

Choosing to retreat this time, I move away from the door and take the stairs. Elevators give me the creeps, especially after the whole kidnapping thing. I smell the perfume before I see the owner. I need to find out who told her slathering it on like that helps. All it does is make her more identifiable.

'Company,' I caution, slowing my pace enough to get a good idea of how many are waiting for me. A fiend provides the answer. A few dozen and some of them are police officers. Why do people always do this before I can eat food? My stomach is full on growling, and the persistent sounds coming from it aren't swayed by the fact that there are bad people waiting a few feet away.

This time though, she isn't getting away from me.

Taking the last few steps I plant a smile on my face and stroll casually around the corner. Most of them startle when they notice my presence, that puts a real smile on my face.

"My boss has a message for you." She says it with a lot more bravado than she's feeling. Only a blind man couldn't see how she's hiding partially behind the large shifter in front of her. She pulls out something wrapped in yellow fabric out of a brown envelope, and tosses it to me. I catch it and open it up.

A single finger lay in its folds.

This isn't a surprise so I keep the smile on my face. Phobe was right, it's a finger. Wrapping it back up, I tuck it in my pocket. It's not important anymore, and I won't let them scare me with it. A severed finger is useless to me. We can't reattach it after this long.

"Okay, what's this supposed to mean? Is it like a snack or something?" This isn't the answer they were expecting. I'm surprising them left and right today. This is fun.

"He says if you don't turn yourself over to him when he summons you, the next body part will be his head," she sneers out. I really, *really* want to rip her face off.

Why not?

Moving before she can react, I grab her and yank her away from the safety of her people and sling her up against the wall. The impact shakes brick dust down around her, and I'm on her before she can scream.

"Coward, that's all you are and all you'll ever be," I whisper to her right before burying my claws in her face. Bracing my other hand against the wall, I pull and rip it clean off the screaming woman. Satisfaction is thick and filling, and I look at the torn skin in my hand before turning and tossing it to the shifter she was hiding behind.

He catches it reflexively, with wide eyes and a gaping mouth, some of it even splatters into the maw of surprise. Turning back to the vampire, I punch through the bones of her chest, past the bone splinters that tear into my hand, and wrap my fingers around the muscle that will end the life she doesn't deserve to have. Meeting her eyes, I smile and pull her heart, still beating, through the hole my fist created.

She's dead before she hits the ground, my Magiks killing her before her heart stops beating in my hand. Turning to face the rest of the mob I lift it and take a nice juicy bite out of it. It tastes awful, but the point is made. The shifter comes at me first.

Black shadows rush in, and everyone standing behind him vanishes in a chorus of screams that are suddenly cut off. Godsdamnit, Phobe is ruining my fun. Punching the shifter mid-air, I turn away from him to Phobe standing on the stairwell.

"Why did you do that?"

"You're barely healed, I'm not about to let you get injured again so soon." Why'd he go straight to the logic part of it and make perfectly good sense?

"We still have that one." I motion with my thumb over my shoulder. "He can probably give us some information."

"You'll live longer if you stop perpetuating this ridiculous self-destructive behavior. Or do you want to die and you're too afraid to tell me?" His sudden anger catches me off guard.

"Eh?"

"That's what it looks like to me, to all of them. It's like you are searching for your death with no thought to what it will do to those around you." I stand there and blink a few times. Feeling like a complete dumbass but not entirely sure what to say, I keep blinking. "You think you're failing, but you're not and this is all—" he sweeps his hand wide. "Due to greed for power. Unfortunately, you and your Feyrie are caught in the middle of it."

Well, then, that's a rather emotional speech for him and leaves with no idea what to say. He's so right that it makes me want to punch him and kiss him at the same time. The fact that he hit home so hard, by saying I feel like a failure, and that I didn't realize how self-destructive I have become...

The sob breaks out of me violently, shocking us both, but it is what it is. Now that it's started I can't seem to stop it. I try cramming my hand over my mouth, pulling my shirt up over my face, but nothing stops the next one or the next one. Soon there are so many I'm a blubbering mess and find myself doing the only thing I can. I slide to the ground with a meaty plop and bawl my fucking eyes out.

There's no way to gauge how long I sit there, sobbing and leaking like a squeezed sponge, but at some point, warm, strong arms wrap around me, and it's not the ground under my butt anymore. He pulls me onto his lap and holds me until I cry myself right out.

There are no words because none need to be said, no pointless comforts or false promises... just his presence and the knowledge it will always be there for me. Nuzzling my snotty face into his shirt I sigh and take a deep breath of Phobe's unique scent. This beautiful monster is all mine. Smiling in a super sneaky way, I blow my nose on his shirt and slip out of his grasp.

"Iza, that's disgusting." He's standing and holding his shirt out from his skin with a look of dismay on his face.

"You've had worse on you." I grab the shifter and sling him over my shoulders.

"You two are the weirdest fucking couple I've ever seen." Adriem comments from the stairs. I shrug, yeah that's us, and it's something I'm perfectly okay with.

16

PHOBE

THE SHIFTER IS PROVING USELESS. HE HAS NO IMPORTANT INFORMATION at all—except the location of where they are holding Jameson. To Iza this is useful, but not me. I'm tired of seeing her hurt over the vain, selfish creature. He doesn't deserve to have someone care enough to go through this for him. If he survives this he better treat her accordingly or I'll rip out his guts and use them to decorate her bedroom. Her feelings of guilt about him be damned.

Leaning down, I put my face in front of the shifter who keeps giving Iza death looks. He had unrequited feelings for the vampire, who was using him as a lackey for her own gains. He was her dog to command, nothing more.

"Be a good puppy and tell me who your master is, or I'll take that small manhood of yours and feed it to you," I say softly, letting my eyes show him that I mean what I say.

"You're going to kill me no matter what I say."

"True enough, but," I smile, and my face continues to stretch, and it keeps growing until I can see the shine of my white teeth reflected in his eyes. "The way you die is still in question." When his pupils expand from small pinpricks my teeth turned them into, he comes to a quick decision.

"He calls himself the Light, and everyone is afraid of him. I can't understand why because when he's in the Guides body, the man wears lacy shirts with these fancy collars from like the fucking eighteen hundred—" He pauses in his rants and looks askew at my teeth that are still on display.

Clearing his throat, he continues, "All I know is that Kael, that dude that she killed," he nods his head towards Iza, who is leaning against the wall next to the bathroom door. "Was terrified of him, they all are." He sneers and says, "Shar was his lover, he'll want to avenge her." He turns his hate-filled gaze towards Iza.

"Does he know anything else?" she asks me instead of him.

"No, that's the extent of his knowledge," I say. His thoughts are only full of dreams of torturing Iza in revenge.

"You going to eat him?" I nod. Turning, she leaves the room, and after a few seconds, Adriem follows her.

"Hey! What does she mean to eat me?" Those vengeful thoughts have turned to macabre images of people eating people. I smile more broadly. The first shadow touching his leg makes him jump. Clamping my hand over his mouth I push his head against the chair and slowly start to enjoy my meal. It's not that he is satisfying in any way other than the more primal one. Instead of him being able to hurt Iza, I get to hurt him.

The moisture of his tears against the hand muffling his screams is a bonus. This diluted creature thought he was going to survive to fight another day, to live long enough to kill everyone close to Iza before raping and then killing her.

All he's doing now is pointlessly begging.

♥

AN HOUR later Iza is still gone, but she's not far away. She's one room over, arguing with Ruthie about feminine products to help with the girl's moodiness. I can't help but be a bit amused by the conversation. Ruthie insists that she isn't menstruating and Iza argues that only menstruating women act like bitches. Ruthie acts offended, and then Iza laughs at her and offers to give her chocolate.

Turning on the TV, I decide to give them privacy in their conversation, when it turns to talk of maxi pads and tampons, which Iza still calls tam-poons. Although, now I think she does it purely for reactions from others. The hurried steps that follow the slamming of the door, precede knocking on my door, makes me shake my head. I open it, and a red-faced Michael slips past me and sits on the bed with a huff.

"I'm sorry Phobe, but I can't handle that anymore." I shut the door and sit in the chair next to the TV.

"Breaking news, our media affiliates are informing us that some type of energy barriers are popping up all over the world and cutting off communications and contact with towns and small cities. So far only the United States, England, and Russia have reported these strange barriers and have sent the military in to investigate. We have a reporter at one of the sites currently but are unable to get in contact with him or any of his crew. The military is refusing to allow anyone to go near the barriers and ask that we remain calm until they can determine their cause." A youthful newscaster reports with a pale face. The worry she's feeling comes out in the rapid was she's talking.

"Government officials are reassuring people that they have everything under control while advising people to remain in their homes and to report any suspicious behavior."

The forward force is here, scouts will already be working in conjunction with the first wave of invaders. The energy barriers will be hiding their base camps and the portals needed for them to bring more through. There have been sightings in major cities, and sightings are now being taken seriously because people are disappearing by the dozens, climbing towards hundreds.

Food for the scouts, prisoners for information… it could be many things.

Before Iza came along, I was their forward scout, giving me insight into what they'll do next. The base camps are typically followed by the second wave which is the elemental warrior mages. Usually metal, earth, and fire workers. Given that this world is mostly water they'll probably throw some of them in as well. I would. After them will come the weather mages. They're brutal when they invade, they'll kill millions.

These human weapons, no matter how large or how many missiles it can shoot, stand no chance against a mage that can break down the components of your missile into dust with a wave of their hand. The only ones who can stop this are in the Sidhe and this hotel.

Iza has already decided to help the humans, and with her help, they might stand a chance because she and I are a package deal and I love eating mages.

"Those Schoth people are coming through, aren't they?" Michael asks quietly.

"Yes, unless we stop them," I answer, watching the emotions chase themselves across his face.

"Can you stop them?" I can tell by looking at him that he wants me to say yes, but that would be a lie.

"Maybe." I choose to tell the truth.

"Are you as badass as Iza thinks you are?" His face flushes, but he holds my gaze steadily.

"Yes. You could be as well. The Schoth fear your people."

"Why?"

I remember that he was orphaned young and was probably not taught much about his true abilities. "Your kind eat Magiks, that's why you go for the brains of your prey, it houses their power. You're also immune to most types of it, and only the strongest Schoth can stop you before you get to them."

"Seriously?"

"Seriously."

"Then how did they kill so many?"

"It was not them that killed most of them." And I leave it at that. "You have spent so long trying to fit in with the vampires that you've limited yourself based on their weaknesses. Yours are not theirs, but you're not infallible either. You have to learn, and then you will be able to use the arsenal you were born with."

"Can you teach me?" I consider him a moment. He will never equal Iza in skill or abilities, but he can be equal to some of the Nightmares in strength. He would be a valuable asset to Iza in the coming times.

"Yes, but you won't like the way I teach."

"I don't like a lot of things that I have to do, that doesn't stop me from doing them." He's sincere in his desire to learn, no matter the method. Yes, a good part of it is loyalty to Iza and belief in their cause, another part is his desire to protect Ruthie because he loves her. Something that frustrates him because Ruthie is always in doubt of it.

"We'll start after Iza finds the imp and returns to the Sidhe." He smiles in excitement and then turns back to the news. Michael is smart for his age. He's also braver than most males I have met, and I have met thousands. Iza chose well in this boy.

The door opens, and a frustrated Iza strolls in, the small frown between her eyes and the clenching of her jaw indicates that she lost her disagreement with Ruthie. I'm not sure how one can argue about menstruation, it seems like an argument for argument's sake.

"She threw my chocolate gift at me. I'm at a loss, how else can I make her less bitchy? Especially when she refuses to accept that chocolate is the magical food," she muses, shaking her head as she plops down on the bed next to Michael.

"She's bitchy about everything. Lately, nothing I do is right anymore," he mutters.

"She keeps telling me it's a girl thing, and I'm a girl and don't understand all of it so don't feel bad, Michael. The Google God says this mood should only last for seven to ten years and then she'll be our smiling Ruthie again." She reassures him and pats his shoulder. Not understanding that she's not truly reassuring. Seven to ten years to Michael is infinite.

She fastens her eyes on the TV and sees the news. Her reaction isn't one of surprise. Iza understands the Schoth in some ways better than even I do. Her cell phone chimes and distractedly she looks at it. The minute her thoughts turn dark she gets my full attention. Through her, I can see the text message.

. . .

I'M GUESSING you disposed of my messengers. I shall then make the offer myself. Your life for your mage's and everyone else in your Sidhe. It is the only way he and the rest of your flock will survive any of this.

HE PROVIDES an address and time for her to meet him. The address is here in this town we are currently in, Melborn, and the time is an hour from now. Iza, forever dangerously impulsive, made up her mind the minute she read the message. Her life for all of theirs. To her, it's a simple choice with no in-depth thought required.

The fool believes that they'll keep their promises.

"Michael, go," I order. Without questioning anything, he's up and out of the room in seconds. The resounding slam of the door shutting pulls Iza's eyes to mine.

"It's the right thing to do, Phobe. One life for all of theirs." It. Is. Not.

"Are you insane? These people aren't honorable. Why are you even considering such a thing?"

"For some reason, this man wants me dead," she pauses and shifts mental gears. "He's killing them one at a time anyhow. This way I can earn them a little more time."

"To what? Hide and run like scared rabbits for the rest of their lives?"

"To live, Phobe. We're all living on borrowed time, something everyone knows. If I do this, they can have a little more." She's made up her stupid, bleeding-heart mind. I can't have this. She can't do this.

I won't allow her to do this! I cross the room in two strides and grab her shoulders and pull her up to me. Holding her face even with mine I shake her a little.

"This miserable world… all of these miserable worlds are better with you in them. Someone like Jameson or one of your special children might make ripples, but you're a tsunami, Iza. You matter more than any of them, you're needed—" I shake her again. "They need you. I need you!" My voice tapers off, and I realize that I'm yelling. Grabbing my composure, I release her and cross the room away from her, more to stop me from yelling again than anything else. The fact that I did pisses me off.

Iza is standing there with a smile on her face and her eyes sparkling in humor. How is this situation amusing to her? As she watches me that smile grows and a laugh parts her lips.

"You like me," she teases, running at me and jumping into my arms. I hesitate, unsure of why her amusement exists. To stop wondering, I dive into her thoughts.

The little twit is happy I care enough to yell at her. Shaking my head in wonder at how her mind works, I bury my face in her neck and breathe in the smell of her. If only I could take this moment and extend it forever, to always have her like this—happy and in my arms.

Fuck, she *has* made me into a sentimental monster.

"We're still going to meet them," she whispers against my skin.

"You're not—"

"No, I won't trade myself… but we're still going," she insists.

I never once doubted she would, but I wish she'd learn to lie better.

17

IZA

We show up late because being on time seems too desperate. I'm not at that stage yet, a finger getting cut off isn't a big deal. Well, to Jameson it might be, but I can think of worse things they could've sent me. Especially the one thing that got him into this mess, to begin with. On second thought, maybe him losing that will teach him a lesson about thinking with something other than his brain. We can hope this whole experience taught him something—with Jameson you never know.

He's a bit on the delicate side. We'll be lucky if he's mentally stable after this mess. I wasn't, I'm still not, not really, but I do what I can.

Phobe's eyes are on me, so I walk in the door first. This way if anyone nabs me he can nab them, or eat them, whichever works for him. I'm only half-surprised when no one tries to. Instead, there's a gathering of people at the center of the large, mostly empty room.

Jameson isn't here.

The Guide, who's staring at me rather angrily, is. On either side of him are Schoth mages, each of them powerful enough that the hum of that awful Light Magiks from here is static against my own. Those two combined can kick my ass, if I'm not careful, I know it with absolute surety.

The Guide is a different story, there are so much Magiks entwined with his that isn't *his*, it's a bit confusing. Someone with a lot of power to spare is helping this fucker, someone who can and probably will kick my ass… if not kill me. Internally I shake myself. I won't waver. I promised Phobe I wouldn't trade myself, I'll stick to my word, but it's hard not to be the martyr my guilt tells me to be.

Common sense won out too. They won't keep their promise, they won't leave the other Feyrie alone. Not unless I'm in the way to be the world's biggest pain in the ass to them. This thought makes me smile, and that smile is what they see first.

The Guide frowns harder and the mages with him tense.

"Are you here to trade yourself?" Rolling my eyes at his question, I stop a few feet away and cross my arms.

"Na, I figured I'd still stop by though. Have a bit of a staring contest and see if your dick is as small as I think it is." Watching the emotions chase themselves across his face as I talk is quite enjoyable. For someone with so much power, he's a bit of an idiot. Speaking of idiots. "So, what happened to my dear uncle? Is he out parking the car?"

"He died on the floor like a dog, as your mother died. Like you'll die!" Spittle forms little white peaks at the corners of his mouth as he yells at me. This only makes the entire thing more fun for me.

"That's a better death than he deserved. It's a shame my dad wasn't able to do it, but I imagine that he's having a bit of fun with him right now. Just like he'll have with you one day soon." He goes to step forward but freezes as he walked into a wall. With a shake of his head, he steps back, and I know then that someone stopped him.

The smell of the Magiks is similar to those affecting Rido and Val. A sickly-sweet smell that reminds me of decaying meat. The hair on my arms stand up as the Magiks inside of me rebel because of the presence of the other. Its Light Magiks but not at the same time—it's more and different but similar enough that its source is hidden away by the present mages. Curious, very curious.

Watching the Light Magiks make small movements across the skin of the Guide, to and fro like the waves of the tide, makes me doubt it's him. The Magiks are doing that because it's being forced to stay on him, which means the majority of the power he possesses isn't his. The Magiks you're born with, lash or swirl around you and are solidly anchored to your soul.

He's weaker on his own than I realized, if I can find a way to strip him of the Magiks that aren't his, he'd make an easier target. I'd be able to get my fucking hands on him and beat the smirk right off his face. The owner of that Magiks is the real threat, the boss—the one who made Kael afraid. I know by looking at this little bit he's laid on the Guide that I can't beat him.

He's like Phobe but stronger. I don't think any of us can beat him, at least... not fairly.

'If you eat him, how big of a jumpstart does that give your battery?'

'Bigger than the two mages with him.' I go to step forward, but his finger in my belt loop stops me. *'I can't get to him now, Iza. He's... protected from me.'* The menace is practically dripping off his words. Phobe isn't happy about this at all, but he's chewing on it, and eventually, he'll have an answer. He's creepy good like that.

It still sucks, because a plan later doesn't help me save Jameson now. Why does everything have to be so complicated? It's easier when I can kill them and move on, or Phobe can eat them, and then we move on.

Pain flashes through my head and the room darkens as black spots fill my vision. To keep myself upright I take a step back and as subtly as I can, lean against Phobe. Lightheaded, and feeling suddenly nauseous, it's the only way to give into the tilting sensation without actually falling over. That might ruin my tough girl image, falling on my face.

'This isn't the appropriate time for your jokes. Your weakness is still evident no matter how much you try to convince yourself otherwise.'

'Well, nothing can be done about it.'

'You could return to the Sidhe and fix it entirely.' How dare he make sense right now! I need him to be angry and ready to take the whole world on.

'You can take your logic and shove it up your ass.' I say instead of what

I'm thinking.

'I will still take the whole world on for you, Iza. Never doubt that.'

Keeping the smile on my face, I stand on my own, gritting my teeth to fight past the cold sweat I break out in. I can't let them see how sick I am. I can't let them see how worried I am. I can't let Phobe see it either.

I don't doubt he'll fight them all for me if he needs to, but at this stage, I'm starting to worry about his survival. If his *brother,* who isn't his brother, is the enemy—I'm pretty sure he is, all the neon arrows point to him and say, 'This is the bad guy'—he's got a distinct advantage over Phobe. He wasn't imprisoned and kept weak for... well, forever. This entire situation gives me the worst feeling in my gut that I can't shake no matter what I do.

"Are you ready to trade yourself, girl?"

I turn my full attention to the Guide. "Na. You can keep him. He's not worth all of this hassle." As nonchalant as possible I shrug and turn to walk away.

"What about your precious Sidhe?"

Without turning, I say, "Well, since you're not at it and haven't taken anyone else... I'd hazard a guess that you have no fucking clue where it is. See ya." I keep walking and am almost to the door when he stops me.

"Are you sure Michael and Ruthie will agree with this decision?" Those words stop me dead. "The girl came along after we clobbered the boy a bit. She's a timid thing, isn't she?" His chuckle sends a chill up my spine and pisses me off so much that I almost lose what little bit of composure I have. The ingrained refusal to give him the response that he wants is the only thing that stops me. "You have a day or two to think about it before I start cutting pieces off them too."

Silent, I walk out and as soon as I'm out of sight, break into a run. Pulling out my cell phone I call Adriem; thankfully he had the sense to add his phone number to my contacts list. He picks up on the third ring.

"Hello, lovely lady—"

"Go to kid's rooms and check on them."

"They're not here. Ruthie said something about them going to the pool downstairs," he answers. I hang up on him and dial Michael's phone.

"Now do you believe me, Iza?" The voice of the Guide comes through loud and clear. I hang up on him too.

Fuck. Fuck. Fuck. He has the kids, that motherfucker has the kids! I run until my legs burn, until I'm standing in front of the hotel and see a worried Adriem leaning against the railing in front of our rooms. I jump up to him and go straight to the kids' rooms. Both of them look normal. There are no strange smells, no signs of a scuffle. Ruthie's bed is even made.

I start pacing in the hallway. He must have taken them on the way to the pool. I'll agree to the exchange if he releases them first, that way they have a chance to get going to the Sidhe before he gets his hands on me. Any power I have in this deal is done the minute I give myself over.

"You're not trading yourself, not even for them, Iza." Phobe's voice brings me out of my turbulent thoughts and smack dab into reality.

The phone rings and I answer it immediately. "Iza, you have to come, or they'll kill him!" Ruthie's raised voice silences anything I was going to say. "They beat him up bad, nothing I did helps… he fought them so hard. Iza you have to save us!" she pleads.

Phobe reaches over and takes the phone out of my hands. "How did they capture you?"

For a second she sputters, and blubbers then start crying in earnest again, until finally, she says, "We were going to the pool… they came out of nowhere."

"Did you fight them?" Phobe asks.

"Of course, she fought them, give me the damn phone," I demand, holding out my hand. He holds my eyes a moment and then does as bid.

"Ruthie, where are you? Do you know?"

"They said if I tell you they'll hurt him more. I'm sorry Iza. Just come and save us." The line goes dead. Angry, I almost smash the phone in my hand but catch myself at the last minute. That was a dumb impulse to have to fight. This is the only way for them to contact me.

Irritated with myself I shove the phone in my pocket and turn to Phobe.

"Why did you ask if she fought?"

"I was curious, is all." His fiery eyes hold mine a moment then he shifts gears, "I heard the sound of lots of people walking and talking in the background. Where is a place that this would be?"

"They have a mall a few miles up the road," Adriem says, coming to join us outside of Michael's room. "It's a place that humans like to gather and shop and talk loudly and often. Mom loves places like that." I know what a mall is, I'm half-dragon and malls represent something that's incredibly important to dragons. Shiny things.

"It's a place I wouldn't look for them, normally. Who holds hostages at a mall?" I muse out loud and head towards the car we rented. The one I'm not allowed to drive. Instead of saying anything I get in the back seat and wait. I have to admit that they're smarter than I hoped. Holing up in a place like that is a good demonstration. Right under my fucking nose, under all those human's noses.

"We're not that far from there," Adriem says, as he gets into the car. Phobe remains silent and gets into the back seat beside me. When his hand slides around mine and lightly squeezes I almost cry, almost. Biting my lip hard enough to make it bleed, I manage to keep the tears at bay.

Crying won't get them all back. I'm not even sure it'll make me feel better either. I think everything will just make me angrier, and angry me doesn't like to be patient and do the smart thing. Angry me likes to kill things first and ask questions later.

Keeping my silence while Adriem tries his best to reassure me, I keep my eyes on the traffic as we drive and hold onto Phobe's hand like the lifeline it is. No one is following us, that I can see, but I wouldn't put it past them. They have vampires and shifters working for them. Hell, they have someone close to me working for them, or getting possessed by them—whatever the case may be. I still haven't found out who, and at this point, I'm not even sure I will.

'We will because it is not the type of secret that can be kept indefinitely.'

'What do you mean?'

'Eventually, the meat suit starts to decay because the soul it was made for is gone.' That makes a weird kind of sense. Also strikes me as a way to stop this from happening all the time with creatures who can body hop. Good to know there is a check and balance system. I wish there were one for the asshole doing all of this.

'There is.'

'Oh, yeah? What's that?'

I look over at him as I ask the question, his eyes are flames when he smiles and says, *'Me.'* Slowly he raises my hand to his mouth and kisses the back of it. *'No matter what happens, there will always be someone like me to counter him. Always. It is how things work, and nothing can break that except for the being who made us all.'*

'Wait... are you telling me that there's an actual god?' Does this mean someone listened to all my silly prayers as a child? That the feeling in my heart that told me there was something greater out there... something more, was right? Instead of answering me, he kisses the back of my hand again and that soft look, I so rarely see, fills his eyes.

The look he only gives to me.

Putting my hand on his lap, still clasped tightly in his, he turns away from me to stare out the window. Well, I won't be getting any more out of him, but honestly, this right here? Him holding my hand, and silently sharing his heart with me? It's enough, it's incredible, and it's all mine.

Sighing deeply, I mentally brace myself when we pull into the massive parking lot for the mall. My eyes narrow on the gobs of humans walking around—laughing and enjoying their shopping day. Today might solve more than one problem. With the invasion coming, one they will see firsthand what they're up against—they need to be aware, and they need to be prepared. I think the best way of doing that is to give them irrefutable proof.

One witness with a camera was a start, let's go for hundreds.

"Why do I have the feeling that you're up to something... you have that look on your face," Adriem states while turning off the car and looking at me over his shoulder. I shrug, he'll find out soon enough.

'I wish I could argue with your logic but as fucked up as it is... it's correct.' Phobe says, climbing out of the car. Since I don't have anything else to add, I follow suit and trail after Adriem as he walks into the mall. Phobe goes off in his search, while Adriem and I head towards the largest concentration of people in the mall.

The human holiday, Christmas, is a few weeks away and they've decorated everything in sight for it. There are bells and ribbons and strings of shiny stuff they call tinsel. I love the Christmas trees, lit up with colors exploding all over them. Some of them look like a unicorn vomited on them but they're still spectacular, and I wanted one. I had planned on having a big Christmas at the Sidhe. Now I won't have any.

Which makes me want to strangle the Guide even more.

"Hey lady, you can't cut in line!" The child's voice pulls my eyes downward. I find myself looking into the very human, blue eyes of a little girl. Her hair is blonde and slightly curly, even tucked under the bright green, knit hat she's wearing. She smiles up at me, showing that she's missing one of her front teeth. How completely, adorable.

"What line is this?" And indeed, there is one, that stretches ahead of us for quite a way. A mix of stressed out looking parents and bored children make up the majority of it.

"The line to see Santa. I'm going to sit on his lap and ask him for a new tablet." She looks so damn pleased about it, too.

"So, the fat man that gives you presents is here?"

"Oh ya. Anything you want because he's magical." Anything I want?

"Sitting on his lap activates the spell?" I knew he came down the chimney to eat your cookies and leave you coal and sometimes socks, but I had no idea he could grant any wish.

"Uh, I guess?" She looks rather bemused, but I don't have time to explain it.

I pat her head and start moving towards the front of the line because I'm sitting on that fat bastard's lap. The spell will give me the kids, Jameson and fix all of my problems. I'm careful not to hurt anyone, but I move more than one belligerent parent—fairly so, I'm skipping the line—out of my way. Finally, at the front, I go to walk up the three small stairs that lead to the old fat man sitting on a throne when a man with fake ears wearing green pantyhose puts his hand on my chest to stop me.

"Santa is taking lunch. We'll be back in half an hour." I look up at him, he's tall for a human elf, I grab him by the shoulders lift him out of my way. I aim for the fluffy chair off to the side and hope he falls on it. He didn't do anything wrong. He's just in my way.

Locking my gaze onto Santa, I head right towards him. He's looking at me with a little frown and surprises me when he turns and runs. Seriously, runs. This old man is in good shape for someone who eats cookies every day. With a growl, I tackle him and pin him down.

Rolling him over I say, "Look here fat man, I need to sit on your lap to activate the spell to bring my friends back. Now, get back on that freaking chair so I can!" His eyes are practically bugging out of his head, and his face is all red. "Are you going to have a heart attack?" He shakes his head but he's now profusely sweating, and it stinks.

"Ma'am, you need to get off Santa right now." I look up and find myself surrounded by law enforcement. Wait, they don't have guns... what are those called?

They are called security officers, and although they don't have guns, they do have pepper spray and tasers. Both of which you hate. Phobe says, from nearby. I look behind the first two guards and see him standing with his arms crossed, looking at me like I did something dumb.

I look down at Santa, who is looking up at me with terror filled human eyes, then back at Phobe. Okay, so... maybe I did something ill-advised.

"You can't grant real wishes, can you?" He shakes his head so hard his beard wiggles. "Why do you tell children this then?" He shakes his head again.

"Ma'am, don't make me ask you again, I will use force." The same guard warns again. Annoyed, frustrated with the entire situation, I look up at him and roar as loud as I can. The color drains out of his face so fast it looks like a bottle of water emptying. The glamour falls off me, little by little, not all the way but enough to scare the living shit out of them if the smell of fear is any indication.

"You spray me with that awful shit, and I'll use you to clean the floor where Santa just peed himself, do you understand me, human man?" I straighten and pull Santa to his feet. "Go change your pants and make those kids happy, or we'll see if you can actually fly." After staring at me for two solid seconds and blinking like a startled owl, he takes off running.

"That video was real?" One of the other guards asks, unsure of whether to run or use the taser his hand is resting on.

"Oh, of me killing the vampires? Yeah, that was real. You should throw me a parade or something. That mess of bloodsuckers was killing people left and right. That entire building was full of human corpses." I'm ranting now, and I don't care. Looking around me, I see all the cell phones now pointed at me, the looks of fear and wonder mixed on many faces. Doubt on others.

"Look, there are monsters invading this world, watch the news—where the towns and people are disappearing... they're doing that, and soon they'll be here. Guard yourself, read your lore. Prepare. I can't kill them all alone. I'll need your help." I can't seem to stop myself from talking either, so I quit fighting it and go with it.

"Aren't you a monster?" someone asks.

"Yes, but I won't eat your children, they give me heartburn." There are a few snickers but mostly still the acrid smell of fear. "I'd love to tell you that I'm a shining angel with pretty little feathery wings and a halo... but I'm not. All I can tell you is, I'll fight for you, I'll die for you if I have to, but I and those like me are all you have to stop the Schoth."

"I told you it was something invading. No one ever listens to me." Someone else says from the crowd.

"Take your pictures, your video... here, I'll show you what is fighting for this world. Adriem." He steps to my side, and that fast turns into the prehistoric monster he is under that human looking skin.

"Mommy, it's a dinosaur!" Adriem hears the small voice too. He lowers his great head and snorts on the child who laughs merrily. Then he shrinks back down to his human form.

"What are Schoth?"

"Yeah. Are they monsters, too?"

The questions start pouring out, and I mentally shake my head. I think I expected more mayhem than this… staid acceptance. Humans can be very surprising at times.

"The Schoth look like your human elves. They're all pretty and sparkly and will cut you up and eat you with a side dish. Never be fooled, ever. They'll send in the things that do look like angels. All shiny and golden, so beautiful it hurts to look at them… those are the things you should fear. Not all monsters look like monsters. If you're an innocent, call out for a Feyrie, we will help you." With that I turn and walk away, leaving the stunned guards staring after me. The flashes of cameras, the murmurs of people as they follow me is satisfying.

"Did you find anything?" I ask.

"No. Nothing… if they were here, they aren't anymore." Adriem answers.

"I found where they were… come." Phobe grabs my hand and steers me towards a hallway that leads to an exit sign. Instead of opening to the outside, it leads into another hallway, that ends in a storage room. In it is two chairs, each with cut ropes on them. I find Ruthie's phone on the crates next to the chairs.

Looking at the two chairs in the room and knowing by the smells that one held Michael and the other Jameson. "Why did they have the guys tied up, but not her? That's strange." I muse. I can only smell Ruthie near where I'm standing.

I flip through her phone and find nothing of interest. Not that I expected to but looking doesn't hurt anything. The entire thing looks like it's been erased, no pictures, no texts, except the single phone call to me. That had to have killed her. She was always taking pictures of her and Michael.

Tucking the phone in my pocket I look around at the chairs.

There's no blood, but I can still smell the former occupants, they haven't been gone long. From the looks of it, they ditched this place as soon as she called us. This was a wasted trip—well, not entirely. Now people can't deny monsters exist, so they might stand a chance.

"They gave her food, but none was given to Michael or Jameson," Phobe says from near where I picked up her phone. I look over at him and see the food wrappers on the floor. It's her favorite restaurant's logo on the labels. I'd recognize those papers anywhere.

"Bribing her maybe?" Adriem asks, picking up one of the wrappers.

"Ruthie isn't a fighter. I thought—no, I hoped that she might be, but in all our training sessions she ended up getting mad and whining, instead of fighting back. I love her but she's more princess than a warrior, that's for sure. They're probably using her to control Michael because he'll do what they say just to keep her safe. Honestly, he's also the one capable of doing damage out of the three of them," I answer, pretty sure I'm right. Michael is still learning who and what he is, and a mage isn't a problem for him—if he accepts what he can do. That's why they took him out first and are using Ruthie to keep him compliant.

I pegged her as a fighter, in the beginning. It's something I was wrong about. I never expected her to give up entirely and worry more about her nail polish than her ability to defend herself. The TV and Google God says that this is typical behavior for a human teenage girl, and even though she isn't fully human, she's more human than I'll ever be. Even Alagard said this happens sometimes. He said some people are not meant to do more than look pretty. That mindset isn't one I understand, but I do accept its existence.

It could also be her trauma was so significant that this is how she copes.

"Stop beating yourself up over the strange behavior of the girl. It's the bane of humans, their children, at this age. They've had thousands of years, and they still don't understand themselves."

"The change seems so sudden, though. Do you think she's the one being possessed?" I hate asking the question, but it needs to be asked.

"No, there are no signs of possession... I saw her when the attack initially happened, and it wasn't her." He shoulder bumps me, his version of a quick hug. "The grateful child you rescued was just a facet of her character, Iza. Everyone has traits that are undesirable."

"Oh, really? What are mine?" He opens his mouth to respond, in the honest, forthright way he has when Adriem coughs loudly.

"That's a trap man, don't fall in it!" he warns him.

I smile, I can't help myself. Phobe's mouth shuts, and he gives me a dirty look. I savor this moment, and carefully store this memory away. Seeing such emotion from him is rare and special.

This is one of my ways of coping, by holding onto the good memories with the tenacity of a kraken. They feed the spark inside of me and keep me going. They help me keep smiling. They're what makes me keep living with joy in my heart. Phobe gives me a deep look and then turns to kiss my lips softly. He's gone before it registers in my fuddled brain, but the warmth of his mouth still lingers.

Another memory to tuck away.

A sudden yawn spurns me into action. "I don't see anything else useful, let's go—I'm tired." I'm still always tired, even with the ring on. I don't like telling anyone. If I tell Adriem he'll fuss at me. If I tell Phobe, he'll find ways to cockblock me all the time from doing shit.

He's the only one who can, and he knows it.

On the way back to the hotel I manage to fall asleep with my face plastered against the window. When the door opens, and strong arms catch me, I keep my eyes closed and let him lift me up against that chest I love so much. He grunts in amusement, fully aware that I'm awake, but still carries me.

Tossing me on the bed is unexpected, but I giggle as I bounce across it. That doesn't stop me from kicking my shoes off and snuggling into the pillow. I'm still tired. He slides in behind me and wraps his arm around me and shoves the other under me. Pulling me against him, he buries his face in my hair and sighs.

"Rest, Iza. I will always watch over you," he whispers. Safe, comfortable, and so tired my eyes burn, I give in and let sleep claim me once again.

18

PHOBE

To this day, the fact that I like to watch her sleep still surprises me. Her mouth is normally hanging wide open, like in the car, but this time she's sleeping peacefully. The sleep of an exhausted person. Iza thinks she's sneaky enough to hide the fact that she's still sick, even wearing the ring. Something needs to be done about it. Either she needs to return to the Sidhe, or we have to find another way.

Self-consciously I pat the small velvet covered box in my pocket. The annoying ringtone of her phone spurs me to grab it before she wakes. She needs to rest and recharge and get as strong as possible. I look at the screen and the 'unknown number' displayed on it. Sliding the circle to green, I put the phone to my ear.

Michael screaming is the first thing I hear. The annoying voice of the Guide comes over the line. "Good, you answered. It took me taking half his fingernails to make him scream. As you know, I have a collar that will make your dear Iza mortal. Once she's mortal, I'll kill her, slowly. But... if you trade yourself to me, I'll let these brats go and leave your woman alive. Meet me on the docks at the lake to make the exchange. You for them." The line goes dead.

I almost squeeze the phone into a ball of metal, but refuse to give into that small loss of control. Pausing only long enough to take the sim card out, I then get the satisfaction of it bending and breaking in my hand. Tossing it away I climb to my feet and go to Adriem's room. He opens the door on the first knock.

I hand him the sim card, "Iza needs a new phone, I broke the other one. Let her sleep and get her lots of food when she wakes up." He nods, and I turn and walk back to our room.

Kneeling on the floor next to her I caress her face. She'll trade herself for those two kids. There's not a single doubt in my mind. She loves them like they're her children. The idea of them being hurt because of her is something she cannot live with for long. Losing them will bring forth all that pain she has stashed in the back of her mind. It will snuff out the life inside of her, the life that makes me smile—the life that gave me life. It will end the sound of her laughter that still has the power to make me… happy. Take that light out of her eyes that makes me want to do anything in the world to please her. I've seen those eyes with no light in them before. It's not something I can do again.

Iza is the only thing that makes life bearable, she's the key to me feeling like I'm alive, and whole. She's what makes everything—anything worthwhile. I refuse to exist without her. I refuse to allow them to take her from this world. Leaning forward, I kiss her mouth, ignoring the burning of my eyes and the wetness that trails down my cheek to drip onto her face. I put everything I feel for her, every single fucking thing, into that kiss.

Standing, I open the box and place it on the pillow next to her face. The opal flickers in the light, looking much like her eyes do when I'm inside of her. A wedding was something I was planning on giving her. Such a simple thing for all the pleasure it would bring her, as it would also give me another solid tie to her.

Selfishly, I can't give her up—to anything.

With one long, last look at her, I turn away, my form twisting and changing into a replica of the woman lying on the bed.

LIFE'S GOAL all along was to put me in this position. I should have seen it sooner. Instead of mentally flagellating myself I look for evidence of him. The lake is small, which makes it easier to find the van that sticks out in the fresh snow. The stark white color with the blacked-out windows makes it look suspicious without trying to. The muffled curses and shouting from the inside of it, doesn't discount that.

Outside it stands a varied bunch of shifters and vampires, with the token Schoth thrown in. The Guide stands off to the side. His bodyguards are scattered around him, none of them dressed for the cold weather and looking like they realized it too late. He's wearing a fur coat, something not commonly worn by the inhabitants of this world —at least, in this country. He looks like the moron he is.

Making my way towards them, I fall into the walking pattern of Iza. Iza walks like a man, making mimicking her easier. The smirk is easy too. I've seen it enough to know it by heart.

"Well, well, you showed up."

"I told you she would. Iza's a fucking softy when it comes to us," Ruthie says, climbing out of the passenger side of the van. The thoughts in her head aren't nice ones. The grudge she bears for Iza, predominant and the selfish, hormonally driven obsession she has for Michael is the reasoning she gives herself for doing it all. She wants what Iza has and has convinced herself, with help from the manipulation of the Guide, that she can have it all if Iza is gone.

Ruthie is the spy, and, in her thoughts, I discover the identity of the one Light has been riding. Motherfucker.

"Now where's the blonde man that we're expecting?" the Guide asks, looking at his fingernails nonchalantly. Then he stiffens, and his eyes roll back in his head. "Oh, the one you want is here? Okay, yes..." he starts mumbling to himself. He opens his eyes and looks at me.

"He says if you fight it, he'll kill her."

The net closes around me before I can move, one that holds me solid in its grasp. I know the feel of that power, the taste of it, and even though I can fight it, I don't. If he says he will kill her, then he will. Light is many things, but he's a creature of his word. He'll leave her alone if I go peacefully.

"Let the two men go; I was ordered to keep my word. This is what I came here for." The doors of the van are opened, and Michael and Jameson are dragged out and tossed into the snow. Both of them look awful, covered in dirt and blood. Jameson is unconscious, but Michael isn't, and he's staring at Ruthie with hate-filled eyes.

Focusing all my power, everything I can get to on Michael, I send my shadows into him.

'Don't move boy, listen to me carefully. As you can see, Ruthie is the spy and Nika is the one that Light has been possessing. Iza must know, do you understand me? Don't let her know you heard her confession, play dumb. Get her to Iza; this is something she must deal with. Understand?'

'But how will we save you?' The question is faint but clear.

It's a testament to how easily Iza and I communicate, him asking that one question causes him pain.

'There will be no saving me.' Something I knew the minute I decided to come here. Iza is more valuable than I'll ever be, and my life is nothing compared to hers. Meeting Michael's eyes he gives the barest hint of a nod and closes his eyes. Ruthie didn't see him looking at her in such a way. For the moment her deception is still in play.

Until Michael gets to Iza.

Rough hands grab me and toss me into the smelly van. The last thing I see is the smirk on Ruthie's face right before she starts smacking herself in the face and crying. This is going to break Iza's heart, and I won't be there to hug her.

The Guide slides in the van beside me and momentarily freezes. His eyes change from a dull gold to a bright, familiar white and meet mine. "Hello, brother."

19

IZA

The stabbing feeling of something being wrong drags me from sleep. Sitting up I stretch and look around the room. No Phobe, no Adriem... no anyone. That's weird. The feeling in my stomach intensifies, something isn't right. Climbing to my feet I leave the room and go to Adriem's room, but there's no answer. Michael and Ruthie's rooms are empty as well.

"What are you doing up? You should be resting," Adriem says from the stairs.

"Where's Phobe?"

"He said he had some errands to run and sent me to get you a new phone." He hands me the phone box and waits for me to open it and turn it on. "I put the sim card in it already, so you should have access to all of your contacts and everything." When I turn it on, there are ten missed calls.

Curious and concerned, I call the number back.

"Adriem? Phobe? You have to hurry because they have Iza. She came and traded herself for us!" The dread intensifies. There is only one person who can fool people by pretending to be me. Only one. I mute the line and look at Adriem.

"Pretend that I'm not here, understand?" He frowns but nods.

He puts his ear to the phone and says, "Hello?"

"Oh god, Adriem, they have Iza, and they let us go. You have to come and get us." I can hear her clearly through the phone as she recites the address through bouts of sobbing. I want to run to her and comfort her, but my gut tells me it's important for them all to think I'm captured. That instinct concerns me.

"We'll be right there to get you. Stay put," he reassures her and ends the call. Without missing a beat, he asks me, "What's going on, Iza?"

"Someone who looks like me showed up to make the exchange." Every word out of my mouth makes my stomach sink lower. The skin all over my body feels like it's going to crawl off. The low pounding pain in my head is getting steadily worse, and the wrong feeling is making my stomach do flip-flops. I'm going to break Phobe's jaw—again—when I get ahold of him. How dare he go in my place... that fucking asshole, that... wonderful man, who knew he was walking into a trap.

My eyes burn, and I rub my palms into them. They'll hurt him when they find out he isn't me. Yes, I know he heals incredibly fast, but pain is still pain, and I've got this feeling of surety that it won't be the same as before. That whoever is running this shit show, can genuinely hurt him.

Gah, that idiot. Why did he do it after telling me I couldn't? Shaking my head, I stomp into my room for my shoes. Something on the bed catches my attention. When I see it, the sudden weakness in my legs sinks me to the bed, and I pick it up.

My hand is shaking so hard I drop it, then pick it up again, bringing it up to my face to stare at it through the blurriness of my eyes. It's a ring.

Carefully, I take it out of the box and hold it between my fingers. The tears are scalding as they trail down my face. Burning their way down my chin and under my shirt. He left me a ring because he was going to ask me to marry him, he paid attention to our conversation. I only showed him a foolish dream I had about us. A dream of a white dress and baby dragons throwing flowers all over the place.

He got me a fucking ring.

"Iza?" Adriem calls softly from the other side of my door.

Swallowing the sob that wants to push its way out, I wipe my face with my sleeve, and shove the ring on my finger. Ignoring the sting of it scraping across my knuckle, I keep going until it rests at the bottom of my finger. The blood will just mark it as mine.

Taking a deep breath in, as I get up, I exhale and gather the shreds of my composure around me like armor. I can cry later, when he's here, and his arms are wrapped around me. Bitching about how I'm an idiot for worrying about the immortal Phobe. I'll try my best to kick his ass too after I kiss the shit out of him.

"I'm coming. Let's go get the kids and figure out how to get my stupid boyfriend back," I say as I open the door and walk by him towards the car. This strikes me as too easy, all of it. They gave up their hostages once they had 'me.' It isn't sitting right on my mind. For once in my life, my worry is outweighing my anger, I have to get through this weighted, nasty feeling that makes me think the world is going to end—my world is going to end—maybe then I can get mad enough to break some shit.

♥

When we pull into the parking lot of the lake, Ruthie comes running to the car. She stops when she sees me and stands there looking confused. Her face is a little beat up, her lips swollen from a smack or two. Maybe her stay with them wasn't as easy as I first thought? Michael is slowly walking towards us with an unconscious Jameson slung over his shoulder. Adriem grabs Jameson and rushes to get him in the car. Surprisingly, Michael heads straight for me, walking right past Ruthie like she isn't there.

Silent, he wraps his arms around me and hugs me so tight it's hard to breathe. I hug him back, confused at what he's doing, Michael has never been physically affectionate with me before. With his mouth right next to my ear, he whispers, so low that I barely hear him, "Ruthie is the one who sold us out." The world falls out from under me. Ruthie? "Nika is the one getting possessed. He wanted you to know."

He pulls away from me and stands there for a few seconds, his much older eyes holding mine. Speaking volumes about what happened while they were prisoners. Michael's world has been turned upside down, his heart broken. Poor kid. Turning, he goes to the car, giving Ruthie—who's trying to latch onto him, a wide berth.

I stand there staring at her, afraid to speak because of what will come out of my mouth. Beautiful Ruthie? The fragile girl I pulled from a trunk and rescued from a pack of shifters that wanted to turn her into their sex chew toy? The girl I buy anything and everything she asks for? The girl I love like family? She deceived me—us, so convincingly that no one knew or even suspected? Then again, why would we? I brought her into the Sidhe; I vouched for her, I loved her. Gritting my teeth, I fight the confusing emotions sweeping through me, that are quickly turning into one solid mass of rage. They have Phobe because of her, they tortured Jameson and Michael, because of her.

An eighteen-year-old girl that I love and gave a home to... betrayed me, and for what? If it's something utterly stupid, which is unfair because any answer she gives will be considered utterly stupid, I'm going to punch her right in her back-stabbing, hormonal face.

"How are you here? I saw them take you," she finally says, hesitantly approaching me. Now her brain is working; I can see the thoughts chasing themselves across her face. I'm not sure if her thinking is the best process, she didn't once consider that Michael might see what she did as wrong.

"Do you truly hate me so much, Ruthie?" I ask softly, stepping towards her. Wisely she takes a few steps back, and I stop. If I get any closer to her, I'll hurt her, and I'm not sure how I'll feel if I do that.

"What are you talking about? Of course, I don't hate you." Her eyes are wider now. Fear is leaking out of her and filling the air around her. It's true, I can see it in her eyes, the deceit of the words she's getting ready to give me. The web, faint but still very much there, twangs, notes of discord and anger, all directed at Ruthie. I'm not the only one feeling the sting of betrayal.

I look to Adriem who's standing a few feet behind her, his eyes glowing with anger. Michael must have said something. "Adriem, grab her and," I grit my teeth as I say, "Put her in the trunk." I fight to keep my voice calm, to keep from taking those last few steps and shaking the piss out of her. "We're going to the Sidhe. I can't get Phobe back in this condition." Adriem grabs her and drags her to the back of the car.

"I didn't do anything wrong! Let go of me! Iza, make him let go of me! Michael—Michael he's hurting me! Save me!" Unable to deal with the noise from her and the noise in my head at the same time, I walk up to the car and punch her in the face. She goes limp in his arms and he tosses her in the trunk. It shuts with a resounding bang.

Stopping next to the passenger window I say, "Are you sure, Michael?" I've got to ask because I think part of me is still in some weird state of shock and disbelief.

"Yes. Phobe saw it too. While I was getting the shit knocked out of me, she was laughing and eating burgers with them. Plotting the entire thing, while professing that she was doing it all for me." He pauses, and the muscles on his jaw stand out, he still hasn't turned to look at me, but I can read his body language just fine. "This all started because she thought you were taking me away from her and her rightful place in life. They used that to get to her, and she ate it up like a starving dog." Michael says it with such venom that I'm surprised he's still wearing his human face. Ruthie achieved the opposite of her goals, he hates her now, and because she hurt him so badly, it's the kind of hate you don't get over.

Sensing he's done talking for the moment, I get into the car next to Jameson, who's out like a light. Despite how pissed off I am with him, I give him a good once over. He looks rough, like run over by a truck rough, his face is one big swollen bruise on top of another. Carefully, I tilt his head around to see better. I'm pretty sure his jaw is broken in multiple places, it's hanging at an odd angle. Good chance he's missing some of his teeth too. That's not counting the ring of scabs on his neck, where the collar was. Jameson's Magiks aren't strong, but he's a good healer and can heal himself with ease... whatever was around his neck stopped him from doing that. A problem we'll address later. Jameson needs to be healed first, and the Sidhe is the only place where that's going to happen.

"Iza... I'm sorry." Michael says, his voice thick with unshed tears. "I had no idea about Ruthie. I feel like this is my fault."

"Nothing about this is your fault. This is her fault, so stop blaming yourself," I reassure him. "As far as Nika goes, it's not her fault either. It's all to be blamed on the motherfucker doing it." I wish her being the one possessed/used, whatever phrase you want to label it with, surprised me more than it does. Since I met her something hasn't felt right, now it all makes sense. The sad thing is I doubt she even knows it's her.

It explains the fight with Rido, too. Two dragons fighting would cause the destruction I saw. I know what I'll be doing with Nika—for her sake and everyone else's. I doubt she's even aware of what's going on, but like some mateless female dragons, she's gone off the deep-end. Her erratic behavior over Jameson was the first sign of many, but because of how she's connected to my mom, I chose to ignore a good chunk of it. Mostly because I was under the false belief that it wasn't hurting anyone.

As cold-blooded as it sounds, Nika isn't needed anymore. Arista can heal Jameson and Michael.

My eyes fall again on Jameson and the dried blood on his jaw. It makes me think of Ruthie. I imagine she's going to be sporting a nice bruise where I popped her one. A sharp pain shoots through my chest, so I rub it and, in the process, have to admit that it feels like my heart is breaking a little. I wish I could deny it, pretend like it didn't happen —make it go away. The desire for a way to go back in time and live like it used to be—with movie night and shopping for shoes—is incredibly strong. Why couldn't she stay the girl with pink hair who looked at me like I was the best person in the world?

Where did it go wrong?

Almost like he read my mind, Michael says, "He's been working on her awhile, Iza. She started going off into town by herself... we were fighting because I thought it was another guy she was going to see, and it was, but now I can see that it wasn't a boyfriend." He sighs. "They talked about their meetings right in front of me."

"Was she spelled at all?" If they Magiked her, I can forgive that and not have to do what the Magiks are demanding I do. What the Feyrie will demand I do.

"No, he played to her insecurities. Honestly, if not him, I think someone else would've gotten her going eventually. I genuinely think that this is always how this was meant to turn out, Iza. People like Ruthie are never happy with what they have. They always want more and more and are never satisfied with anything." He swallows noisily and then continues, "I saw it early on, but I love—loved her too much to accept it." Michael sounds so old, and part of me is proud of him, but another part wishes he wasn't hurting either. That same part wishes this was all a bad dream that I'll wake up from any minute.

"We'll get to the truth of it when we get to the Sidhe." That's if I can keep myself from strangling her before then. "Call ahead and have everyone brought back from the other place and then send the children someplace safe." Since I know who the culprits are now.

The worry for Phobe that I keep trying to bury boils to the surface. If something happens to him, I'm not sure how I'll react. I'm not sure at all. Adriem starts the long drive ahead of us, and I lean my head against the window. Now that I have some facts I can start putting the pieces together, it gives me something more to do than worrying about Phobe and mourning the loss of Ruthie.

20

IZA

The minute we drive into the borders of the Sidhe my skin prickles and energy floods my system. Closing my eyes, I bask in the wonder of this enriching feeling of coming home. After a long, draining journey, some of the weight comes off my soul and the tears rolling down my face are left to fall. I refuse to allow myself to feel any shame for this, especially with everything else going on. The web was getting dimmer every day, it flares to life and I gasp from the rush of it.

There's one that is noticeably absent. I can't feel Phobe anymore. Not even here, in the seat of my power. The dark line that runs through the center of the web is dim and silent. My heart rate jumps, and I bite my lip to keep from having a breakdown. The warmth running down my chin pulls me out of that web and back to the car. With my sleeve, I wipe away the blood and turn to look at Jameson, who's stirring beside me.

He's been making weird moaning noises for a while now, but I was tuning them out. Now he's thrashing around in what I'm guessing to be a nightmare. I feel a little twinge of pity for him, those types of memories will never go away. They fade into the back of your mind waiting for you to be weak enough to allow them to come out and rob you of sleep.

These dreams of his are the result of his stupidity. He'll have to deal with it like I have to deal with mine. In a way, this is Jameson growing up.

Turning away from him, I watch the Sidhe come into view. Standing tall against the snowdrifts around it, the familiar white paint and big windows draw me out of the car while it's still moving. Running, I head right towards the wall that opens and welcomes me in. To me, it's like running into the arms of my mother. Taken to the very heart of the Sidhe, the warm touch of the Magiks flow over me and embrace me in safety and comfort. For this brief time, I can let my guard down and let my battered soul breathe.

"I need your help. This ring… it eases the sickness—but not enough. Because I'm as weak as a baby, they took him from me." Gritting my teeth, I continue, because the Sidhe is listening, "They took him, and I have to get him back, he's my soul… he is the reason life has color again." Speaking into the blackness, I'm floating in I wait for the Sidhe to respond. The sad notes whisper through my mind and encourage me to say the rest of it, "Ruthie… she betrayed me to them. She got her kind killed. She tried to have me killed. All because of someone's dick!" The word echoes back at me, and through the snotty tears, I laugh. Hoarse and rough, it sounds like someone much older than me.

The music of the Sidhe flows through me, and I receive the answers I need. All around me roots raise, all different sizes. The Sidhe is offering me a solution, and I'm taking it. Closing my eyes, I exhale long and deep, feeling the pulse of power inside of me once again, the comfort of my home. The tip of each root piercing my skin stings, but I've suffered much worse, and the result is more than worth it. Each pain means that a small piece of the Sidhe enters me. In essence, the Sidhe is turning me into a physical part of it, a limb that can be away from the body. Changing me into something unknown, and it's completely acceptable because I need to be stronger for what's coming.

As I'm gently lowered to the ground, the Sidhe twists and shapes around me depositing me in the front room. Everyone jumps to their feet when I open my eyes and look at them. I can understand their confusion. I came through the ceiling. Any other time I'd have laughed, but not today—there are no laughs left in me.

Looking around at those gathered, taking note that someone listened and sent the children away as I requested, I think on what I need to say. I'm glad the kids are gone because Knox would be here and yelling at me for leaving. I imagine he would also be confused about what happened and why I have to do what's next or delay what I have to do next as long as possible. My heart is at war with my mind on this one.

Feyrie law dictates that betrayal of Feyrie kind is a death sentence. One that I have to carry out on the perpetrator, in the absence of the king. Who at this point hasn't been crowned and is the dumbass who went and got himself captured.

My eyes seek out Ruthie, who's sitting on the loveseat, sandwiched in between Auryn and Licar. She looks squished and uncomfortable and looking at her makes me sick to my stomach. Neither of them look directly at her either, but both of their eyes are glowing red. A quick look around the room shows that no one is looking directly at her. Everyone knows now, I'm sure. Gossip is alive and well in the Sidhe.

Jameson is gone, I assume with Arista and the other healers getting worked on. People have heard about Nika too since she's standing with Adriem, who is in a position to stop her from leaving the room. She looks lost to the world, and pale-faced. Michael is standing slightly behind her, watching me. He's cleaned up, and his poor face has barely any bruising left on it. The look on it is all serious business, and I can tell he's doing everything he can to not look towards Ruthie. She keeps looking at him with a frown between her eyes.

She still hasn't realized the depth of what she did, the idiot girl.

Giving up on having the right words to say I turn to Nika, and say, "Nika. Are you aware that someone has been hijacking your body and using you to kill people?" When no surprise enters her eyes, I see that she suspected something was off, at least. That annoys the fuck out of me. "You should've come to me. You know that, right?" There is not one single ounce of guilt in my next words, "For now, you're going to be imprisoned. I can't trust you—understand?" She nods and hangs her head.

"Jameson is safe, and that's all that matters," she says then falls into silence. No one says anything in her defense, because there's not much to say—it happened. Until it can be stopped she needs to be somewhere she can't hurt people.

Roots spring forth from the floor and wrap around her, dragging her down to a place that the Magiks won't reach her. Not even a wannabe god can find her there. She'll be comfortable and taken care of while she sleeps. At least, she had the dignity to accept her current fate and my opinion of her climbs a little. Hopefully, I can figure out how to save her—if not I'll kill her or leave her sleeping. There are no other options available.

Slowly, I turn to Ruthie. "Give me every single fucking detail. If you leave even one small, itty-bitty thing out, I'll beat you within an inch of your life. Heal you, then do it again. Do you understand me?" Ruthie opens her mouth to argue then closes it. I'm dead serious. I might consider Ruthie a child in some ways—a foolish belief on my part, but her actions were those of an adult. She got people killed, and Phobe captured. There's no leniency left in me for her, only a stabbing pain in my heart.

"You were supposed to be the one they took!" she yells, then crosses her arms, face mutinous.

"And?" I prompt, taking a single step towards her.

"They planned on killing you because somehow killing you empowers the Light side and they'll be able to more easily take over the Earth and others." She was willing to betray me, knowing they'd kill me. Yeah, she made adult decisions, so from this moment forward I'll treat her like one.

"You're okay with that?" I ask. She shrugs and continues to give me dirty looks.

"The Guide's power is only temporary. Once the battery in his necklace dies, he's afraid you'll beat him. He's coming after you because he knows how big a pussy you are now." She's going for smug, but the shaking of her hands shows how afraid she is.

"Where was this bravery you're pretending to have when you were asked to betray your people?"

"I wasn't betraying them. I was getting rid of you." She's so obstinate about it that she hasn't truly looked at what she did. Getting rid of me is betraying them.

"Why?" I have to know. There's got to be more to it than that. She gets Michael and an old house that won't listen to her. She starts to cry, and for the first time since this awful day started, I think they're real tears.

"You're going to take it all away to fight some stupid war. Our home, our men—all of it, for your shitty war. He told me if I helped them that they'd leave everyone alone that I asked them to, and we'd get to live out our lives in the Sidhe... that I'd get to be in charge." What a petulant, selfish way to repay the kindness of the people here, to believe something so flawed, and untrue, for purely selfish reasons. Nothing in life is ever that easy, nothing comes without strings—especially when dealing with people who want to kill you.

"You idiot, without me the Sidhe will kick your ass out. If it didn't murder you outright for betraying everyone. It thinks and feels for itself, I have nothing to do with it, and no one can control what it does!" I pat my healed hair to calm it down. It wants to wrap around her neck and squeeze. I can feel its murderous intent. "The war is coming, whether any of us want it to or not, and we all have to fight, not just the men. How they convinced you of that idiocy, I'll never know."

The more I think about it the madder I get. She fell for the manipulation tactics of complete morons. "They won't stick with any deals or promises, they'll kill anyone who represents any kind of threat, and that's *every* single Feyrie here—including you! Believing that nonsense shows how ignorant you are of the real world." How stupid is she to entertain that she could be the Shepherd without any kind of ability to do so, that people would listen to her? "You let yourself be blatantly manipulated by a fucking tool. I'm ashamed to know you right now." Roots fly out of the floor and grab her.

"She does not sleep. I want her to sit here, stared at by everyone while she thinks about all that she's done." I feel the music of the Sidhe and Ruthie is dragged screaming into a cage made of the same material of the Sidhe. She's not getting out of there any time soon.

"Iza… you know the laws," someone says from behind me. The voice eventually registers, it's Auryn, and she doesn't sound happy about it. Still, I say nothing to her. Ruthie's life is forfeit now because she didn't just betray me, she betrayed everyone. That's treason, and the sentence for that is death. Killing her is not something I'm in a massive hurry to do. Regardless of what she did, she's still that girl I pulled out of a trunk.

One problem at a time.

"I have to get Phobe first, then we'll worry about punishing people, okay?" No one argues, not that it would change anything if they did—I'm going to go after him no matter what they think.

"Iza." Hearing my name spoken so softly grabs my attention as nothing else has. I turn, and Jameson is standing, pale and shaky, in the doorway. He's sporting new scars and missing a finger, pretty sure he's a good twenty pounds lighter too. Otherwise, he looks mostly intact. Looking at him leaves a bad taste in my mouth.

"I'm glad you're alive, but I can't look at you right now. Ruthie's backstabbing bullshit and your dick might cost me everything, and that makes me hate both of you a little. Go do something productive before I kill you myself." I'm not sure where the words come from, but they're true, and I won't apologize for them.

He looks sad and ashamed, but it doesn't move me one bit. For once in my life, I'm laying blame where it's due. After staring at me, his brown eyes flicking over my face with a defeated look on his own, he turns and limps out of the room. There's nothing left in me to spend on sympathy for stupidity. Not one single fucking drop.

"What are you going to do?" Auryn asks.

"Kill things until someone decides to give me the information that I want." Turning on my heel, I head towards my room. I need clean clothes for this and weapons, lots of weapons. Already I feel ten times better than I did when I got here. Separation sickness won't be an issue again. The Sidhe made sure of that.

Absently I rub my chest, right over my heart. Normally, I feel fullness there, because it's where I feel the bond between Phobe and I. The lack of it is disturbing and giving me anxiety so bad that I might need to find a paper bag to do that breathing exercise. Killing things will help, though. Lots of stuff. I want to make bloody snow angels in their guts. Growling under my breath I grab the leathers out of my closet and start stripping.

On TV a lot of people wear them to look sexy, I'm wearing them because they stand up against claws and teeth. A lot better than cotton and jeans. These are thick, hardy and flexible enough to not restrict me from moving the way I need to move. After zipping them, and filling the various pockets and loops with knives, guns and other odds and ends, I put on a plain leather jacket.

The boots were a present from Phobe. They're resting on my bed, new and untouched. A perfect fit and designed for high movement and durability. They're steel toed and heavy enough that if I kick you in the face with these on—it'll hurt. Giving a mean smile to my reflection in the mirror, I shove my phone and wallet into my inner pocket, zip the coat and head out the door.

There are a million places to go and not a lot of time to do it, if I start with the vampires I think I'll get more answers. They seem to be neck deep in the fucking mess, maybe—

"Iza... you need to come out here." The seriousness in Adriem's tone is enough to make me want to stop and vomit. I hate that tone, it means it's something awful, and I don't wanna fucking know! Taking a deep breath, I close my bedroom door and follow him to one of the main family rooms. There's a TV the size of the wall in there and on it is the smug face of the Guide.

"What the fuck is this?" I demand.

"They call it face-timing, isn't it lovely?" My eyes narrow on the man's face, the inflection in the voice isn't the same as before. The eye color isn't either... fuck... he's being ridden. This isn't the true face of my enemy.

The camera swings around and Phobe's battered face comes into focus, a concerning sight to see. There's also a webbing of Magiks wrapped so tightly around him that it's cutting into the darkness that makes him what he is. He isn't healing, at all, something I've never seen before. They've got him strung up on a metal pole, eyes full of fire and glaring hatred at the Guide.

Those fiery eyes turn to the camera, and when they meet mine, I know he can see me. For the first time since I've known him, they fill with something so unbelievably soft it takes my breath away. That emotion hovering like a drop of water is so far beyond love, there isn't a word for it, and it pulls my heart right out of my chest. *Kill them all, Iza.* He mouths to me, his eyes filling with... apology.

"I love these kind of human inventions. They give you freedoms you wouldn't normally have. For example," the Guide-possessed person starts talking again and shoves his face in the camera, "I was going to draw things out, make you suffer, simply because that idea appeals to me... but, you tend to come out on top. Even in horrible circumstances. Plus, I made a deal. However, I can't leave things to fate. It gets messy when you do that." My heart is beating so fast I can hear it in my ears. My vision narrows on that screen like I'm looking down a long tunnel. "I'll settle for the suffering I can get from making you watch while I do this."

He turns the phone back to Phobe, and all the hair stands up on my arms when I see the flash of light. Phobe's eyes widen but stay on the screen, looking unerringly into mine. I know that look, I've seen it before—I just never thought to see it in his eyes. It's goodbye. Nononononono. It's impossible!

"Now you have to admit that I am the supreme being, *brother.*" The Guide says with such hatred in it. It gives me chills.

Phobe laughs a full-on belly laugh that brings the barest hint of a reluctant smile to my lips. It's a sad smile, the last one I'll share with him, but I won't keep it hidden. He wants to see, I know it.

"You're no brother of mine." He turns to the Guide and smiles, all monstrous teeth, then continues, "The light can be extinguished, but darkness is eternal." Those words seem cryptic, and I decide to hold onto them, maybe because I'm desperate to have something to hold onto. "When you're wiped from existence—because it will happen—you will only be remembered as a wanna be gold who didn't get enough hugs from his mommy." I have never loved him more than I do in that moment. Phobe is channeling me, my sarcasm, my mouth. The smile changes into that rarely seen happy smile. Looking into the camera unwavering, as the light flashes again, I watch in horror as the body that holds him begins to unravel. All the while, he keeps smiling for me, just for me.

Helpless, I stand there and as the man who means more to me than anything—than absolutely anything, is turned into nothing but smoke. There's a flicker of blue in the heart of it, that's gone so fast I barely catch it. Towards the edge of the screen, one of the stone-faced shifters steps forward—with familiar eyes so blue they glow—and snatches a piece of smoke out of the air. When I blink, he's already standing back in his position, amber eyes blank.

Why is Life there doing weird shit? Why didn't he step in and save him?

Clenching my hands so tight my claws bury themselves to the root in my skin, I face the Guide when he puts the camera back on him. "Wow, what a show! A genuine shame that there will never be another. I'm afraid he was one of a kind." He considers me and then shakes his head a little. "I didn't expect the sentiment he showed you Shepherd. It looks like it's you who made him weak enough to die so easily."

"If you hadn't locked him up for a thousand years, he'd own your ass, fuckface. His fist would have given you a second asshole, that's how hard he'd have owned you. That's how hard I will." I vow it right then. I will annihilate all his ilk, his little helpers. Every. Single. Fucking. One.

"Little girl, I'm not afraid of you. You're only real weapon is no more." He smiles and waves his hand towards the empty pole that once held Phobe. "I will accept your surrender now." The only thing that gloating bastard will accept is my foot up his ass.

"You're pissed off that Phobe's Magikal dick is bigger than yours," I say, smiling a toothy smile and crossing my arms over my chest. Pulling on every shred of inner strength I have, I make myself relax and not give away one iota of the wrenching grief inside of me. This motherfucker isn't going to see my pain. The only thing he'll see coming from me is the knife in his face.

"I'm going to enjoy killing you," I say with a light voice and an easy smile.

"I can say the same," he grits out between his clenched teeth.

I hold up my pinky and wiggle it at him. His eyes flash, and the call cuts off. Taking two breaths, my knees give out, and I hit the floor, hard. Phobe is gone, my beautiful monster is gone. He wasn't supposed to be able to die. He was supposed to be indestructible. This… this—was never supposed to happen.

Grabbing my head with my hands I scream out my sorrow. One long, lonely roar, while I kneel there letting the tears fall, uncaring of who's watching me. For once, I let the grief fully have its turn, let it consume me and burn through my body like acid.

Every moment we shared, every kiss, every hug. Every single fucking laugh is scorched into my memory. The look in his eyes, in the end… will haunt me forever. The emotion in them was so earth-shattering, so deep, that I could drown in it happily. Gods, I want to die with him, I want to see him again… I will see him again.

Pushing the pain, the worst pain of my life, down is harder than it has ever been, but I do it. Resolve hardens in my stomach like a stone. Climbing to my feet, I wipe off my cheeks and look at the stunned faces around me. Alagard, looking a bit lost for words, hands me a tissue, and then looks away—trying to hide the sympathy in his gaze. I blow my nose and pocket the tissue. Clearing my throat, I look at the somber faces around me.

From years of practice, as the pain claws my guts to bits and slowly but surely shreds what's left of my heart, I make myself appear calmer than I am.

Forcing myself to talk in a normal tone, I say, "I suggest everyone gets a good night's sleep. Go have dinner, hug your families, because war is coming." I turn towards the cage in the center of the room, which lights up, showing Ruthie bound and gagged by the Sidhe, glaring at me. Without a word, I reach through the bars and wrench her from the cage.

Screaming in pain she curses and kicks out at me. Ignoring it, I pull her face to mine, and I show her the real me, the one she never sees. I show her the monster that I am, and I growl at her. My heart is no longer interfering with what I need to say to Ruthie.

"They killed him because of you," I spit out, so furious with her about her part in everything, that it takes me almost biting the tip of my tongue off to keep from ripping her head from her shoulders.

Pale-faced she begins to cry and goes limp in my grasp and starts blubbering over and over, "They said they wouldn't kill anyone except you."

How does that make it any better? I had no idea that I'm worth so little to her, that our time together as a family means nothing to her. I look at her with all the Magiks in my possession, but I can't find any evidence of a spell. We did suspect one of the kids of being possessed, initially, but not of outright backstabbing shit. Never would I have accused her of such a thing.

"How can you be so different?" I say between my clenched teeth, right in her face. "I saved you from a life of slavery and degradation. I gave you a fucking home and love. I cared about you when no one else was willing to. Did it matter at all?" I yell louder, shaking her hard enough to make her teeth rattle.

"Everything was fine until you decided to play hero!" she yells, and time freezes. My helping people made her turn against me? Why didn't the Magiks tell me?

Wait, did I ever check her or was I dumb enough to be fooled by her? Looking at her with tears in her eyes and the dislike—the anger, all directed at me makes me take a deeper look at our interactions. Other than movie night, she avoided me most of the time. I always thought it was because she was chasing Michael.

The Magiks show me the truth now, show me the slippery slope she was on even in the beginning. Yes, Ruthie suffered, but instead of becoming stronger for it she became bitter, yes—she's technically loyal to the dark—but not in the way that she should be. The strand connecting her to me has started to decay and rot like a corpse. Like our relationship. The minute I made a choice she didn't like she decided to sabotage me at the first opportunity. In her own, soured mind she thinks she deserves to have all of this given to her because her step-daddy was an asshole.

Wow, life must be a never-ending disappointment to her.

"She loved you in her way, but some people are easy to lead to corruption, and she's one of them." The voice belongs to someone else I want to tear into almost as bad as Ruthie, Life. I drop her on her ass and turn to him, ready to do exactly that, but the sad look in his blue eyes stops me. "Iza, if you kill her now, you'll never forgive yourself." That kindly look on his face makes my heart hurt more because he might be right. He continues, "I'm so sorry, Iza... I—I broke my own rules, and I meddled, and hopefully, one day, things will be better than they are now."

Frowning, I step towards him, reconsidering my stance on hitting him in that fake, wrinkly face of his. He's up to something. I don't know what but it's something I won't like. "What did you do?"

"The only thing I could do to help you both, but I'm afraid that it won't make things easier. Remember, darkness is eternal." With that mysterious bullshit said, he vanishes. Standing there, staring off into space, some of my rage banks itself, and I can think more clearly. How the fuck did he get in here? The music of the Sidhe fills my head.

"You let him in here? Why?" The music comes again. Why is the Sidhe adamant that he's trying to help me? "Can we not let them in here, please?" A sadder tone sounds acceptance of my wish.

"Who the hell are you talking to?" Ruthie demands from the floor. Didn't she see Life? That's interesting to know.

I turn my full attention to her. She isn't going to like what I do next. "If you'd kept your mouth shut, I might have left you there for a while longer." I grab her by the hair and toss her in the center of the group. "Do with her what you want, but she doesn't die, not yet. I have plans for her." Auryn steps forward and crosses her fist over her heart in salute.

"As you wish, my lady."

There's nothing I can do right now to vent this… mess inside of me, but there will be—I know I can find some of the ones working with the Guide. First, I need to sort myself out. I head to the lake, something about the water always seems to calm me down, even when it's frozen.

The fiends are mourning, I can feel their sadness, even though they're trying to protect me from it. When Phobe disappeared so did his forlorn, and with them, even their male children. My poor fiends. I send my love to them—I feel even more sadness for them. Swallowing the knot of grief that's threatening to overwhelm me again, I sit next to the lake with my legs crossed and stare out at the ice. I miss the rippling of the water, watching it chase itself to the shore. Something about the rhythmic movement is soothing, almost like a song of the spirit, or a magical heartbeat. Slowly, it starts to melt, and the first wave laps on the shore. The Sidhe is trying to comfort me.

Deep breath in, deep breath out. A few tears still manage to slip through my control but not the heart-pounding feeling from before. Nope, that's buried and will remain there until I kill the motherfucker that took him from me. So I think, because more tears slip out.

I have to hold onto that small spark of faith that says he isn't dead. Darkness is eternal, right?

21

JAMESON

It's hard to watch her, someone who is normally so strong, so brave—sneaking off to cry at the lake. It kicks you right in the guts. She's done it every day for the last two weeks. I want to comfort her, to help, but she won't look at me. Not without her eyes going black and anger filling them. Up until I was taken, I didn't think her opinion meant much to me. I was wrong, it means everything, and now it's not very high.

I fucked up, bad.

At least in that, I'm not alone. Nika is in a coma somewhere in the depths of the Sidhe, while Ruthie is in a cage in the family room. The Nightmares punish her every day, at the same time of day. They all gather, and each throws a handful of small pebbles at her. For five solid minutes, the entire group of them stand there and throw pebbles —the size of the tip of my pinky finger, at her—reducing her to a sobbing, bloody mess. Arista comes in, her delicate cheeks red with anger, strange to see on her normally serene face, and heals her. She only ever says one sentence to her, and that is, 'You don't deserve to be healed.' Ruthie throws tantrums for a few hours afterward, and the process starts the next day again.

The pebbles are symbolic of the people who died as a result of her betrayal. The anger of the lost souls. Their choice in punishment is a bit poetic really.

Today, I decide it's time to ask her, "Ruthie, why did you do it?"

She jumps to her feet, still healthy because Iza makes sure they feed her, and runs to the bars closest to me. "Jameson! Oh, my god, Jameson, get me out of here! They throw rocks at me all the time, and it hurts." I stand there and stare at her until she shuts up.

I ask again, "Why did you do it?" I know the stupid reasons I went and got myself captured, but what are hers?

"Because she gets everything she wants. The keys to the kingdom, the money... even Michael. He's supposed to be mine," she whines.

I scoff. "You think Iza had an easy life? Gods, you're dumber than I am. They tortured her for years... awful things, Ruthie. Things that you wouldn't survive the easiest of. She grew up in prison!" I shake my head and continue, "Over and over they did terrible things to her, her entire fucking life, and you think she doesn't deserve to have something good?" I realize that I'm yelling at her, but she deserves it, she deserves the rocks too. There's no guilt on her face, no remorse. She's not plagued by the nightmares and shame like I am. "If she kills you, you deserve it."

"I'm a kid—she loves me, won't kill me." The confidence in that statement is astounding and possibly true. Every time Iza looks at her, through the blooming hate, I see a flash of love. Albeit one that shrinks a little every day.

"You're not a kid anymore, Ruthie." If I were her, I wouldn't count on Iza not killing me, either. I wake up with that very real fear every day and try to stay out from underfoot. Phobe was captured, because I was captured, because I'm a fucking idiot. I was captured because Ruthie played spy and told them the magic words to get my moronic ass out of the Sidhe. A vicious cycle that played out and cost too many good people their lives.

"Will you let me out, Jameson? I'll run away and—"

"And what? Cause more deaths? Even if I were inclined to, and I'm not, Iza would string me up by the balls and, quite frankly, because of what you did, I don't think you're worth going through that for," I say and turn away. I thought I'd feel more sympathy for her, but I don't. Despite my inability to do the right thing, I care what happens to Iza... to these people.

More so now.

Speaking of Iza, I go to the closet at the front door and put on my coat. This time of day she's forgotten to eat and is at the lake, sitting in the muddy, wet snow, staring off into space at the water. Water that somehow thawed and is warm to the touch. No one bothers her anymore, not after she beat a few of them up, but everyone watches her from a distance, and now I feel like being a weirdo and doing it, too.

The snow is high and gets into my boots, but I keep wading through it, resolute on reaching the lake. Someone had the foresight to put lights up to illuminate the path for those of us that can't see in the dark. Which I'm increasingly thankful for as I fight the wind that seems determined to blow me back to the Sidhe. She was out here a few days ago wearing only a shirt. I'm not entirely sure she had underwear on.

It's heart wrenching to see someone, who is normally so strong, be a shadow of their normal selves. Other than cursing and pushing people to train she doesn't say much of anything. The cakes the goblins have baked for her go untouched, any food they make her is. I'm not sure if she's eaten anything, she doesn't look like she is. Her cheekbones are sharp, her cheeks sunken, and her skin is pale. None of us know what to do about it anymore. Phobe's death seems to have taken the life out of her.

We need to figure out how to put it back in her, or we're all doomed. Up ahead of me a dark figure stands out against the white backdrop of the snow. Other than them being dressed head to toe in black, I can't make out any more details about them. Tall, on the lean side, dark hair that matches the clothes. No winter clothes. For half a second, it looks like Phobe, and then the person vanishes. I rub my eyes and look again, but no one is there. Gods, now I'm seeing things.

Determined to follow through and check on her, I shake my head and keep going. When I come around the corner of the small picnic area, I find her, sitting on the table, her bare feet buried in the snow. She's wearing shorts in this weather. Does she not feel the cold? Picking up my pace I take off my coat and wrap it around her shoulders.

"I don't need it, Jameson. Take your coat back before you freeze your ass off," she says in that emotionless monotone voice that gives me the creeps. I listen, and take my coat back. Sinking into the warmth of it again I sigh in relief. I tried. I didn't come out here to piss her off and have her kick my ass.

"Do you need something?" she asks.

"Everyone is worried about you," I blurt out.

"Yeah. So?" Since I don't have an answer for that, I hold my tongue, almost literally. I'm biting it to keep my mouth shut. There are a million things I want to say or ask, but the majority of them will probably upset her, and I don't want to do that.

"I want to go into town. Would you like to come?"

Her request surprises me, and honestly, no, I don't want to go, but my mouth says, "Yes. I can do some needed shopping." I have no willpower at all, and when it comes to sticking to my guns with Iza, I'm a pussy.

"Get the car ready, please. I'll be along shortly," she says in that same creepy tone.

Bowing, something I can't say I've ever done before to her, I turn and half-run back to the Sidhe. Once inside, I yell for Adriem to get the car ready and wait for him outside. I'd rather be cold out here than pacing inside where people will ask questions.

"Why am I getting the car ready?" Adriem asks as he comes outside. He gets in and starts the car.

"Iza requested it."

"Oh, well, then. Where are we going?"

"She only said into town." Why doesn't he ask her himself instead of grilling me?

"For?"

"You ask her. I'm not." Maybe now, he'll get the point. I climb in the car and pray for the heater to work soon.

"No, we'll take her where she wants to go. I think asking her a bunch of questions will piss her off." Duh. A few minutes later the back door opens, and Iza gets in, silent as usual, but at least she's dressed.

"Where to?" Adriem asks after staring at her a long moment in the rear-view mirror.

"Town," she says with finality. Roughly translating to, stop asking me fucking questions.

"Okay then," he mumbles under his breath and puts the car into gear. I think that's the smartest choice, do what she says, and you get to keep your arms.

Plus, this is the first time she's left the Sidhe in weeks, maybe she's finally starting to recover. We can all hope, but my pessimistic side, that didn't exist before I lost my finger, thinks that there's a reason she wants to go there and none of us will like it.

22

IZA

I didn't expect to get a call from Armpit. I didn't expect I'd care to answer it either, but I did. Jarvis, the putz, claims to have information that I'd want because I'm hoping it's the kind that leads me to things I can stab, I'm meeting him. He picked a local restaurant that I've never been to. I'm assuming he's going to have men stashed everywhere. Humans are fragile. If they piss me off, I'll show them how fragile.

I still owe them for their attempt to take the kids.

My eyes move across the two men in the front seat before looking back out the window. The roads have been plowed, and snowdrifts are several feet high on either side, its ugly—piling it up that way, but necessary to get cars through. I wonder what this place looked like before humans came here. I bet the trees were thick and the forest floor looked ethereal with the snow blanketing it.

Jameson clears his throat, for the fiftieth time, and tries to look at me sneakily. He sucks at it, and I kind of want to flick his ear so he'll stop giving me those cow-eyed looks of pity. At least, it pulls me out of these morose thoughts I keep falling into. It's a constant thing now. I stare off into space thinking about shit that has nothing to do with anything.

When Jameson came and poked at me, I was thinking about who invented socks. Anything to keep my mind off— "We're meeting the idiots of armpit. He'll bring a crowd because he doesn't like to go on dates solo."

"You call them armpit?" Jameson laughs and chokes it off when no one else in the car laughs with him.

"We're going to Brandi's diner, off of main street," I say, as I turn to look at the two men hunched over like abused dogs. "I haven't beaten either one of you yet, so quit acting as I did."

"It's 'yet' that makes me nervous," Jameson quips, smiling at me, then immediately looks back out the front of the car.

Have I become the boogeyman for them to fear me in such a way? I only slung a few persistent people around who tried to physically bring me into the Sidhe. It's fucking annoying of them to act this way, and if they don't stop it I'm going to give them a reason.

"Why do they want to meet you?" I was wondering when Adriem would get around to asking. It's a bit unlike him to go along without any kind of comment.

"I'm assuming because they want to bribe me with information, so I'll go investigate their missing towns," I tell him truthfully. I see no reason to lie.

"Are you going to?" Adriem has a bit of hope in his voice. He's not a stay at home type any more than I am.

The last news report said that they've been finding bodies of people from the towns out of contact. All of them missing their hearts, that smells a lot like Blood Magiks to me. The Schoth are spreading quickly. Video of sirens taking victims at a lake in New York is all over the world. Their guns aren't working either.

Would it be so bad to check on the people? Fuck Jarvis and his bullshit, but the other humans—the ones being held or killed, they don't deserve this. A not so nice smile tickles my lips. I'd get to stab something, after all.

"We might look into it, but not for fuckhead. We'll do it for the people who are suffering." Going head to head with the Schoth sounds fun. Leaning my forehead against the cold glass, I look back out the window. I can sneak in and make a mess, maybe free some people.

"Okay, a road trip will be nice," Jameson says, a bit of excitement in his voice. Up until this moment, I didn't think on how he probably needs to get out of the Sidhe too. Ruthie isn't the only one people are shunning, Jameson is getting it a little. Not so much anymore but it was relatively bad in the beginning. Honestly, I couldn't find it in me to care at the time. Not sure I can find it in me to care now. He fucked up. I didn't kill him. That should be something positive in his eyes.

Ruthie is still in the cage. I haven't spoken a word to her since the day I pulled her out of it. No one wants to execute an eighteen—freshly turned eighteen—year old girl. Especially one they've shared meals and laughter with. I'm dreading it. I won't lie to myself about it. It's easier to leave her in the cage than deal with the dilemma of whether or not to kill her. Eventually, I'll have to do something with her.

Doesn't mean I won't avoid it as long as possible.

We pull up to the diner, and I see Jarvis right away. He's standing in front of the door, looking at his phone. Looking around the parking lot, I spot the twelve men he has stationed outside. Considering it's winter time, the 'construction workers' they're posing as looks incredibly out of place. How can they fix anything when they can't see it because of the snow? Plus, they're way too clean, working in slush and muddy snow won't keep your boots looking brand new.

The ones in the diner probably stick out like sore thumbs too. Amateurs.

"There's at least eight of them out here," Adriem says, sliding sunglasses onto his face.

"There are twelve," I correct him and get out of the car.

Jarvis sees me immediately and opens the door for me to precede him. Without returning the blatantly false smile on his face, I do. Inside I take a corner booth with my back to the wall, facing the door. Adriem slides in beside Jameson, across from me. Jarvis jabs at him until he moves over so the smaller man can fit in the seat.

"Thank you for coming." The smile he gives me is real, although it's more of a grimace than an actual smile. He hates that he had to ask me for help. "I honestly didn't expect you to show up," he says, resting his elbows on the table and steepling his fingers under his chin. This is his intimidation pose. I wonder if it works on anyone who isn't in his payroll.

"You mean after you tortured and tested captured Feyrie and lied about having the wingless?" He raises his eyebrows and shrugs. "Yeah, I wouldn't have bet on me coming either, but you have something I want."

"Ah, yes. Information." He takes a manila folder that the 'waitress' hands him. Opening it up, he turns it towards me so that I can read the contents. There are several photos taken from the satellites the humans have cluttering up their orbit, I'm guessing. The house is located in a rather wealthy looking area, if going by the size of the houses are any indication.

As I flip through the pictures, I see every angle of the outside of the house and even a few of the insides through an open window. It's a vampire nest, and nest is a stupid word for a bunch of bloodsuckers, but they are drawn to them whether they want to be or not. Several of the people lounging outside at the pool aren't vampires. They look too tanned and healthy. That means they're shifters. This is the right place.

The included printouts list the addresses, estimated occupancies, and other bits of important information. It also lists where they go, what they do when they're there, where they grocery shop and what kind of toilet paper they buy. Jarvis is thorough. I'll give him that.

"What do you want in return?"

"I need someone to go in and assess the threat these creatures are posing to this world." Well, that was something I was thinking of doing anyhow.

"How many people have you lost?" He wouldn't come asking for my help without having tried to do it himself and failing.

He stalls by clearing his throat and adjusting his tie. There had to be a lot of them for this kind of behavior from someone like him.

"The last count was two-hundred and forty-seven. Not counting civilians, which numbers in the thousands."

"Do you know the exact number of civilians?" Jarvis's goons are all private mercenaries. The military isn't even going in. They're keeping their distance and observing the phenomena. Can't say I blame them, going by how many of his men are dead, I don't doubt that they are aware of, it would be foolhardy to send in valuable military to die too.

"Not at this time, no." As expected, he doesn't strike me as the sentimental type, more like the type that will sacrifice the few for the many—but in a shitty way. Like when they keep sacrificing until it turns into many.

"Okay, we'll go in, however—I and my people are not yours to command or control. We do things our way, on our time and by our rules." Conversation done I stand up to leave. Jameson and Adriem stand as well, and we file out of the diner.

"Four," Adriem says.

"Seven, you two need to learn to be more observant."

"How do you figure seven? I counted twice," he argues.

"The large woman sitting at the booth next to ours was wearing postal uniform. Considering she was also wearing high heels, I highly doubt she's a mail carrier. The teenagers sitting at the counter had chocolate pie in front of them, but neither one of them took a bite or looked at their phones. Instead they watched the traffic outside. How many teenagers you know prefer traffic over their cell phones?" I explain.

"Shit, I see it now. How did you learn to be so observant?"

"Survival," I answer and get in the car. When Jameson shuffles between the passenger door in the front and the door opposite me in the back, I almost smile. He looks like someone is jerking him around on a string. After a few looks of worry at me, he makes the decision and gets in the front immediately striking up a conversation with Adriem about how Jarvis reminds him of a guy on the chocolate movie. The car salesman specifically. Picturing the character in my head, I bite down on my lip to stop another smile. He does resemble him. Damn them for making me want to do something besides be angry and mope.

"When we get to the Sidhe, I want you to call a meeting. We'll choose who goes with us and take a small but lethal force. And no, Jameson, you're not going." I watch him visibly relax from his puckered butthole position. Just because he was kidnapped and tortured a little doesn't mean I think he's ready to fight Schoth.

"What about Ruthie?" Adriem asks a bit cautiously. I choose to ignore the question and look out the window. He still keeps talking. "Iza, people are starting to complain."

"Then have them kill her." He holds his tongue from further comment. None of them want to kill her either.

23

IZA

When arguments break out about who's going with us to investigate one of the incursions, I end up screaming for them all to shut up. This is ridiculous, this bickering and yelling over something this important. Some of these people are hundreds of years old, but you'd never know it from their behavior.

"Auryn, Licar, Alagard, Adriem, Michael—Arista, you're going with me. The rest of you will stay here and guard the fucking Sidhe. End of story." The silence is deafening.

"Let me out of here, Iza!" Ruthie demands from her the cage that's shrunk to the size of a doggy crate. The mood I'm in leaves no room for her shit right now. Whispering a request to my annoyed hair, a piece detaches itself and slithers down my shoulder to my hand.

"Can you keep her in check?" It rears up like a cobra. Turning, I toss it at her. With a small splat it hits her face and as she's yelling and clawing at it, attaches itself to her scalp then proceeds to bite her. She's lucky it's not using venom—even my hair doesn't want to kill her. This whole reluctance thing is frustrating, she did something awful and got people killed.

Phobe was killed.

Gritting my teeth, I turn away from her and pause at the door. "If she tries to escape, kill her." It's an order for everyone remaining.

"You can't do this to me!" When she starts yelling again, I walk out the door. Of course, I can do this to her. Considering death is the only other alternative, I think she's getting the easier end of the stick. A stick I should beat her fucking ass with.

Annoyed with myself I shake my head and prepare for what's coming. I need to see the outside of the shield to know where to look for a weak spot. All shields have them, might take me smacking it a little first. A lot of it depends on the strength of the mage who created it.

The drive to get to the chosen encampment is close to six hours. I pack my gear in a duffle bag because sitting with knives and guns strapped all over me in a car crammed with people isn't comfortable. Alagard's elbow has made itself a home in my rib cage, while Licar—who's in the front seat with a sleeping Auryn on his chest, has pushed the seat so far back to sleep that I have no leg room. They insisted on riding in the same car when we have more than one car to use.

Is this their way of getting me back for leaving them with a squalling Ruthie?

At least, I can ignore the snoring from the old dragon. I've gotten so used to the sounds of it because sleep hasn't been my friend. Instead, I wandered the Sidhe late into the night. While doing this, I developed the habit of checking on everyone while they slept. This is the reason that I know Jameson sleeps less than I do, most nights. When he does fall asleep, it's in the library while pouring over information on the Guide. He's trying to find a way to kill him, an answer I could give him if he asked.

Strip away the Magiks protecting him and slit his fucking throat.

He's more juiced up than he was the first time I fought him and as long as he's protected by the motherfucker that killed Phobe, I can't touch him—no one can. He's too strong, layered with protections on top of protections, and anyone who tries to get him will die doing it. Looking at it straight on, it appears impossible. Ruthie, however, gave me some information that I needed without even meaning to tell me.

The key is the necklace, if we can destroy it, we destroy him. Something I'd like to do rather messily. I think I'll do some wall art with his intestines, maybe use his skin to make a hammock. One that I'll make Ruthie sleep on, so she never forgets what she did. I truly believe her being alive and aware of everything going on, will ultimately be a worse punishment than any kind of death—no matter how violent. Death gives closure. I don't want her getting closure. She doesn't deserve it. When Michael finds love again, he's a good boy—man—so he will find it, that will be the icing on the cake.

"That look on your face does not bode well for some unfortunate soul," Alagard muses in a sleepy whisper.

"She's not an unfortunate soul. She's an asshole."

"Ah, I see. You know," the scratching of him rubbing his beard fills the pause. "I'm a bit proud of you for not bending under the pressure of old laws."

Looking over at him I chew my lip while thinking about what I want to say. When I decide I shrug and say, "Some old laws are okay to follow, like letting an enemy honorably defeated in battle become dinner or die in their way of choosing. But the Feyrie who made most of those old laws are dead and gone. Their time has passed, they did things their way. This is our time, now, which means our rules. It's only fair that we do things our way, and people learn to adapt because that's way more important than following old outdated laws. It's the only thing that will save the Feyrie as a whole."

"You've put some thought into this." The surprise in his voice is almost insulting.

"Of course, I have, I want to survive—I want to see the Feyrie survive and I'm willing to crawl through a lot of shit to ensure it. However, everyone needs to be willing to crawl through the shit with me. This isn't a one-person journey because I'm no one's fucking martyr." Done with the conversation, I turn back to the window.

After discovering what Ruthie did, hearing what people said, and the entire clusterfuck that came with it—I'm not going to keep sacrificing alone. They can all freaking bleed with me. Isn't that how teamwork works? All for one and all that camaraderie bullshit. I'm tired of it always being Phobe and me on the front line while everyone else sits at home having tea.

No, now it's just me.

When I first accepted that I would be this Shepherd person, I foolishly convinced myself that I had to stand in between the Feyrie and all the bad guys. I don't think that's what this all means, it's not the song the Sidhe sings to me. The Feyrie need to stand up on their own, too, they need to fight for themselves. I'll lead them to it. My job is to make them strong enough for the task and letting them sit at home and hide is not helping them achieve it. The time for peace is over with. I gave them all that I could. This world isn't safe anymore, our enemies are here, and this is only the beginning.

This is the world we make our stand in.

"You left them with instructions to train, Alagard?" I ask.

"Of course, war is on the horizon. Although, not all of them are built for fighting. In my day, they would have been weeded out and used as servants or something menial, but at your suggestion I have them catering to their other strengths."

A good example is Florenta, who is not physically strong, but she's super smart and great at getting people organized, and this is why I put her in charge of schedules, tasks, and other adult stuff. Essentially, she's taken over for Jameson and doing a better job at it. Which also frees him to work on his strengths, potions and spell crafting. The bastard can turn anything into a potion, and although he can't use spells for shit, he can create them.

Arista has become the head healer and is responsible for training and taking care of injuries and illness. She's got a sharp eye for spotting anyone with healing abilities. It's why I brought her with me, to heal, we're going to need it potentially. We have to move in fast, silent and brutal. My favorite part of all of this are the brutal bits. I'm going to enjoy them immensely.

"What do you think we're going to find in there?"

"Scouts for sure, and at this point potentially their assassins—they send them out to infiltrate the ruling bodies of the places they invade. Probably some other Light Fey too, they use them primarily for muscle." I sigh and keep going, "This is the easy part. The shit doesn't truly hit the fan until the mages get here." They're the heavy hitters, I've seen what they can do. I'm also looking forward to killing a few of them when the time comes. Who am I kidding? I plan to kill as many of them as I can get my grubby hands on.

Let's call it cathartic slaughter.

When I stay silent, Alagard takes that as his cue to go back to sleep. My attention turns once again to the passing scenes outside, losing myself in planning our mission, because I don't want to think about anything else. Only what I need to be thinking about. Not about a man who had dimples when he smiled. Biting my tongue, hard, the sting of pain pulls me away from those thoughts and back onto going into the shielded zones.

A few hours later when the sun is kissing the horizon and suffocating the darkness with the light, I feel a twinge of loss as the sky gets brighter. Needing to look away from something that reminds me too much of more painful things, I study the occupants of the car. Adriem is driving with Licar and Auryn in the front, while myself, Alagard, and Arista are in the first row back seat, Michael has the farthest backseat all to himself. I'm not sure how it ended up this way, and it's something we'll remedy on the trip back.

My mouth is dry, and I chug the bottle of water that I've been holding in my lap like a baby. Empty, I crumble it, using the noise it makes to get everyone's attention.

"We'll be there soon. Michael, Auryn, and Licar, you'll be coming in with me. Adriem, you, Alagard, and Arista will wait at the entry point. Do NOT come in unless I tell you to. Arista be prepared for injuries, lots of them. Everyone understand?" There are several nods, but no one says anything. My eyes automatically go to Michael who's the least experienced present. His face is resolute and set in hard lines. He's ready now for what's to come. Michael needs an outlet as much as I do.

This is one of the reasons I brought him with me. The other is to keep him from killing Ruthie because there's a part of him that wants to and it's growing. One day that part will be stronger than the one that still loves her.

The shield comes into view ahead of us, swirling shades of gold and yellow sickness. The earth knows it doesn't belong here and is keeping it from infecting the soil. Looking at it closely, I can see the space in between the bottom of the shield and the ground. There's our way in.

Thank you, Mother Earth.

The military sentries posted on the road, oddly enough, wave us through without issue.

"Park over there, because that's where we're going in," I say, pointing at one of the larger spaces to the left of the road. When they park the car, I climb out without waiting for it to come to a full stop. Everything I need is on me, and they can catch up.

Unsurprisingly, there are no guards patrolling the perimeter. Arrogance, and the belief that there's nothing here that can hurt them made them slack in this task. Stupid of them, very stupid. Smiling, I run at the shield and at the last second drop to my side and use my momentum to slide through the space that's barely big enough for me to get through.

Climbing to my feet, I watch Auryn climb underneath in a disjointed way that she shouldn't be able to move her body, but does because this form is not her true one. Licar pulls himself through and to his feet, then kneeling down, he pulls Michael through. Turning away, I look in the direction that I smell Schoth and death. So much death that I can hear the buzzing of insects that infest the corpses.

"Licar, Auryn, circle round and meet me on the other side of the town. Take out any Light Fey that gets in your way, with prejudice. If you spot surviving humans and you can get to them, free them," I order.

"What about you, my lady?"

A smile splits my dry lips, and my hair stirs around. "I'm going through the middle, of course." With a nod at them, I take off running, because not only can I smell them, I can hear them. They're throwing a party at their prisoner's expense if the screams are any indication.

Michael's heavy breathing from behind me makes me speed up. He's getting a workout today.

The first house we reach is outside of the small town up ahead. On silent feet, I creep around it to look in the windows. The first thing I see is a baby bed, the second thing I see is a dead woman on the floor. Blood has turned this place of joy and love into a horror movie of painted teddy bears. Grabbing the window seal and digging my claws in, I pull myself up enough to look inside the baby bed.

It's empty.

Dropping to the ground, a sixth sense makes me look down at the basement window at my feet. A youthful face peeks out of me, that of a teenage girl and in her arms is a baby, one that's very much alive. With my finger to my lips for her to keep her silence, I point at the back door. A few minutes later I hear the creak of it opening, and I pull her around the side of the house.

The sleeping face of the baby eases some of the tension.

"Go that way, straight that way. There will be a group of people standing there, tell them Iza sent you. Okay?" She nods and with a few furtive glances around her, runs.

"How did she know to trust you?" Michael whispers.

"For some reason, human children always do."

"I can see it," he says with a nod.

Deciding not to comment, I'm not sure what to say anyway, I head to the next house. The occupants of it aren't so lucky. Every window gives me a view of a dead body. A half-naked human woman demonstrates that the Schoth aren't only murdering them. As we move unerringly towards the center of town, I check every single house. A few have survivors that I quietly send into the arms of my people waiting outside. Most don't.

The children weren't spared, either.

Hardening my resolve, I decide killing a few here isn't enough. Oh, no. I'm going to kill as many as I can.

♥

THERE WEREN'T many Schoth or their Fey kin that could put up much of a fight. Not only were they gluttoning themselves on their human victims, but they're also drinking highly potent ale. This works out for me, but I'm a little disappointed.

Looking over my shoulder at Michael, I ask, "You hungry?"

Jumping from my hiding spot, I land on the chest of one of the Schoth scouts lounging on the hood of a car. The impact crushes his breastbone and stuns him enough for me to slice him from groin to belly button. With a little stomp, his guts pop out and ooze down his hip.

Now, that's fun.

Michael's eyes glow, so blue they're almost white, and his other face shows itself. He's on someone before they can do more than yell out in surprise. Good, purge the rage. The few humans that are coherent enough to run in the direction I tell them to, do so with scars that will forever be on their bodies and soul. The ones who are too injured or traumatized to do more than sit there screaming, I leave for now. This won't be a camp for Schoth anymore when I get done with it, and someone can come in and help them in a way I can't.

Taking part of the Sidhe inside of me gives me resistance to Light Magiks that I didn't have before. It's still hurts but doesn't weaken me as badly as before. The small freedom is exhilarating.

Hours pass, hours of blood and pain-filled screams, and the useless begging of the dying Schoth. Until there's none left to kill. Standing on top of a pile of bodies, I look around at the destruction, not all of it caused by me. Casually discarded corpses of humans who didn't survive the invasion of these parasites are everywhere.

My adrenaline high wavers. Some are so young that I have to look away from them. The shield around us flickers and goes out which means Auryn and Licar found the source of it. When the steady thwump thwump of a helicopter approaching reaches my ears, I know it's time for us to take our leave. The humans can come in and deal with this.

Jumping off the bodies, I start walking in the general direction of the car. When the others join me, I remain silent, but I do look at each of them to assure myself of their welfare.

Michael's face is covered in blood and gore. He fed well. His injuries are minimal, and he'll heal overnight. Auryn is splattered with blood, but I see no evidence of injuries to her. Licar is spotless except for his hands and mouth. I look down at myself. I'm covered in all sorts of gunk.

Today was very *cathartic* and that morbidly makes me want to have a chuckle about it. Do I feel better? No, not really. Did it feel nice to kill them? Oh yes. Perhaps I'll share my philosophy that killing makes you feel better with the others, because whoever said vengeance wasn't sweet, never tried it.

Now I need to visit the rest of these places—this way I'll get all their attention.

24

JAMESON

Michael spoke to me about their trip to the Schoth base. He spoke of how wonderful it felt to finally get a taste of dealing justice for all the wrongs committed by them. He told me how Iza was spinning like a death tornado and killed with a smile on her face, laughing and dancing like it was a party instead of a fight. He is in complete awe of her, and it concerns me.

Not that they killed people, but that Iza isn't... Iza. She's quiet and withdrawn, she rarely speaks to anyone. When she smiles, it's so cold that it makes you need to stand next to a heater. Phobe's death has turned her into a stranger, and I'm not the only one who noticed. They all have.

I can't remember the last time she asked for a pie.

She's out at the lake again, and I don't plan to bother her, no one is. Instead, I'm sitting in the dining room listening to a few of the Feyrie having a 'secret' meeting about the condition of their fearless leader. For some reason, they haven't noticed me sitting on the fringes of the room, listening.

There aren't many familiar faces in the gathering, Auryn and the other Nightmares are out doing other things. Arista and the ones who run in her circle are in their wing of the Sidhe doing whatever it is they do. These are mostly new people, ones who tend to complain a lot.

Most of them are on Iza's secret shit list. For some unknown reason people think she doesn't pay attention to anything, they forgot to read their history... our history. The more they talk, the angrier I get, the idiocy leaving their mouths is infuriating. How dare they do this!

"She allowed the girl to live after she helped murder people. Face it, Iza is useless now. We need to do something about it." I can't remember the man's name, he's relatively new and a shifter.

Preparing to stand, I open my mouth to tell them exactly how I feel. A firm hand on my shoulder stops both actions. Startled, I look up and find Iza, with her solid black eyes on the gathering of people. The shit has now officially hit the fan or will when they notice she's here. Going by her relaxed stance, it's one of those situations where you give someone enough rope to hang themselves. Except in this case, she'll hang them with it.

"Who are you suggesting, Gary? I don't think any of us are capable of doing what needs to be done." Someone says from the crowd.

"There are plenty of viable candidates that have political experience," Gary says.

"And you think she's going to hand you the keys and walk away?" one of the male dragons, one that came while I was gone, asks and smirks at Gary.

"She doesn't know what planet she's on, let alone who's leading the Feyrie," Gary argues.

"Are there going to be donuts and coffee at this meeting?" Iza calls out, walking towards Gary, who now looks like he wants to disappear into the floor. As she walks by the dragon who spoke up, she smacks him in the back of the head, hard.

"Iza, we uh—didn't know you were here," Gary says, coughing a little when he chokes on his spit.

"Yeah, I see that. So, here's the deal," she turns to face the group. "If you agree with douchebag here, you can leave. I'm done defending myself or my decisions. At this point, if you're unhappy, go out there and die, because I won't save you." She points towards the door and then crosses her arms to wait.

People shuffle around in their seats, but no one moves, except Gary. When he realizes no one is following him, he stops and then drops into a chair looking like a child that's been scolded.

Iza scoffs, "You should all be ashamed of yourselves right now. You come here, you eat for free, you live in luxury, and when one thing doesn't go your way, or I make a decision you don't like, you want to mutiny? That's not even a thing. I'm not Captain Ahab. I will slit your fucking throat for betraying me, do you understand?" She says it in such a pleasant tone that I don't think most of them realize how serious she is.

Gary does, his face is white as a sheet.

Iza is tired of people backstabbing her, and I can't blame her. Look at what she's given up helping the Feyrie, what she's lost... what she went through to be strong enough to be here. Gods, we're a bunch of ungrateful assholes.

"You're not going to let them get off so easily, are you, Iza?" The words pop out of my mouth and when she smiles that scary smile, for the very first time—I smile back at her. Turning she snaps Gary's neck without batting an eye.

"I don't care about what the rest of you do, but the Sidhe does." The room around us rumbles. "I'll leave you all to it, good luck," she says in a singsong voice. As she walks by me, she grabs my arm and drags me from the room. The door slams shut behind us and then the screams start.

The question almost leaves my mouth, but I stop it. Opening that can of worms might end up with me in that room, too. Admittedly, being dragged through the Sidhe by a woman who weighs eighty pounds less than me and is probably close to a foot shorter, is a bit emasculating. When she tosses me onto a couch, without breaking stride and goes out the front door, it's a bit worse.

Still not opening my mouth.

"Wow, she tosses you around like a ball. Doesn't it piss you off?" Ruthie snots off from the cage.

"Nope, but you running your mouth does. If you had any sense, you'd start wising up and be thankful you're still alive."

"I told you, she won't kill me."

Looking up at her and seeing the gloating face from between the bars makes me blurt out the truth, at least what I'm guessing Iza is doing.

"She's keeping you alive for a reason, and once you've served that purpose..." I make noise deep in my throat and run my finger across it. The warmth of satisfaction in my stomach when the color leeches from her face is worth it.

Dusting at the muddy handprint on my sleeve, ineffectually, I sigh. There are holes in the material too, from her claws. I think I need to rethink my wardrobe choices, especially after I start weapons training. Something that no one thinks I can do. I'm going to prove them wrong.

"You're still as superficial as you ever were. I see how you're looking at your clothes." I look up at Ruthie again and smile.

"Yes, yes I am, but I'm not the one in a cage." Looking down at my watch, my smile gets bigger. "Oh, it's that time of day again." Right on time, the door opens and the Nightmares file in, each bearing a handful of small pebbles. There are times that karma comes and bites you in the ass. I realized it the day they cut my finger off.

A quick glance down at the nub flashes a memory through my mind. Gritting my teeth, I force it away and focus on the TV while Ruthie yells in the background.

Yeah, karma comes for all of us, but I still feel like I got off easy. And every single time I look at Iza, knowing that her soul is gone, a little part of me hopes she'll kill me. The guilt that wrenches my stomach like I'm on a boat and seasick, and almost brings me to tears, would go away then.

25

IZA

A MUTINY, WHAT KIND OF IDIOTS PLAN A MUTINY IN A HOUSE? I'm starting to think these earthbound Feyrie aren't worth saving, then I think of Knox. Well, some of them are. The Sidhe is dealing with the current pains in the ass. A fact that I find very... amusing. The Sidhe doesn't step in often. Typically it lets me deal with the issues. It shows its displeasure, like when it took all of Jameson's furniture away, but it doesn't outright punish like it is right now.

By the volume of their screams, that I can hear even at this distance, they act like they're being tortured to death. The wusses, that's not the case at all. A scream hits a high note and sounds out right nasty, well, maybe there's a little torture going on. The Sidhe is in their heads, giving them visions of their worst fears. Some of which is rather unwise. The Sidhe is letting me eavesdrop into their minds. Whose worst fear is to be covered in peanut butter and licked by small fluffy dogs? Oh, wait, it's Fred's worst fear. I wonder if his mother ever shut his head in a door as a baby, slammed it a time or two on top of it. It would explain that fear, and maybe some of his other peculiarities. He shaves his toe hair, ONLY his toe hair. Not his face, or legs, or even his man bits. He's obsessive about it, has sexual fantasies about shaving other people's toe hair.

The Sidhe is singing the songs of laughter. The task amuses it, and my thoughts. Shining its bright light on the pieces of my fractured soul. Sighing, I lean my back against the rough bark of the tree and ignore the wetness from the melting snow under me. Bending my legs, I rest my elbows on my knees.

They're not wrong, I have kept to myself and away from most of them. Looking at Ruthie reminds me of everything I've lost. Looking at the ones who want to 'mutiny,' makes me angry about the losses.

The Sidhe warns me right before I feel the familiar, warm, and completely unexpected presence. "Ah, dove. I'm so sorry," my Dad says in a tired voice. I'm on my feet and running to him before I can think about it. He grabs me out of the air and the smell of cold and dark jerks at that door everything is hiding behind.

"You got out."

"Yes, I think someone helped me, I'm not sure who. The shield disappeared, and I came here the second I realized it." He squeezes me in a hard hug as he talks. I'm not in a hurry to let go, either.

"They took him from me, Dad." The giant sob burns my throat and takes away any will to speak. Dad rocks me and murmurs as he rubs my hair and lets me cry it all out. When the sobs space out and become only those hiccupy things, and the faucet of tears has finally turned off, my dad sets me away from him. With gentle hands, he lifts my chin to meet my eyes.

"Now, what else has been going on?" I look into his beloved face, the one I needed to see and thought I wouldn't be able to. The dark circles under his eyes are new, and there are some scars on his face now, small ones, but the soft look in his eyes, the love shining so brightly there gives me much needed strength.

So, I tell him, all of it.

♥

"The father in me wants to tell you that it gets better, that the pain eases with time and you can find that kind of happiness again. I don't want to give you platitudes, Iza. Neither one of us accepts them." He pats my leg as he says this.

Somehow, he ended up on the ground with me, sitting in the snow and mud, talking. Since being reunited, we've always had talks, but this one was a whole new level and shows me exactly how much our relationship has grown. Up until now, I didn't realize how much I need him in my life.

"What are you planning on doing?" he asks, after both of us quietly contemplated the lake for a little while.

"I'm going to kill them."

"I assumed as much. What's your plan to do that, exactly?" I toss a handful of snow at him.

"First, I'm going to start taking out their outposts here." He nods along with me as I talk. "Then I'm going to get strong enough to get that fucking necklace off of the Guide so that I can smash him into little bitty pieces."

"And what about his master?"

Meeting his eyes, I shrug and say, "All I can do is fight until I can't anymore, Dad."

"I don't want to see this kill you, dove. If they can hurt Phobe…"

"It's okay, I know that I'm not at that level, but giving up isn't part of my nature. Since I got half of it from you, it's your fault." He smiles and pats my leg again.

His face grows serious. "Tell me what Phobe said to Light again?"

Staring at the ground, drawing circles in the snow, I swallow the lump in my throat. Verbatim, I repeat the words that pull at my heart. He nods in acceptance and turns to look back at the lake. "And you saw the One-God there?"

"Yes. I have no idea what he was doing, but it pisses me off he didn't try to help. He stood there and let him die."

I feel his mood turn more somber. "Are you going to execute her?" The seriousness of his tone makes me look at him.

"What would you do?"

"Betrayal cost you and me both your mother, and it also cost you

Phobe. How many other lives has her selfishness cost or will?" Logic, I hate logic at times like this.

"What if I'm not sure I can do it?"

"There's no shame in that, Iza. You love her. She's family to you." He pauses and grasps both of my shoulders. "Remember your mother's soft heart, Iza."

Her soft heart and what it cost her, is what he means. My mom refused to believe that Kael would betray her, which he did many times, and ultimately murdered her. I can't lie to myself though. I don't want to kill her. Killing her will take away something vital inside of me. Inspiration hits me, a way to have justice dealt, pacify the Feyrie, and not have to sell the last of my soul.

"I'll put her to trial. The Feyrie can decide." Then she can have her day in court that she keeps yelling about. They can decide her fate and deal with the consequences of it since they're so keen on doing it.

"If it were anyone besides one of your kids, you'd kill them yourself." He's not wrong, so I say nothing. "I think that given the circumstances, you're making the right decision." He gives me one of those one arm hugs that Dads are famous for and then climbs to his feet. "Will you be okay?" he asks me softly, holding his hand out to pull me to my feet. I shake my head at his hand and shrug.

"I'm guessing that you're being called?"

"Yes, I'll return as soon as I can, they're sending constant attacks against me. Against the dead, I have to protect them." I understand now, I didn't used to, and I resented it a lot, but now that I have my shit job—I get it. "I love you, dove," he says as he's fading out of existence.

"I love you too, Dad."

Hugging myself, I lay my head back against the tree once again. Being around all of them is hard, it's hard not to resent them, all of them. A small, petty part of me blames the Feyrie as a whole. Phobe was there for me. We didn't ask anyone for anything. We survived on our merit. I came here, and it cost me everything.

These feelings have to be worked through before I can care enough to bother with them again. Grief is an odd duck, but it's possible to work through the negative bullshit it brings with it. I might still blame them, but I don't want to kill them anymore.

If only Ruthie knew how hard it was *not* to kill her, she might sing a different tune. The fact that I want to keep that spark of goodness inside of me prevents me from giving into the dark, the monster. It wants to pull her apart and then pile her pieces up and dance on them while they burn. The dark part of me wants to burn them all.

Thankfully, it's controllable and has lessened significantly over the last few weeks. The reason I come out here is to work through it, control it. The impulse was harder when the idiots were planning to toss me out. Even the Sidhe was quiet on that one, waiting simply for me to make a decision.

I can't promise I will always be able to control the urge. The anger, the rawness of my emotions from losing Phobe are simmering in the background behind my control. The fire is getting hotter. For now, my will is strong enough to keep it contained, because I want to.

For now.

26

IZA

Iza

THE MUTINEERS ARE NOW SITTING at a table isolated from the rest of them. The Sidhe has marked their table with one word. Backstabbers. I didn't realize how smart the Sidhe was, not really. The idea of it is there but seeing this diabolical display confirms it. How refreshingly wonderful. Also, they're all naked. No idea how they ended up that way, but no one is going to help them remedy the situation. Their clothes were taken by a more powerful force than anyone here.

Even if I could return them, I wouldn't. Let the fuckers spend a few days naked and guilty of something. Might teach them some humility and gratefulness.

"Ha, it marked their table too?" Jameson asks his voice still holding that little nervous wobble he's had since I brought him back here.

"Yep," I answer, staring at him. His color is better today, but his eyes are the same. Reaching inside of myself I look for the sympathy that should be there and find a small spark. Less than before. In fact, every time I look at the empty chair beside me, it shrinks a little more.

This is what I'm fighting, I can't want to kill them, I can't stop caring for any of them, but I can be angry.

No one can take that away from me, not even me.

"You hate us all, don't you?" Jameson's perceptiveness catches me off guard.

"Sometimes," I say honestly.

"I can't say I blame you." I watch his maimed hand. "If I hadn't have gone…"

"This would have played out another way, eventually. All of us will end up dead fighting this fight." It's nothing but the truth. War means death.

"Is this something you even want to do anymore?" Tilting my head, I think about it as I stare at him. I don't want to, not really. I'm somewhere in the middle. "You know, I wanted to tell you about a saying I read." He leans his elbows on the table and moves closer to me. "Darkness can't die, everything started with darkness and will end with it." Then he's up and gone, moving to another table where they greet him in a friendlier way.

Well, Arista does. She likes him because she's got horrible taste in men. He also gave me something to think about. It's entirely possible Phobe isn't dead-dead and is floating around out there in the worlds somewhere. In the scheme of things, technically if he were, he's still dead to me. In that form, he'd have no idea who I am or care about knowing me. Darkness has no thoughts on such things. I know this because he told me what it was like for him before he became something else.

Before he was mine.

Climbing to my feet, I push the full plate of food away and leave the house. The lake is calling me again, and I think I need it right now. I need to think and to think I need quiet. I can't keep being this way, not towards the innocent ones. I knew what I was signing up for, so I have to work through this hateful bullshit and get over it.

I just have to figure out how to do that.

27

LIFE

IZA HAS ALWAYS BEEN A CREATURE I LOVE TO WATCH. WHETHER IT'S HER quick smile or open-mindedness about how life works, or the way she leaps into every aspect of life, I'll never know for sure. Something about her pulls me back to her, makes me help her when I can, made me break my own rules for the first time in creation. The result of that offense is looking at me with eyes full of nothing but chilling cold. A fire that freezes your very soul in place, while demanding their will to be met.

Even I'm affected by a stare like that, but that is not why I'm giving in to the demand.

Turning away from it, I watch the sad woman, who was once a vivacious child, stare off into a lake that melts for her because this odd place... loves her. I was unaware of how alive, and sentient the Sidhe had become. Not that I created it, no one did. The Sidhe came to be all on its own, and there's not another one like it in existence, anywhere. No Light equivalent, either. The Sidhe chooses its shape, its companion, and where and when it exists.

Iza's influence on it is astounding and unprecedented. She has a way of making things, powerful dark things, adapt to her instead of her adapting to them. Like Phobe for example. She changed an ageless creature with no emotion, into someone who laughed at her terrible jokes. A creature that liked to watch her sleep and loved her with every cell of his being. That laughter inside of her pulled on him, changed him.

I sigh, there are many battles ahead for her, but the one inside of her I cannot help her with. Iza is the only one that can decide if she wants to remain the Shepherd for the Feyrie, if she wants to wield the Dark Magiks to save them. Or if she wants to walk away from it all. I'm pretty sure that if she does throw them all out, the Sidhe will remain with her, especially since it gave up part of its—soul is a good word for it—to keep her healthy when she is away from it.

Never has the Sidhe made such a sacrifice or a bond with another. The Magiks inside of her will not choose another while she lives either. I think they might agree with her rather low opinion of some of the Feyrie. Like the naked ones back at the house. Those Feyrie are loyal enough to the dark to survive the Magiks but dumb enough to perhaps not survive Iza.

I wonder if she realizes that she's changing and that whatever she is to become is more than she was fated to be? Iza does like to break out of the mold and drive on the sidewalk when it comes to the road of life. She is what she is and makes no apologies for it, but she struggles, too. Much like she is now.

Iza has this light inside of her that, somehow, she protected and nurtured while growing up under terrible circumstances. It gives her compassion, sympathy, and makes her heart fill with laughter, even in the darkest times. The light is in danger, her grief—her feelings of guilt and anger, are smothering it. She's fighting it, trying to protect it from all of this, but she is struggling with it.

If she loses it, she is a danger to everyone—but that isn't what concerns me. It's what it will do to her, to that light she held onto despite impossible odds. Therefore, the next step has to be taken to ensure that light remains and although, a bit more battered, Iza remains who she is.

The survival of this world, my favorite among them all, depends on it.

28

IZA

A nest of vampires sprinkled with shifters brought me to the roof of this building. Looking down at the traffic and the people below is a bit surreal. If I had to guess, I'm close to six-hundred feet in the air. A fall like this would probably kill me because you can't heal if your brain is soup spilled out on the concrete.

"Iza, what are you doing?" Adriem's voice snaps me out of it.

Giving myself a good mental shake, I turn and walk away from the edge, but for the entire drive home, it haunts me. The uproar when I get to the Sidhe doesn't help my mood, either.

When I walk into the dining room, everyone is talking at once and loudly.

"ENOUGH!" I yell. Immediately the noise stops. "What's going on?"

"Did you tell Jameson that Ruthie was to go on trial?" Someone demands, I look at the dragon and half-heartedly search for their name. Vernon.

"Yes, do you have a problem with that?"

"Don't your Feyrie laws require her execution?" My Feyrie laws?

"Technically, they demand yours, too. Since you participated in the discussion about electing someone else." He sits down and shuts up. I walk towards him and my Magiks that have been slumbering wake up. Roaring into existence they brush up against Vern and makes itself known.

The Dark is angry.

Frozen in place, with only his eyes moving frantically around, looking for help, he stands there while the Magiks invade his mind and soul. They're searching for the real reason he's doing this. Digging, digging… oh, there it is. The Magiks don't hold back. It shows me everything.

The conclusion is, Vernon is a greedy moron.

"You think that I get paid for this job?" Throwing my head back I laugh. He's treating it like a human job, like a mayor or something. In his head are dreams of riding in to be the hero and organizing the Feyrie, of sitting at his fancy mahogany desk while making executive decisions. With his attractive secretary who wears short, tight skirts. The worst part of it is the dream of hobnobbing with rich people.

The Magiks release him, and he sags in his chair. Weakly he says, "You have money."

"That money is my own. Even if you 'took' my job, you wouldn't get it. You'd just get killed, dumbass." I'm still chuckling. I can't get the image of him sipping tea and laughing with what he determined the Schoth to be. Rich businessmen who look like characters from a movie. Leaning down I put my face in front of his.

I let my glamour drop and let him see the way my face changes and how my hair moves and weaves on its own. I can see myself reflected in his widened eyes. Smiling, I laugh when his eyes widen even more.

"Today I killed a dozen of your kind, without breaking a sweat. I beheaded a dozen more vampires and enjoyed it. This would be your daily life, Vern. Killing and fighting. There are no big desks and hot secretaries. You still want it?"

Vehemently he shakes his head, and I straighten and turn to the rest of the room and ask, "Anyone else?" No one says anything. "I know that I've been unavailable, but I lost the man I loved because of stupid decisions made by the very people I'm trying to protect. Then you have people like Vern here. His late buddy Gary met his maker a bit early on. I've run into so many of you thinking you can do a better job or dreaming about power and money. I'm not sure I want to try and save any of you anymore." The Dark streams out from me, touching everyone. My eyes burn, and I know they're black as I look around at all the startled faces. I take a deep breath and continue, "Get your heads out of your asses and wake up. WAR IS HERE!" As the Nightmares closed ranks on the gathered people, their growls echo in the room.

These were chosen to stay for a reason, some for their fighting abilities, some for their doubt and deceit. Now is the time of reckoning for them. I'm tired of the stupid fucking games. Continuing as the Shepherd is something I have continuously wavered on and won't any longer, if it's not me doing then it's some idiot like Vern or Gary trying. I'll keep trying for the Feyrie as a whole, for people like Knox and Arista. Ones who have no one to stand up for them, but I won't be nice anymore.

Turning and pulling my arm back I punch Vern right in the mouth. "If you try to backstab me again I will make you a casualty of war, just like I did Gary." Turning back to the others I cross my arms. "Ruthie will be put to trial." Deciding honesty is best I keep going, "I can't kill her, I love her too much. It's only fair that her fate is left up to someone else."

Almost immediately people start to look uncomfortable. The smile I give them is nothing short of mean. "It's time for you to get your hands dirty, I'm not your fucking scapegoat anymore. Understand?" The last word is growled out, and my smile gets bigger.

"When do you wish for the trial to start?" Jameson asks.

"Now is good." As furniture moves and changes shape on its own, I'm pretty impressed when we're left with a courtroom. The Sidhe is amused still, the notes of its song are colorful and encouraging. Ruthie's cage rises from the ground into the witness box.

"Who is the judge?" Jameson speaks up again.

"Me, of course," I answer matter-of-factly.

"The executioner?" Ah, so this is the heart of the worry on his face, he's afraid I'll pick him.

"If one is needed, all of you."

"Iza, what does that even mean?" Poor Jameson looks so confused, and a bit sick to his stomach.

"This is a trial. They were so eager for me to kill her, so now I leave it up to them to determine her punishment. Whether it be death or something else." This way they get to make the final decision into what is done with her and deal with the responsibility for it.

Climbing into the judge seat, I bridge my hands and lean forward on the mahogany desk—that amuses me to no end—and wait for it to begin. When everyone turns their head towards me in expectation, I shrug.

"All of the facts against her must be presented, and she needs someone to defend her. Haven't any of you seen those law shows?" I know they have, everyone from this world has. "Any volunteers for prosecution?" A bunch of hands go up, that's interesting, so quick to condemn her. I look at the only one who didn't raise their hand. "Jameson, you'll be prosecuting." He's learning because he doesn't look surprised that I picked him.

"Vernon, you'll be defending her." He looks as happy as Jameson does.

While they talk and huddle together in their plans to do things, Vern whispers to Ruthie in her cage. I can hear their entire conversation. He's telling her to admit it and be done with it, while she's calling him names. Nothing unexpected at all.

My stomach rumbles and I discover that I'm hungry for the first time in days. I eat sometimes but not a lot and only to keep myself from getting ill. Healing or not, I still need food. On the desk, in front of me, a plate of barbecued ribs pops into existence. The goblins know me so well. Without hesitation, I dig in, suddenly ravenous.

Seeing people get what they deserve makes me hungry.

♥

Two hours later and after a lengthy monologue by Vernon on how an eighteen-year-old girl couldn't possibly be intelligent enough to be that deceptive, I catch myself fighting to stay awake. How idiotic is he? Jameson decides to be the one to point it out to him, and I have my first proud moment in a while.

"You're wrong, we all know it, and I have no idea why you've gone with that as her defense. Honestly, we're not here to say she's guilty—we all know she is. We're here to determine her punishment. Shall we move onto that?" Several murmurs of agreement follow his little speech.

Now we're getting somewhere.

My gaze falls on Ruthie, and her smug expression is no longer there. She looks like the scared kid she is, and she should. "You realize what you've done yet?" I ask her. My question silences the room.

"Fuck you." Well, I'll take that as a yes.

"At least this way, I won't be the one to kill you. That's something you should be thankful for." I look back to the group of people in the center of the room, discussing what is to be done with her. Ruthie is pretending to ignore them, but her eyes keep straying there. Looking at her doesn't hurt as bad as it did, I know she did it without any doubts. That doesn't stop me from loving her, but it stopped me from hoping this is all wrong—that she didn't do it.

There's no denying she did, and quite happily.

The group of people scatters back to their seats and Jameson stands up. He's the one who volunteered to read the verdict. Clearing his throat, he says, "Given her age, we have voted against execution." Looking at Ruthie I see the smile on her face, but Jameson continues, "However, we vote for her to be blinded and branded a traitor." Whoa, I didn't expect that one. The smile drops off her face.

"That's no big deal. I'll heal," Ruthie snaps.

"There's more, Ruthie, just wait," I whisper to her.

"As we all know, each of us has different abilities. Shifters—like Ruthie, heal quickly. There are ways to stop that, and our final ruling is for her to have her Feyrie nature stripped completely from her. Ruthie will be made human." Her gasp of shock is pleasing and heart wrenching at the same time, but it does appease the more bloodthirsty part of me.

"As you wish." I stand, and the Magiks come alive once again. Turning to face Ruthie, I give her the finger and watch the ethereal black claws appear—my Magiks making itself visible for all to see—and tear into her aura. Her screaming gradually slows down, and the claws leave her, kneeling on the floor of her cage—the sockets of her eyes empty and bloody. Completely, and utterly human now. This punishment is worse than death for her, fitting for what she has done. As I watch, the Feyrie symbol for betrayer appears on her forehead. It will be invisible to human eyes, but any Feyrie would know it.

The cage dissolves, and Ruthie is free to leave this place because it's no longer her home.

"Escort her out, leave her in town with some money and her clothes and precious shoes that she was willing to do all of this for. The Sidhe will never welcome her again."

"Michael!" she yells.

He steps out of the crowd and comes to stand in front of her, I expect to see pity on his face as he looks down at her, but instead, I see resolve and dislike. She doesn't matter to him anymore, that bridge is burnt.

Without a word to her he turns and walks away, closing that chapter of his life. Looking at her, I feel like the right thing has been done. Yes, she's blind and human now, but she's alive. She will remember why she's alive, and I didn't have to kill her. That sin will not tarnish my soul.

For that I am thankful. When Auryn comes forward and drags her to her feet, there is no pity for her there either. Tuning out her screams and pleas, I step down off the judge's podium and go in search of a shower. I stink.

29

THE UNKNOWN

"This form is not the same one I wore before?" I ask, looking down at the hands that seem familiar, but only in glimpses of memories, I don't understand. Instead of being flesh and blood, they fade in and out of reality at my command. My body is only solid when I wish it to be, made from the fabric of the realm I was born to.

The old man, who is not an old man, frowns at me and his bushy white eyebrows wiggle. Why do I feel like someone I know would find this entertaining? It is one of the many foggy memories, tickling at the edge of my consciousness but not coming through. Instead, they leave me confused and frustrated with my inability to make them make sense. Most of them are wrapped up and tangled in with the ones about the woman with the red hair, the one whose face I see everywhere I look.

Iza. I knew her name before Life told me, but I feel like I should know more than her name. When I close my eyes, I can smell her skin, and hear her laughter echoing in my mind, but then it slips away like water through my fingers, and I'm left again with the incomplete memories.

"It is identical in appearance to it. I simply made it from the planar essence of the NetherRealm versus flesh and blood of your previous one." Life explains patiently, his frown deepening. "This body is more suited for you than the one you had before."

"I don't remember very many things clearly... the woman, her presence is sprinkled in these bits and pieces of memories. Why?" The part of me that is visceral, primal in its wants and needs—focuses on her constantly. Circling the memories of her in a predatory way that's more protective than preying. She's special, somehow, this woman with red hair.

"Your memories will return to you, albeit slowly. I've never done this before, so I can't tell you exactly how things will happen, I can only make educated guesses." My shadows brush him but cannot read him.

"Do I want them to return? Can I not simply go on my way and forget about this woman and the confusing feeling she arouses in me?" Would it not be simpler to do such a thing?

"Ask yourself if that's something you can do. Can you walk away from her without a second glance?" Annoyed with him, I lean against the wall and allow myself to think about it really. The monster I am protests, vehemently. The area in my chest... where a heart should be, protests violently as well.

What was this woman to me?

"How long was I trapped as a mortal creature?"

"Well, over a thousand years. Light made sure that you were locked up tight, I merely looked for the key." He sounds bothered about this. It seems that Life has truly become the softy I expected him to be eons ago. Strangely enough, it suits him.

To weaken me and eventually kill me was Light's intention. Him, I remember just fine—the three of us came into awareness together and in our way of communicating, considered each other brothers, of a sense. Light was always the more turbulent of us, always wanting more power, more creations. More. More. More.

While I simply wanted to do what I did and be left alone.

"I don't remember you being this talkative before. She's been a good influence on you." The amusement is sudden in his eyes and takes me aback. Exactly how much influence did this creature have on me? Is it her influence that makes me ask questions when logic dictates that, if I can't read his mind, it's through questions that I can find my answers, instead of leaving and not caring?

He continues talking, "The 'original' you would simply eat someone frustrating you."

"I can't eat you, leaving me stuck asking questions. Duh." I answer, not understanding why I added the duh. It came out on its own. His laughter surprises me, and I step back from him. Why is that word so amusing to him? It's a word, a stupid one at that.

"A good influence, indeed. Iza has a massive sense of humor, something you were painstakingly slow in coming to possess yourself." His smile fades, and he turns serious again. "What else do you remember?" Why do I need to remember to function? He says they'll return. Can they not return while I'm out there, in the world? I'm tired of staying in this place and hiding. It goes against the fabric of my nature to hide.

"There are flashes but nothing solid enough to use." I refuse to admit that they are mostly of her. The longest, most detailed pieces of memories always revolve around her. Snippets of conversation, flashes of battle. Erotic images of her legs wrapped around my waist, while my teeth tear into her skin and her claws are buried in—I blink to clear the images. This is a memory that affects my entire person, while similar ones I remember don't.

I shiver, those memories are new.

"I have a feeling you're going down a thought path that you might need to be alone for." His amusement is back.

"She is my lover?"

"Oh, brother... she is way more than simply your lover. Iza is a force to be reckoned with, and you adored her for it."

"Chaos... that is what I sense about her. Her mind, her actions—the very essence of her is chaos." Strangely, these things draw me in more. Because of this, I'm incredibly annoyed with myself.

"Yes, that's something that I always admired about her. Don't snap judge that chaos, she's got a sharp mind—your Iza."

She isn't my Iza, but it feels like she is. My instincts say she is, the images of her and I locked together in passion says she is. The Schoth torturing us...

I can't do it. Can't leave him. I just can't. Those thoughts in her voice, her sad, beautiful eyes looking at me from the stairs—from the point of her finding escape. Instead, she turned back around and came to 'rescue' me. That stupid woman.

She gave up her freedom for me. No wonder the other me loved her, to sacrifice something precious for someone so unworthy of it, is that incredible. Why do I feel like I have had that thought that before? Frustrated I shake my head. There are too many memories to sort through. A lot of them belong to the food, while others are from lifetimes before Iza. This body isn't as limited as the one I possessed before, but because of its newness, still has its own limitations.

I have no heartbeat, and for some reason, having heartbeats seem important. I have to have answers why a creature like me loved. I have to find her and see her and ask her why. Find her and touch her face, taste her mouth again. Feel her in my arms. Bloody hell, my brother is right, I can't walk away, she's *mine*.

"I'm going to find this Iza creature." I can feel her out there. A bond that needs to be completed is within my reach, waiting for me to take it. I will not. Instead, I'll use it to find her, and when the time comes, then I'll complete it. To possess her, to touch her, yes, I will complete it then.

"Phobe, I am not sure this is such a good idea."

I say nothing. It is not his decision to make. Instead, I ask, "Why did you save me?" Growing a body for me took some of his life force, doing it with such speed took a bit out of him. I'm stronger than I have ever been, but he is not.

"You demanded it." Perhaps, but that is not why he was there.

"You were there to collect my essence. I imagine that I couldn't demand such a thing at that point."

"Honestly, I should've never let it come to this. I should've never let him do what he did. At the time, you were so strong and dangerous, and foolishly I believed it was the only way to protect our creations from you."

He isn't wrong. I have memories from before that are more intact than the recent ones. I wanted to devour it all and would have. He was right to stop me, and wrong at the same time. If not for my imprisonment I wouldn't have met the woman who, as confusing as it all is, is a big part of my thoughts. Whole memories or not, she is in all the pleasant ones. She made the creature I was happy. She made him feel and... love.

Can she do that for the creature I am now?

Decision made, I walk out of the small cabin that has kept me hidden while I rebuilt myself. Smiling for the first time since I awakened, I let the night take me as I dissolve into smoke.

30

IZA

The buildings of the town look like a brick skeleton from up here. The streets are dirty and slushy from the recent snow. The few people out and about look miserable and cold. I think it looks quite beautiful. Dead and melancholic, it fits my mood perfectly. Standing on the very lip of the ledge I look down at the ground below. This is the tallest building in town, and although it's not a skyscraper, it is tall enough that once again, I've spent a few evenings up here. Solitude seems only to be achievable when I hide.

To get up here I had to beat Adriem unconscious, I normally might feel a bit bad for it, but this time he got in my way and I didn't appreciate it. Jameson plastered himself against the wall and tried to talk sense into me. The idiot even hit me on the head with a flower pot in an attempt to knock me out so Adriem could grab me.

Why they put up such a fight, is asinine. I didn't come up here to commit suicide.

It's a shame Jameson's tooth won't grow back. I told him it'd match his missing finger. Why the hell he thought a flower pot would stop me, I don't know. I'm a little bit proud he tried though, second time since I found him almost dead. Which makes me reluctantly smile, damnit.

Sighing, I step down off the ledge. I would never contemplate killing myself, it feels like a betrayal to life. No matter how selfishly I want to be with Phobe, suicide just isn't the right way to go, not for me. I owe myself a glorious death, with the bodies of the Guide and his buddies at my feet. There are still too many things I need to do, people I need to cut up into teeny tiny pieces.

The problem is that I feel so fucking alone. Being surrounded by people at the Sidhe makes it worse. I miss my dad, who must still have his hands full, or he'd be here kicking my ass. I miss Ruthie, well, the person I thought she was, who's now wandering around the town trying to get sympathy for her sins. Not as poignantly as before, but the bite of it is still there, mostly when I see Michael.

I miss the kids that are well hidden, even from me. The last report I got informed me that Knox is still mad about being sent away, he won't even talk to me on the phone. Auryn told me that he wanted to greet me at the Sidhe, but I couldn't risk leading them to the kids. The wisest solution was to have them moved before I got there. No one told Nika either. In fact, no one knows except the ones who took them.

The children can't fight in this coming war. They'll die. No matter how tough or how many fancy moves they're taught, they'll still die. I can't have that, especially not after losing—I swallow the tears. I'm not sure that the ache will ever go away. When you love someone, the house inside of your heart is full. Flowers bloom bright and colorful in the garden of life that you plant together. The moon shines brightly down on the garden that grows into something so fucking magical it can bring you to tears from the strength of it. It's so rare and precious that you want to lock it up and protect it from everyone.

Love gives a dead heart like mine, life. The hope I have that he'll come back to me, keeps it beating.

When hope is completely taken away, the moon stops shining and the garden you so carefully cultivated with emotion and memory, dies. That happy, full house starts to fall in on itself, and all you're left with is the rotting wood of grief. Hollow, lonely, and empty of anything resembling life. Eventually, you start to die inside too. Walking around in a haze of utter misery.

This is a stage of grief and one I must go through.

Fuck. I turn away from the ledge and find myself staring at the very face haunting my every breathing moment.

"Phobe?" Gods, I'm fucking hallucinating now. Phobe is gone, he's gone, and I can't get him back, ever.

"Why do you cry?" My legs almost give out. My heart is beating so fast in my chest it feels like it'll burst from it. What the ever-living hells is this? Cautiously, I stare at this creature with his face, because he's freaking real, I can feel it. From head to toe, he's similar, but there are some differences. He doesn't look as young. He looks more in his late twenties than a fresh-faced nineteen-year-old. The face is identical though, and those eyes—while the same pumpkin color—

—Those are the eyes of a stranger looking back at me.

He approaches me, stopping inches away from me to stare down into my face. This man smells like Phobe, too, deep earth and the cold night sky. The energy of him feels achingly familiar, sending shivers down my spine. Slowly, he lowers his face to touch his nose to my cheek.

His breath tickles as he says, "I know you... your face, the way your eyes sparkle in the moonlight—the smell of you. The intoxicating taste of sweet darkness in your blood exploding on my tongue." He smells me, running his nose from my jaw to my temple. "I want to..." he pauses and does it again. "Devour you." He steps forward, bringing his body flush against mine and I freeze completely, feeling his arousal against my stomach. "Every instinct inside of me says you're mine. Is this so, Iza?" He draws my name out in a verbal caress, and my body responds to it immediately.

A million emotions crash through me at the same time. Euphoria because Phobe is standing in front of me. Despair because this isn't the Phobe I lost, he's... different. Lust because he smells, talks, and looks like my Phobe and my body craves him. Fear, because I have no idea what the fuck to do. Breaking through my temporary paralysis, I take several steps back from him, I need the space.

"How—" I clear my throat and lick my dry lips, "How are you here?"

"Life grabbed my essence as Light ripped it out of the mortal body and grew me a new one." Wait, I don't understand. "I don't have all of my memories, they're returning but very slowly. You're the subject of most of them." I can feel him digging around my mind, and he's much more forceful than he normally is— was.

"So, you're not the same Phobe who died." I pinch myself in case I did jump, and this is some sort of weird death dream. Nope, that hurt. Shit.

"Yes and no." What does that fucking mean? "Once all of my memories return, perhaps I will be, but until then I am who I am now." He takes a step towards me. "You didn't answer my question."

"I belonged to him, yes. You? I'm not so sure about you." I'm not so sure about me either. I'm afraid to hope. I'm afraid that the man I love is standing in front of me and isn't the man I fell for.

"That's something we'll remedy. Now, tell me about this stick in my ass. In this memory, you laugh, and I find myself liking your laugh." I bite my lip to keep from laughing now. How confusing is this shit? I mean it's him but... it's not. How am I going to cope with this?

"You perpetually have one up there. I simply offered to remove it." The words are shaky and hesitant but until I know what to do or the right thing to say I'm hitting default mode. Until I get answers, I can use this. I can use this and be close to him and maybe, just maybe he'll remember it all and I get him back.

"I have things to do," I say, more confident than I was. I don't have things to do unless you count killing people, then yes, I do have lots to do.

He cocks his head to the side in a familiar movement. This version reminds me of the one I first met. Except a little more... well, a little more dangerous.

"I enjoy killing things."

"I don't need your help," I say it half-hearted.

"That is too bad, Iza... I do not plan on going anywhere."

ACKNOWLEDGMENTS

One more book to go.

I want to thank everyone who stepped in to help me write this. You're a rock in the storm of life.

Thank you honeykins, you're the reason I wake up on planet Earth.

Thanks Savages, you keep me going.

ABOUT ZOE PARKER

Zoe is the type of person that thinks that writing about herself in third person is giggle worthy. She also laughs at those T-REX costumes that flap about when you run. Zoe has a hard time writing about normal things and has a soft spot for the antihero and the monster in the closet. For all we know they're lonely and trying to make friends. They're just doing it badly. She also likes pickles and peanut butter, yuck.

Www.zoeparkerbooks.com
https://www.facebook.com/ZoeParkerAuthor
https://www.facebook.com/groups/ZoesSavagesquad

ALSO BY ZOE PARKER

Facets of Feyrie Series - Urban Fantasy
Elusion, Book One
Ascension, Book Two
Deception, Book Three
Obliteration, Book Four

A (RH), multiple-mayhem series, The Fate Caller Series:
Cadence of Ciar, Book One
Rhythm of Rime, Book Two

Unsylum Series
Up with the Crows - Book One
As the Crow Flies - Book Two

Printed in Great Britain
by Amazon